Certain... *...d before...*

This was possession, claiming, and Meredith wanted nothing more than to surrender.

Surrender to a potential traitor.

That sharp, shocking thought drove her from him. She shrugged out of Tristan's embrace and stepped back as she raised one trembling hand to her swollen, hot lips. With effort, she forced herself to look into his eyes. He stared back evenly, his gaze smoldering green fire. There was no doubt he wanted her back in his arms as much as she wanted to be there.

If she hadn't been investigating him, she would have given into that desire. But she was.

She had no choice but to gather her quaking emotions. She had to forget how much she was affected by his touch and use his reactions against him. Use the kiss to get more information.

Instead, her only desire was to throw herself back into his arms. Worse yet, let him lead her even farther. Past mere kisses, past his warm embrace.

All the way to his bed . . .

Other **AVON ROMANCES**

BE MINE TONIGHT *by Kathryn Smith*
HOW TO SEDUCE A BRIDE *by Edith Layton*
ONCE UPON A WEDDING NIGHT *by Sophie Jordan*
SINFUL PLEASURES *by Mary Reed McCall*
SINS OF MIDNIGHT *by Kimberly Logan*
WHAT TO WEAR TO A SEDUCTION *by Sari Robins*
WINDS OF THE STORM *by Beverly Jenkins*

Coming Soon

NO MAN'S BRIDE *by Shana Galen*
THE PERFECT SEDUCTION *by Margo Maguire*

And Don't Miss These
ROMANTIC TREASURES
from Avon Books

THE DUKE IN DISGUISE *by Gayle Callen*
SHE'S NO PRINCESS *by Laura Lee Guhrke*
TEMPTING THE WOLF *by Lois Greiman*

ATTENTION: ORGANIZATIONS AND CORPORATIONS
Most Avon Books paperbacks are available at special quantity discounts for bulk purchases for sales promotions, premiums, or fund-raising. For information, please call or write:

Special Markets Department, HarperCollins Publishers, Inc., 10 East 53rd Street, New York, N.Y. 10022–5299. Telephone: (212) 207–7528.   Fax: (212) 207-7222.

Jenna Petersen

From London With Love

AVON BOOKS

An Imprint of HarperCollins*Publishers*

This is a work of fiction. Names, characters, places, and incidents are products of the author's imagination or are used fictitiously and are not to be construed as real. Any resemblance to actual events, locales, organizations, or persons, living or dead, is entirely coincidental.

AVON BOOKS
An Imprint of HarperCollins*Publishers*
10 East 53rd Street
New York, New York 10022-5299

Copyright © 2006 by Jesse Petersen
ISBN-13: 978-0-06-079861-1
ISBN-10: 0-06-079861-0
www.avonromance.com

All rights reserved. No part of this book may be used or reproduced in any manner whatsoever without written permission, except in the case of brief quotations embodied in critical articles and reviews. For information address Avon Books, an Imprint of HarperCollins Publishers.

First Avon Books paperback printing: August 2006

Avon Trademark Reg. U.S. Pat. Off. and in Other Countries, Marca Registrada, Hecho en U.S.A.
HarperCollins® is a registered trademark of HarperCollins Publishers Inc.

Printed in the U.S.A.

10 9 8 7 6 5 4 3 2 1

If you purchased this book without a cover, you should be aware that this book is stolen property. It was reported as "unsold and destroyed" to the publisher, and neither the author nor the publisher has received any payment for this "stripped book."

My thanks go to Miriam Kriss for being my friend and my cheerleader, as well as my "barracuda." Also to Susanna Carr, who said, "What about *Charlie's Angels*?" You were kidding, but you got it right on! And I can't forget Shelley Bradley, who always poses the questions I need to know the answers to. Even though I whine, I appreciate it. Finally, to Joely Sue Burkhart, who pulled out her fine-toothed comb for me when I asked.

This book is for Michael, who listens to me talk and talk and talk, but hasn't run screaming from the room . . . yet.

Prologue

London, 1808

"**L**eave convincing the Crown to me, Charles."

Charles Isley leaned back in the comfortable seat in his companion's theatre box. Through the shadows, he could hardly see her face, though he knew it well. She was, after all, one of the most influential and well-liked matrons of the *ton*. If her equals knew of her daring scheme, they would never believe it.

And that was a key element of her plans.

"Very well, my lady." He gave a nod. "I'll defer to your greater influence on that subject. But that still leaves us with matters to resolve. You wish to form a group of female spies. Widows, so they will not be shocked by the reality of the world of underground criminals; ladies of society, so they might have access to the most powerful people in the Empire. Have you anyone in mind?"

"We will need more than one lady, of course. They can assist each other if they work together. But I want you to approach them individually, so we can keep this as quiet as possible. I have decided on the first lady."

Her ladyship's skirt rustled as she reached for a reticule from a maid who stood beside her shoulder. She withdrew a list of names Charlie had collected for her a few weeks prior, unfolded the page and looked at it. In the dim lamplight, he saw that she had made notations beside many of the names, though he could not make out the words.

"Keep me in suspense no longer, then. Who have you chosen as your first lady spy?"

He heard the smile in her voice. "Meredith Sinclair is a fine candidate from the collection you presented me."

He nodded. "I agree. She is very popular, as well as intelligent. And she lost her husband a few months ago."

"She has always been a shining diamond in society. And she has a certain grace about her, a strength in her movements that leads me to believe she could handle the more physical aspects of the training she will have to endure."

He pulled a small notebook from his pocket and wrote down the lady's name. A thrill of excitement rushed through him as he stared at the swirl of his handwriting.

"I shall contact her immediately, my lady," he said with a smile.

"Very good, Charlie." Her ladyship lifted a hand in farewell as he got to his feet and made for the hallway in the theatre. "Very good."

Chapter 1

1812

Meredith Sinclair held her breath as she knelt before the safe, a lock pick clamped between her teeth and a candle flickering on the floor as she gave the door a pull. Her lips tilted into a smile around the pick as the safe door swung open, revealing two identical velvet boxes.

Withdrawing them both, she pulled a tiny magnifying glass from the pocket of the fitted gentleman's trousers she wore as a disguise and removed the first necklace from its box. She barely held back a gasp of pleasure at the beauty of the piece. The diamonds sparkled in the glow of the candlelight and the amethysts reflected a violet so rich and deep that it was worthy of a king.

She dipped her head and examined the piece. When she didn't find what she had been looking for, she opened the second box, to reveal a necklace that was identical to the first in all ways.

"All ways but one," she murmured to herself with a smile as she found the tiny mark on one stone that indicated a forgery. She replaced the real necklace in its case and put it into her bag, then got to her feet.

Carefully, she slipped from the room and down the dim hallway to the servants' entrance she had paid a disgruntled footman to leave open for her. The home was silent as a grave, its occupants at a party across London, where they were no doubt scouting out their next piece of jewelry to steal. The servants had the night off or were in their quarters.

It was all too easy.

Meredith stifled another smug smile as she made her way into the garden behind the estate. In a few short steps she would be in her waiting carriage hidden around the corner and on her way back home. Another case solved.

The thought had no more than passed through her head when she heard a shout behind her. She glanced over her shoulder to see three men burst from the home in her direction.

"Damn it," she muttered as she started to run.

The door leading from the garden onto the street was still a good twenty feet away.

That was when the first shot whizzed past her ear. Without breaking stride, Meredith looked back to see the second man lifting his gun as the first man fell behind to reload.

She dropped her shoulders and darted to the left as she reached the garden door, just as a second bullet slammed into its wooden face and splintered wood flew in all directions. She grabbed the door handle and pulled . . .

Only to find it had been relocked since her entry into the home not half an hour before.

A wide variety of curses passed through Meredith's mind, but she didn't utter them. For one, she had to save her breath for running, and two, since she was in disguise, she didn't want her pursuers to know she was a woman. That would only complicate matters.

She bounded along the garden wall in hopes she would find something to be her salvation. And then it appeared. A wheelbarrow propped against the wall by some helpful gardener.

"Thank you patron saint of spies," she murmured as she jumped onto the rounded top of the wheelbarrow, balanced for a brief moment, then braced her hands along the garden wall and pushed herself over the top.

She hit the cobblestone below with a jarring force that made her teeth rattle, but was instantly on the move again. Her carriage was parked in sight in the dark shadow of a nearby building, and her driver had turned, looking for her. Likely he had heard the gunfire inside the garden, for his own rifle was raised to cover her if need be.

With a yank, Meredith pulled the carriage door open and dove inside.

"Go, Henderson!" she called as another bullet shattered the glass window on the door. She reached back and pulled the damaged door shut as she flattened herself against the floor in case her pursuers fired again. "Drive!"

The horses had already begun to move before the second order left her lips. They roared forward under Henderson's skilled whip, leaving her hunters behind, their loud curses echoing along the quiet streets.

Ah, the life of a lady spy. Running from gunmen at midnight, overseeing a charity meeting by tea time. Meredith smiled. Somehow she doubted that the gentlemen who protected the Empire were doing the same.

"That is all the old business we have to review," Anastasia Whittig, one of her partners, said as she removed her wire-rimmed spectacles. "As always the Sisters of the Heart Society for Widows and Orphans' charity ball was an enormous success."

Their other partner, Emily Redgrave shrugged. "These events always are. But who cares about some stuffy ball?" She turned her sparkling blue stare on Meredith. "You have new business, don't you?"

Meredith couldn't suppress her wicked grin. She'd been fighting the urge to crow from the rooftops since her arrival. "I do."

As her friends watched, she reached into her reticule and withdrew the box she'd pilfered the night before. Ana and Emily leaned forward in anticipation when she removed the top and held up the necklace that lay within the folds of protective velvet. The jewels flashed sparkles in the afternoon sun.

For a moment a heavy silence hung in the room, but then Emily let out a sigh of delight and carefully took the piece from Meredith's hands. She held it against her throat.

"My God, Merry, it's beautiful! Even more exquisite than the sketches led us to believe," Emily squealed as she turned to the mirror above the mantelpiece and examined herself with the diamonds draped around her neck.

"Yes. I could scarcely draw breath when I took the piece from the safe." Meredith sighed.

Anastasia eyed the two women with a purse of her lips. "Is it wise to bring the jewelry here? It's against protocol."

Meredith looked at Ana with a wry grin. Her friend was talented and beautiful, but she lived by rules *always*.

"I decided to hang regulations and protocol this once." At Ana's gasp of horror, she continued quickly, "At any rate, Charles gave me permission to let you see the fruits of our latest labor. He'll be by to retrieve the necklace in just a few moments and deliver it to the Watch."

Emily spun from the mirror with a scowl. She set the jewels back into their case and folded her arms with displeasure.

"It seems so unfair that we do all the hard work, put our very lives at risk and some ridiculous officer of the Watch, who probably couldn't find his own—"

Meredith arched a brow. "Emily."

Emily shook her head. "Whether I'm vulgar or not, the sentiment remains the same. The Watch will get recognition for the recovery. For heaven's sake, Meredith, you were shot at during this investigation! Don't you feel you deserve some acknowledgment for that?"

Meredith folded her arms. "And just how do you know I was shot at?"

"I have investigative skills, remember?" When Meredith lifted her eyebrows in disbelief, Emily shrugged. "Oh, very well. Henderson said something about needing to replace the glass in the carriage door. But you are avoiding the question!"

Meredith sighed. "Emily, when we were chosen to join The Society we realized what hard and dangerous work spying would be, and that others would always receive the accolades for our efforts."

Emily threw up her hands in disgust and paced away.

Meredith continued, "At any rate, Lady Devingshire's property will be returned and that is what matters most."

Ana nodded. "And if we were given credit for our work, Lady M wouldn't be able to give us new cases. Our lives as spies would be over. You wouldn't like that, would you?"

Emily let out a low sigh. "No, Ana. I wouldn't. I'm being silly, as usual. We did our duty."

"You did, indeed, ladies," a male voice said as the parlor door opened. "And Lady M thanks you, much less reluctantly than the Crown."

Meredith spun toward the door with a wide smile as she watched the middle-aged gentleman enter. Charles Isley was portly through the stomach, and the thinning hair that swept across his bald spot disguised the shining skin beneath. But his rosy cheeks were filled with cheerful color, and his smile for Meredith and her friends was genuine.

"Charlie!" she said as she got to her feet, crossing the room with both hands outstretched. He took them and gave them a squeeze.

"Fine, fine work, Merry," he said with a crooked grin. "Though we could have done without the theatrics last night."

She shrugged as she tossed a smile over her shoulder at her companions. "I had no choice but to jump over the wall. It was that or be shot."

"Quite so."

He tried to look stern, but the twinkle in his eyes was anything but. It reminded her of the night he first approached her and changed the course of her life forever. He'd offered her a place in the small band of female spies being formed by a mysterious woman of power in society.

Within weeks she found herself standing in this very home, meeting the other two women who were to be her partners. The training had been long and arduous, over two years honing their mental and physical skills.

And then the assignments had come. Investigations into treachery in the war against Napoleon. Cases that involved murder. Theft. Even thwarting an attempt on Princess Charlotte's life. The last four years had been thrilling, and it was all thanks to Charles Isley and their mysterious benefactress, whom they only knew as Lady M.

"Meredith?" Charles cocked his head. "I asked if you have the necklace."

She shook away her thoughts with a nod. "My apologies, Charles, I was wool-gathering. Of course I do."

She turned to the table and handed him the box she had set there earlier. Charlie opened it for a quick peek and gave her a swift nod. "Very good. Thank you."

"Don't only thank me," she insisted with a wave to her friends. "It was Ana's inventions that helped me find the correct vault and break the lock. And Emily's meticulous research helped determine which necklace was the forgery."

He nodded. "You know I thank you all. But I'm afraid I can offer you no respite from work this time."

"You have a new case for us already?" Meredith leaned forward with giddy anticipation. She hated the quiet times between cases.

Ana shook her head. "Honestly, Charlie, there isn't any way I could take a field assignment right now. I'm working on a new project here and I shall have to encode my notes on this case for the records—"

Charles held up a hand. "Don't worry, Ana, Meredith will be the one doing the fieldwork."

As Anastasia breathed a sigh of relief, Emily pursed her lips. "That isn't fair! Merry got the last field assignment."

Meredith stuck out her tongue playfully and got the same in return from her best friend.

Charlie rolled his eyes at their girlish display. "Fair or not, this is the only way. Would you like the particulars?"

Meredith nodded. "Go ahead, Charlie. What's the case?"

He pulled his pipe and a bit of tobacco from his front pocket. As he tamped the tobacco into the bowl, he took a seat beside the fire. "I'm sure you've all heard of the upcoming auction at the Genevieve Art House?"

Meredith nodded. "Of course. It promises to be quite an event. It was all the talk at The Society's ball last week."

"Recently there have been two incidents at Genevieve's. In the last, a painting was stolen."

"Is that all?" Emily asked with a burst of exasperated breath. She threw up her hands in disgust. "Whatever happened to defending Crown and Country? I thought *that* was our duty, not to return stolen jewels to a spoiled duchess or find some silly painting for an art house auction."

He shook his head. "There is more to this case than a mere stolen painting, Emily!"

Meredith met his eyes. "What is it?"

Charlie looked at her evenly. "We believe the person who stole the painting is a man of rank and title. A man with whom you had an acquaintance in the past."

Meredith sucked in her breath through her teeth. "Who?"

"Tristan Archer."

The room spun off kilter as Meredith struggled to keep her face benign and unaffected. It took all her training to prevent herself from physically backing away.

"The Marquis of Carmichael?" she croaked out, her voice strained by the effort it took to remain neutral.

"The very one." He watched her carefully, scrutinizing her every move and affectation.

She reacted accordingly, letting out a light laugh that didn't reflect her inner turmoil. "Charlie, that is madness. Tristan Archer has twenty thousand pounds a year at minimum. He is the owner of over five thriving properties. He would have no reason to steal a painting."

He took a puff from his pipe. "That may be so, but this is not the first time the auction house was tampered with. About a week ago Genevieve came down from his apartments above stairs to find the very same painting taken from its place and left propped against a wall. At the time, he believed he or his staff might have done it themselves and simply forgotten. But when he found the item missing, he realized no one would have cause to move the painting."

Meredith nodded as she clicked another bit of evidence together in the puzzle of her mind. "Could a robbery have been interrupted the first time?"

He shook his head. "No. There was no evidence a thief was disturbed in the midst of a robbery. Lady M believes the first attempt was not about *removing* the painting."

She thought of the possibilities, mulling over why a thief would remove a piece of artwork from its rightful place, but not take it outright when given the chance.

Meredith's mouth dropped open as a possibility occurred to her. "Whoever tampered with the painting the first time was *adding* something to it, not taking something away. And whoever stole it was retrieving the information the first thief put there, possibly because the painting had already been sold and he couldn't buy it outright."

"That is our belief," Charlie said with a small nod.

"By God," Emily said from behind her.

Meredith started. She'd been so wrapped up in her investigative process, she'd all but forgotten her two friends.

Ana smiled. "You're brilliant, Merry! But what does Lady M believe was added?"

Charlie set his pipe down and stood to pace to the fireplace. "Any manner of information could have been transferred in such a way. There have been rumblings about traitorous counterspies utilizing such covert methods. Whatever it was, it was sensitive enough that those involved wanted to do it surreptitiously."

Meredith nodded. Her heart throbbed, but not with the normal anticipation that preceded the beginning of a case. This emotion was not the thrill of discovery or the excitement of formulating a detailed plan of attack.

It was dread.

"Why do you suspect Tristan Archer?" she asked softly.

Charles cocked his head at her tone. "We did not choose Carmichael for our pleasure, Meredith. In fact, Lady M's first reaction was as shocked as your own. The man has never shown himself to be anything less than gentlemanly. But Genevieve says the day after he sold the painting, Carmichael came to the art house offering an exorbitant amount of money for the piece."

Emily arched a brow. "And Genevieve wouldn't sell?"

Charlie shook his head. "He refused to renege on the prior bargain he made. Apparently, Lord Carmichael grew very angry and stormed out of the auction house."

Meredith's heart sank. "What more is there?"

"Witnesses saw a carriage bearing the Carmichael crest departing the auction house the night of the robbery. When other investigators questioned his lordship about his whereabouts, he was quite uncooperative and ultimately gave us an alibi that was later proven false. Worse, he has been keeping very bad company of late. There is no getting around it. Carmichael has something to hide. An investigation is in order."

Meredith straightened her shoulders. Duty. She had to remember her duty. She'd sworn an oath and she could not break it. Not for anyone. Not even the man who had saved her life on a dark night long ago.

"Yes, Charlie. Of course."

He nodded. "Carmichael is hosting a ball tomorrow evening. I've obtained an invitation for both you and Emily. While she conducts a quick search of the home, you'll reacquaint yourself with the Marquis and determine your next action."

Charlie took the velvet box containing the necklace Meredith had recovered and long forgotten. With a smile for the three women, he said, "Meanwhile, I'll send over a list of Carmichael's associates for Ana to research. I know you three will discover the truth and intercept any transfer of valuable information. Now, if you will excuse me, I must deliver this to the Watch. Good day, ladies."

Emily and Ana responded, "Good afternoon, Charles."

Meredith couldn't bring herself to answer as she paced to the window and looked outside.

Emily took a few steps forward as Charles left. "Merry, how do you know Carmichael? You've never spoken about him, yet it's clear this assignment and the possibility that his lordship is a traitor upsets you greatly."

Ana nodded as Meredith turned to face her two friends. Emily's blue eyes were focused on her with an intensity she usually reserved for target practice, and Ana had removed her spectacles.

Meredith's stomach clenched. Her sister spies knew her far too well for comfort at times.

"Even Charlie could see you were conflicted," Ana said. "Who *is* Tristan Archer to you?"

Meredith utilized her training to cover the tangled emotions that burned within her. "Lord Carmichael was a friend of my cousin's when I was a girl, nothing more."

Ana's forehead scrunched and Emily opened her mouth to speak, but Meredith rushed on, "If we are attending a ball tomorrow, I have arrangements to make, and so do you, Emily."

"But—" Emily began, her icy blue eyes watching Meredith's every move with rising suspicion.

Meredith needed to get out of the house before Emily and Ana wrestled the truth from her. The truth she wasn't ready to think about, let alone speak.

"Good afternoon," she called over her shoulder as she fled into the foyer, hands trembling. She nodded to the butler as she left, then climbed into her waiting carriage. But once inside, her emotions rushed back, flutterings around her heart that she was normally able to distance herself from. And they were so very, very dangerous. Because the last thing she needed was to feel some kind of tenderness for a man.

Especially one who could turn out to be the worst kind of traitor.

Chapter 2

As Meredith passed through the massive mahogany doors into Lord Carmichael's ballroom, her stomach flipped. With a scowl, she willed herself to calm down. What was she so upset about? If Tristan really was a traitor, the fact that she once found him dashing and handsome did not signify. Nor did the fact that he'd saved her life then avoided her like she was cursed afterward.

She was a spy, damn it! And a good one at that. She couldn't let silly remembered emotions cloud her judgment.

She cast a side glance at Emily. Her friend was smiling sweetly, but she scanned the crowd with focused intent. It was difficult to make out any one person of interest in the jammed ballroom. She hadn't seen such a crush in a while, but late Season gatherings were often the busiest.

"Ana gave you the list of people to look for?" Meredith asked as she flipped her fan open and waved it slowly to circulate the stifling air around her face. Only she and Emily knew a knife blade was hidden within the handle, ready to be released with the slightest press of a hidden mechanism. The fan was courtesy of Ana's inventive mind.

"Yes," Emily said as they moved forward. "It's too bad we can never coax her into the field. Her intellect is stunning."

Meredith nodded. Ana was a master code maker and breaker, inventor of most of the special weapons and items they used in the field. But she claimed to prefer working in the office to putting her life in immediate danger. Meredith couldn't imagine finding comfort behind a desk, deciphering information others retrieved. No, she lived for the thrill of the chase, the heat of the hunt, and the slow piecing together of evidence in order to determine a suspect's guilt or innocence.

"There are so many people; it's going to be difficult to determine who our targets are." Meredith sighed.

She glanced over the crowd a second time, pausing to wave at a few friends as she slipped on the mask of favorite widow of the *ton*. Being popular and sought after gave her entry to locations crucial to their cause.

Emily made a subtle gesture at the crowd. "There is Lord Carmichael now. This is the perfect time for you to renew your acquaintance, don't you agree?"

Meredith turned in the direction Emily indicated and sucked in her breath. Indeed, Tristan did stand a stone's throw away, leaning on a pillar. At present he was alone.

She drank in the sight of him. He was as dashing as ever, dark and handsome like the images that sometimes still haunted her dreams. But this was no vision. Tristan's green eyes flitted up from time to time as he looked at the crowd around him or acknowledged a friend. They pierced even from a distance.

He pushed a strand of dark, slightly too long hair away from his eyes before he took a sip of his drink and turned away. She shivered. How could he be even more handsome after all these intervening years?

"Merry?" Emily hissed.

She shook away her distraction. "Yes, this is the perfect time, I agree." She glanced at the grandfather clock beside the ballroom's double doors. "Let's meet on the terrace in three-quarters of an hour."

"That should give me more than enough time

to make my first search. Be careful." Emily slipped into the crowd, disappearing in a wash of colorful gowns and laughing people.

Drawing a deep breath, Meredith refocused on Tristan. He smiled as he said a few words to a passing servant, and her heart lurched as she remembered, once again, his kindness to her as a child. She didn't want to believe he could be a vile betrayer, despite the evidence of his involvement in the plot to steal the painting. But if he was implicated in one aspect of that crime, she had to assume he was aware of its underlying motive.

But there was only one way to determine the truth. With a shaky smile, she headed in his direction.

Her case had officially begun.

Tristan Archer sipped his drink, but the sharp burn of alcohol did nothing to quell his uneasiness. He couldn't recollect a time when he actually enjoyed a party like this. Even long before his life grew complicated, he hadn't taken pleasure in the frivolous gaiety and social backstabbing that flew at him from every corner. He could easily spend a night talking to a hundred people and not recall having an interesting or meaningful conversation with one of them.

He would have ceased hosting such events and cut down on his attendance if he had a choice in the matter. But a man of rank was expected to host soirees like this one. It was one of the things his father had ground into him during unending lectures about how he was expected to behave once he was Marquis. Even now, after all these years, he could still hear his father's voice. It echoed in his ears so often.

Even if he hadn't been doing his best to live up to his familial expectations, he wouldn't have been able to escape social interaction. These parties had also become his link to unappealing, but unfortunately necessary, elements.

With a sigh, he lifted his glance and found himself staring at Meredith Sinclair. His heart began to race like he'd run a league, just as it always had. She was coming toward him, steering through the chattering crowd with the wide smile that was her most charming attribute. He'd seen it countless times over the years in ballrooms and drawing rooms all over London, but the expression hadn't been pointed in his direction for a very long time. That was his own fault, of course. He had done his best to avoid contact with her over the years.

There was no doubt her smile drew people to her. While most women of their circle hid behind fans and handkerchiefs and demure turns of their heads, Meredith put her soul into her smile. It was inappropriately wide and honest and often flashed at times when most in the *ton* wouldn't dare show amusement.

And now she stopped in front of him, her face open and filled with a light he'd almost forgotten existed. He fought to draw breath against a swell of unexpected emotion and desire as he acknowledged her with a wordless nod.

"Good evening, Lord Carmichael," she said with a little curtsey. After he returned an awkward bow of his own, she continued, "You must forgive my impertinence at approaching you without a formal introduction, but I could not wait to congratulate you on a most excellent party."

He blinked. Party? Oh yes, the buzzing annoyance he had all but forgotten. Of course *she* would enjoy it, as she was his polar opposite. Meredith had always been very popular, but even more so since she'd come out of mourning for her late husband.

He remembered his manners with difficulty and returned her smile with a rusty one of his own. He hadn't utilized it for so long that it felt strange. He could only hope he didn't look as ghoulish as he felt.

He cleared his throat. "No apology necessary, my lady. After all, we do know each other, don't we? There is no need for a formal introduction between old friends."

As soon as he said the words, he longed to retrieve them. After such a long time, she probably didn't recall their brief acquaintance as children, or even the one dark night of near tragedy they shared. The muscle in his jaw popped with the long buried memory, but he shook away the anger that still accompanied thoughts of that evening. Those powerful reactions were exactly why he had fought so hard to stay away from Meredith.

Her face softened and her smile faded with memory. "Oh, that was a long time ago, wasn't it? I wasn't sure you remembered. Certainly, we've not spoken since—" She broke off, and for a moment he saw powerful emotions in her eyes. "—since you last came to my aunt and uncle's estate," she finished with a benign smile that wiped away any earlier reaction.

He dipped his chin. Memories of those carefree days were bittersweet. He had no real responsibilities then, fewer expectations. And no secrets. If only he had realized the prison his life would soon become, he might have savored his youth more.

He couldn't help thinking of Meredith in those days. She had seemed so alone as she followed him at every turn. She even played along as his pirate hostage, dead body, and army private. "Of course I remember, Lady Northam. You were a good sport."

She laughed, but despite the melodious beauty of the sound, he saw very little joy deep in her eyes. Beauty, yes. But that had been a constant even when she was a young woman. The last time he visited her cousin before they went to school, he took note of the changes in her. How her eyes had a certain light that intrigued him. Her smile, which she rarely flashed during those days, captivated him.

The night he discovered her alone in a run-down pub, just a year after that final visit, it was clear other men noticed her blossoming beauty as well. She was under attack when he found her, in the arms of a brute who would take whatever she was unwilling to give. Seeing her like that, tears streaming down her face as she pleaded to be released, had incited such a rage in him that he'd nearly killed the bastard who dared touch her. He'd forgotten everything else, every duty he held to his family, every inch of control his father demanded of him . . . and let emotion rule. When he came to his senses later, he knew he could never let himself go like that again. And that meant avoiding Meredith Sinclair. Avoiding the one person who had ever made him feel so powerfully. He had pushed her away, returned to his responsibilities.

It had been damned near impossible to shut her out of his life. Thoughts of her tormented him. He'd even sought her out once more, after she came of age, but she had already married. And that was for the best. It was better to simply see her from a distance at occasional parties, but avoid getting too close.

With a start, he realized she was speaking to him, and attended to her with more focus.

"I am not sure *you* weren't the good sport as a

child, my lord. I think I must have tormented you with my constant questions and presence."

"You were never an annoyance," he said softly.

She blushed, just a tinge of pink that made her creamy skin warm. Is that what she would do if he dared kiss her? The unbidden thought gave him a powerful start. Where had that image come from?

"I'm glad your memory is so poor," she laughed. "I must say, you were my favorite of my cousins' friends. How have you been? I heard of your father's death five years past, and your younger brother's passing more recently. I was sorry to hear of them both."

He nodded, but he was hardly listening. He could only watch her lips form words. Such tempting lips, they were, indeed.

"My lord?" she asked with a tilt of her head.

He started. "I'm sorry, my lady. Thank you for your kind words regarding both my losses."

"I imagine they must have given you an increased responsibility. And at such a young age," she continued.

He winced. She was being kind, but she had no idea how deeply her words cut. They hit close to the bone. In places he tried to ignore, but that always came to the surface.

He had to wonder, as he always did when these subjects came up: What would his life have been like if he didn't have those never-ending responsibilities?

What if he didn't have such ugly secrets?

He shook away the thought as he straightened his shoulders. He *did* have both those things. And that was why it was better to walk away from the woman before him, rather than lament what he could not have, even if Meredith was now a widow and unattached.

With a second bow he said, "It was a pleasure talking to you again, my lady. I hope you enjoy the rest of the party. Excuse me."

Meredith's lips parted in surprise at his sudden dismissal. It took all Tristan's willpower to turn on his heel and walk away. After a few steps, he allowed himself a last glance over his shoulder. Through the crowd, he saw that she remained in the same spot, eyes wide and fists clenched at her sides.

He sighed as he forced himself to look away. Meredith was a beauty, but she was forbidden fruit. Now more than ever, he couldn't let his emotions rule him as they always did when he got near her. He had to set his renewed attraction aside. The matters that currently dominated his life were far too important and dangerous to allow even the most pleasant diversion.

Meredith watched Tristan disappear into the teeming crowd, and was pulled by two opposing reactions to their brief encounter, each as strong as the other.

Though they had only exchanged a few brief words, she had enjoyed their time together enormously. Normally, she found these parties boring, despite her false laughter and popularity.

With Tristan, even their benign chatter stuck out in her mind. There was a connection there. A bond that had little to do with their reminiscence over the past. Beneath the casual words they exchanged lay a deeper emotion.

Under any other circumstances, she would have allowed herself to hope they would meet again. That they could continue their dialogue another night. Her desire to delve deeper into her attraction to the man terrified her.

Especially since her second reaction to their conversation was equally powerful.

Tristan Archer was hiding something. His behavior had been . . . *off* somehow. He smiled and nodded and said the right things, but in his eyes she saw a flash of desperation. A glint of the emotion that almost always existed in culprits she pursued. Men with secrets were rarely happy and could seldom allow themselves to be at ease, even with those they knew and cared for.

The moment she delved into the realm of his private life, Tristan had thrown manners to the wind and hurried away. It could have been grief that caused him to flee her questions, but she hadn't seen sorrow in his eyes at the memories she evoked.

She'd seen grim resolve. A hard gleam that said he had no intention of discussing anything that could remotely relate to his true self or the secrets he so desperately wished to hide from the world.

Her heart sank.

With a harsh sigh, she straightened her shoulders and began to make her way through the crowd. Emily would meet with her in less than a quarter of an hour. In that time, she needed to eliminate any emotion from her face. Her friend would surely see her regrets and fears if they still existed. And Emily was already like a hound on the scent of a fox when it came to the relationship she had once shared with Tristan.

With a set jaw, Meredith took a glass of champagne from the nearest footman and headed for the terrace. She could only hope Emily had uncovered some clues that would disprove Tristan's involvement in the robbery of the painting. And that those clues would tell Meredith if his reaction to her questions was due to some other melancholy, not the guilty conscience of a traitor to King and Country.

As she slipped into the cool air on the terrace, she prayed that would be true.

And knew, deep in her heart, that it was not.

Chapter 3

Before she spoke a word, Emily's face revealed everything Meredith needed to know. In her friend's blue eyes there glittered the excitement of the hunt. For the first time in four years, Meredith dreaded that flash.

"You found the painting," she whispered as she looked away from Emily's excited expression through the ballroom window. In the distance, Tristan stood at the edge of the dance floor speaking to a man she couldn't see clearly in the milling crowd.

"No," Emily said. "I cannot yet be certain, but I don't believe it's here."

Meredith's body clenched with unwanted

happiness before she could control it. Tristan's
guilt hadn't been proven absolutely. She flinched
at the relief that flowed through her. Emotion
had no place here. Not in her profession.

"What are you thinking?" Emily asked quietly.

Meredith broke her gaze away from Tristan's
solemn face to turn to Emily. Her friend's eyes
met hers with unwavering focus.

"What do you mean?" she asked with an innocent smile.

Emily arched an eyebrow and shook her head.
"You are . . . there is something unusual in your
demeanor. Did you have a chance to speak to Lord
Carmichael?"

Meredith nodded as their short conversation
played over in her head, tormenting her with the
questions it stirred. "Yes. We spoke briefly."

"Did he say or do something that troubled
you?"

Meredith paused as she pondered the question.
Obviously Emily saw some of the truth in her behavior, but she wasn't sure how much more she
could share. A fact that bothered her as much as
Tristan's conduct. Why did she want to hide important facts from her partner and best friend?

She cleared her throat. "His words themselves
were above reproach," she said with a shrug. "But
his manner was questionable."

Emily touched her arm. "And that concerns
you."

"More than it should." Meredith sighed as she glanced into the ballroom again. Tristan was now out of her view, but certainly not out of her mind.

Emily hesitated before she said, "You want to believe he's innocent."

Meredith nodded. She would *not* lie.

"Yes, I admit I do. I should enter a case without any decision made about the character of my suspect, but I *know* Tristan." She hesitated. Did she really know him anymore? "I hate to believe he could betray that which I hold dear."

Emily sighed. "Then you shall not like this. As I was coming to meet you, I saw several people from Ana's list."

Meredith winced. Tristan had been keeping company with quite a few of The Society's most dangerous suspects of late. To know that those same villains were inside his home at that very moment went right to her soul, where it sat heavy.

"And?" she asked. "Because by your tone, it's clear there is more."

Emily nodded with a grimace. "Tristan was engaged in intense conversation with Augustine Devlin."

Meredith's eyes widened until they hurt. Devlin. He was the second in command of a dangerous group of traitors. A man with his hands in so many schemes that he reeked of scandal and ruin.

Her agency and others like it had been pursuing

Devlin's set for years, but had never been able to find sufficient evidence against them, or determine the identity of the leader of their gang. But they were very likely responsible for the deaths and injuries of many good men in duty to the King, both in the military and in the ranks of spies.

"You're certain it was Devlin?" she asked, and couldn't control the tremble in her voice.

"I think after pursuing him for so long that I know the bastard," Emily said through gritted teeth. "Carmichael did not look pleased to be met by Devlin, but he didn't seem surprised. And he didn't snub the man."

Meredith's heart sank, but she straightened her shoulders nonetheless.

"Then there is no avoiding the truth I have been loath to believe," she said. "I must move forward with the investigation in earnest. Tristan may truly be involved in plots that endanger our fellow countrymen. If that is so, he and his friends must be stopped before they can transfer whatever information may have been hidden in the painting."

She rubbed her eyes. How had things come to this? If he was guilty, what had turned Tristan from an honorable man who once defended her life to a traitor?

Emily patted her arm in reassurance. "I am sorry, Merry. I know you didn't want that to be true of a friend."

With a shrug of one shoulder, she answered, "If he has done what he is accused of, he is no friend."

Emily nodded, but she didn't seem sure of Meredith's resolve. "I overheard some talk. Apparently the Carmichael family departs London early next week. Tristan and his mother are bound for their country estate, where they host an annual party. The gathering will last a fortnight. Afterward, they often retire to Bath or other outside destinations. I don't know when he'll return to London."

Meredith's lips thinned. "I must ensure that I follow them to Carmichael. If the painting isn't in town, it is likely there. The country may even be where the transfer will take place."

Emily nodded. "I agree. Did Lord Carmichael mention the party to you?"

She shook her head. "No, and I don't think I could approach him again without rousing his mistrust since we haven't spoken for so long. But Lady Carmichael is here and may be my best chance to obtain an invitation."

Wrinkling her brow, Emily looked at her carefully. "Should I attend with you?"

"Attend the party in Carmichael?" Meredith asked. When Emily nodded, she drew back in surprise. "Why in the world would I want that? You'll be needed here to search the house once the family has left town. And Ana will want your assistance to decipher any information I send from the field."

"Yes, yes." Emily waved her off. "But I'm worried about you. I've never seen you so grim when starting a case. Your expression is positively tortured. Perhaps it would be better if I were there to help."

"No!" Meredith turned her back on her friend in preparation to go inside. Emily's astute observations set her on her heels with surprise. Her friend so easily put words to her own doubts and worries about her involvement in this investigation. "Don't be ridiculous. I know my duty."

"But do you know your heart?" Emily called after her.

Meredith froze, clenching her fists at her sides as she turned on her friend. Slowly, she shook her head. "My heart has nothing to do with this, Emily. Nothing at all. Excuse me, I must see Lady Carmichael."

But as she fled the terrace, she couldn't ignore that the heart she claimed was not part of her investigation was pounding so loudly she could scarcely hear over it.

Constance Archer, Dowager Marchioness of Carmichael, was much the same as Meredith remembered her. Tristan had inherited his dark hair and piercing eyes from her ladyship. But unlike her son, Lady Carmichael was quick to laugh and seemed to enjoy the pressing demands the party made on her time and company. As Meredith crossed the room, she saw the Marchioness surrounded by a crowd of young women and their mothers. All seemed enthralled by whatever tale the lady was sharing with them.

Meredith could see why. Lady Carmichael's face was animated as she shared her story. Her eyes were bright and her hands fluttered like a hummingbird to accentuate her words. Unlike Tristan, there was no sense of melancholy about her or weight of secrets around her neck.

Meredith set her shoulders back in preparation. Garnering an invitation to a party from a woman who likely didn't remember her would be a challenge. She couldn't forget herself or what was at stake. If she lost track of Tristan for an entire fortnight, he could rid himself of the painting before she was able to intercept him. Her chance to prove his innocence—or guilt—would be lost.

She slipped through the enraptured group of women carefully, keeping her eyes focused on Tristan's mother as she edged near. Before she could think of a way to interrupt, her ladyship's eyes fell on her and she gasped as her hands came up to cover her cheeks.

"Oh my! Lady Northam, is that you?" she said with a wide, welcoming smile that tugged at Meredith's heart. "My dear, my dear, how long has it been?"

Meredith pushed away unexpected delight that she had been remembered. "Lady Carmichael, how kind of you to recall me. It has been far too many years since I've had the pleasure of your company."

Lady Carmichael nodded with a wide grin, then shook her head. "Oh, I'm forgetting myself. I'm sure you know these ladies."

Meredith looked around the group. To her surprise, she knew them all. She'd met them at many a party and laughed at their frivolity. They were the debutantes of the current Season, with their mamas in tow. In fact, *all* of them were debutantes.

She arched an eyebrow as she looked from the crowd of young women to Lady Carmichael. Her ladyship's daughters were grown and married, so she wouldn't know the young women through their social acquaintance with her children. Why was she surrounded by them at present?

Unless . . .

Tristan. She found him in the crowd with one quick pass of her gaze. He was unmarried. Evidently, Lady Carmichael was playing matchmaker.

A strong and equally surprising blast of jealousy smashed through Meredith before she pushed it aside with violence.

"Of course, my lady." She gave a nod to the women. "Good evening to you all."

The women nodded politely and said their hellos. Meredith refocused her attention on Lady Carmichael. "I am sorry I haven't spoken to you in so long, my lady. I suppose it has been since the death of my husband."

"And that was many years ago, was it not?" Lady Carmichael asked. "It seems we have been two lonely ships. We have passed each other, but never on the same course."

Meredith nodded. "Indeed. How pleased I am that we navigated to each other tonight."

Her ladyship sighed quietly. "I've told Tristan many a time how I wondered about you these past few years."

Meredith wondered how Tristan felt about that statement, since it was he who had desired the distance between them, but she smiled, and it wasn't an expression she had to force. Her memories of Lady Carmichael were all fond. The woman had been nothing but kind to her during her visits. Almost motherly in her care.

"I have fared very well, ma'am," she said.

"I'm glad to hear of it."

Meredith cocked her head. Lady Carmichael was staring at her with an odd expression. Like she was being sized up. And suddenly she realized . . . she was. The lady's matchmaking had apparently stretched to her as well, despite her six and twenty years and status as a widow. The thought was quite shocking, but Meredith recovered herself as well as she could.

Like it or not, she could use Lady Carmichael's desire to see her son married against her . . . and against Tristan. The idea left a sour taste in Merry's mouth, but she swallowed it.

"I enjoyed a very brief but pleasant conversation with your son earlier in the evening," she said with a shy dip of her head that so went against her personality. Even when she was out in Society, she had never been good at flirtatious games. She preferred to be straightforward. Something she could rarely be in her role of spy. "He is looking very well. As handsome as I remembered him to be so many years ago."

Lady Carmichael's eyes lit with interest and she stepped closer, effectively closing out the conversation she'd been having with the other women. She took Meredith's arm and led her away without a backward glance.

"How nice," she said as they took a slow turn around the perimeter of the room, Lady Carmichael deftly guiding them through the crowd. "You two were friendly as children, were you not? He has often spoken of his carefree days at your uncle and aunt's home." A shadow momentarily passed over the older woman's care-lined face. "He laughed easier then."

Meredith tilted her head. So her ladyship sensed the trouble in her son as well. How much did the woman know about his dealings? Lady Carmichael could be a valuable source of information, if only Meredith could get that precious invitation to Carmichael.

"I believe we all laugh easier as children," she said. "There are no responsibilities, no cares to weigh us down. Now that your son is Marquis, I suppose business keeps him from enjoying too many nights such as this one."

Her ladyship shrugged. "Even when he is out in company, he hardly allows a smile to pass over his lips. I try to encourage him with events like this."

Meredith nodded. Tristan had always been serious and quiet. It did not surprise her that he didn't care for such events. Still, she had to prod on. "Perhaps he does not care for London Society, my lady?"

The trick was to slowly guide the conversation toward the country party. Then she could maneuver her way into the invitation. But it was like piloting some great ship. It took care and slow determination.

Lady Carmichael laughed. "He cares little for country Society either," she said. "Even our annual Carmichael gathering brings him little joy."

"Do you have an annual gathering in Carmichael?" Meredith asked with pretended surprise. "How lovely. I hear the countryside there is beautiful. I'm sure it will do him good. I certainly love the country air." She held her breath as she watched Lady Carmichael from the corner of her gaze.

Her ladyship snapped her gaze to Meredith's

face and her green eyes twinkled. "You are welcome to join us, my dear. We depart Monday next. After so long, it would be a pleasure to renew our acquaintance."

Meredith stifled a burst of triumphant glee. She forced an unsure expression as she lifted a gloved fingertip to her lips. "Monday next? I'm not certain. You know I'm involved in the Sisters of the Heart Society for Widows and Orphans."

Lady Carmichael nodded. "You do excellent work. But our gathering is only for a fortnight. I'm sure you could be spared from your good works for such a short time."

She paused as if considering the offer a bit more, then nodded. "I suppose you're right. If I am to censure your son, even in jest, for his overly serious manner, I cannot live my own life by work alone. I think I *shall* join you."

Lady Carmichael clasped her hands. "Excellent! Oh, Tristan will be very pleased."

"What will I be pleased about, Mother?"

Meredith stiffened. Her skills as a spy were obviously in need of tuning. Without her realizing it, Tristan had approached from behind and was standing directly at her elbow. She fought the urge to spin on him with a move of defense and instead subtly maneuvered to face him.

"My lord, you startled me," she said with a breathy laugh . . . *too* breathy for her taste.

"Tristan, Lady Northam has agreed to join our

little party in Carmichael next week," his mother said with a wide smile. "Isn't that wonderful?"

For a brief moment Tristan's reaction to his mother's news was completely unguarded, and Meredith was able to interpret his every emotion. Surprise darkened his eyes, and an anxiety that knotted her stomach with suspicion.

But along with those expressions was something else. Deep within his eyes, in places so dark she almost turned away, she saw desire. Hot and burning out of control. Desire for her.

A desire her traitorous body answered in kind, despite how shocking that reaction was. And how shocking it was to realize Tristan felt that way toward her. She never guessed his attraction, even in the days when she searched endlessly for it. The years when he avoided her in such an obvious fashion had all but killed her hopes that he wanted or even liked her.

She drew a calming breath and forced the reaction away.

"My," Tristan stammered as he turned his gaze on his mother. "That is quite . . . quite . . ."

"Unexpected, I know." Meredith heard the tremor in her voice. "I hope you do not mind the intrusion, my lord."

He hesitated long enough for her to know he *did* mind. But since he could not know of her status as a spy, she wasn't sure why he would want to keep her at a distance. Especially when his attraction for her was so clear, no matter how hard he seemed to be fighting the urge. But then, she had never understood his dismissal of her.

"Of course not, my lady," he answered with a bow in her direction. "I look forward to your presence there. I hope you ladies will excuse me, I see someone motioning to me."

Meredith nodded wordlessly as Lady Carmichael launched into a conversation about how enjoyable the country party would be with her in attendance. Though Meredith felt herself answering the other woman's questions in every way proper, she hardly paid attention. All she could do was watch Tristan's broad shoulders push their way through the crowd, and feel an excitement course low in her belly.

A thrill that had nothing to do with her case.

Chapter 4

∞

Tristan's face was going to freeze with this unnatural smile plastered to it and, as such, he would never be able to go out in public again. He pondered that idea for a moment and found it less unpleasant than he expected. If such a thing occurred, he would never again be forced to attend stuffy parties or suppers that were actually his mother's veiled attempts at matchmaking him with some admiral's daughter.

Of course, this country gathering wasn't veiled at all. His mother had practically told him outright that a gaggle of potential brides would be paraded before him over the next two weeks, and she did hope he would seriously consider pursuing one before the fortnight was over.

Little did she know just how impossible that request was to fulfill. If she did . . . He winced. How disappointed she would be in him if she knew the truth.

He nodded absently as yet another faceless, nameless, giggling debutante paused in his foyer to briefly curtsey while her boisterous mother cackled her hellos. He shuddered as they were escorted to their rooms.

He was actually in hell. Not that he didn't deserve such punishment for a variety of sins.

"Tristan."

He started at his mother's sharp tone. Damn, he'd been caught wool-gathering again. "I apologize, Mother. Just, eh—"

"It's your duty as host to greet your guests, my dear," she said, her voice gentler than he expected after yet another slip in gentlemanly behavior. When he cast his glance in her direction, he saw a flash of worry in her eyes that she tried to cover. "You loathe this."

He let his unnatural smile give way to something more real as he slipped an arm around his mother's shoulders. God, she was so thin. It reminded him of how fragile his world was. As if he needed more reminders.

"I do not loathe it, Mother," he lied. "I realize

it's necessary. Our gathering here is tradition, and it is my duty to uphold that tradition."

Her mouth tightened. "I do wish you took some pleasure in these events. I hate to feel I'm only appealing to your sense of duty rather than your sense of fun."

Fun. How long had it been since he'd indulged in that? Actually, he knew exactly how long. One year, eight months, and thirteen days. Since he received word of his brother's death. If he concentrated, he could determine the hours and minutes as well. He decided not to concentrate, for his chest was already tight with destructive emotion he had no time or spare energy for.

The false smile returned to his lips as he gave her shoulders a squeeze. "Mother, I promise you, I'll do everything in my power to have fun. You will hardly recognize me as I grin my way through supper, chuckle my way through croquet, and dance my way through every ball in the county."

"That sounds rather . . . terrifying, actually." His mother laughed.

He nodded. "It does, doesn't it?"

"Why don't you just promise me you'll try not to frighten away any debutantes with your stern expressions and that you will make a special effort to spend time with Meredith Sinclair."

His stomach twisted at the mention of her name. He cleared his throat as he tried to keep strong emotions at bay and out of his mother's line of sight. If her ladyship found out how much he longed to make more than a special effort with Meredith, there would be no end to it.

"Any particular reason why I am to reserve my special efforts for Lady Northam?" he asked with nonchalant boredom. "That isn't very fair to the others you've invited. Judging from the sparkling looks in their eyes when they met me, the ladies all have hopes—no doubt fostered by you—that they will leave here as the future Lady Carmichael. I would hate to hear gossip that my mother is misrepresenting herself, not to mention me. Really, I am only trying to protect our good family name."

His mother swatted his arm playfully. "I do not recall raising you to be such an unapologetic cad. If there is another lady who attracts your attention, then by all means reserve your special efforts for her. I certainly do not wish to control your heart. I only hope you'll make some effort to listen to it. You've been alone for far too long."

Before he could speak, yet another carriage pulled to a stop at the circular drive in front of the main entryway. The footman clamored down and opened the door for its inhabitant. A gloved hand emerged, followed by a flash of trim, feminine ankle.

And then the world stopped. Froze on its very axis as Meredith Sinclair stepped from her carriage. Despite himself, Tristan caught his breath.

She seemed to grow lovelier each time he saw her. Today her rich, dark hair had been bound up for travel and tucked beneath a robin's egg blue bonnet, but a few wild strands had broken loose to tangle around her flushed cheeks. Her eyes sparkled with life and vitality as they darted swiftly around the yard and the house, as if she were memorizing each detail. Finally, her gaze settled through the open door and on him. If he thought his heart rate quickened by her arrival, it was nothing compared to the leap he experienced when she smiled gently and moved forward with the grace of a soaring dove.

"Reserve a little time for Lady Northam because you light up whenever you see her," his mother murmured close to his ear. "And I want to see that expression on your face as often as possible. It has been too long since your happiness has been a priority."

Tristan shook away his reaction and managed to close his suddenly gaping mouth. "You are letting some silly romantic notions in those books you read make you forget yourself, Mother," he muttered as he watched Meredith approach the open foyer door. "My expression does not change for Lady Northam and my happiness is of no consequence."

Before his mother could voice the protest he saw trembling on her lips, Meredith saved him.

With a wide smile, she came into the foyer and bobbed out a curtsey.

"Good afternoon, my lord, my lady," she said.

His mother focused her attention away from him, though her forced smile let him know she was not finished with this topic. As she greeted Meredith, he took the opportunity to again examine this last guest.

Now that Meredith stood mere feet away, he caught the faint whiff of her perfume. An intoxicating mixture of lilac and exotic spice. Sensual and forbidden, just like she was.

Damn, but she was an unwanted distraction. Well, not unwanted. She was very wanted. And that was why he wished she wasn't here! He was so close to his goal, so close to ending the pursuits that had plagued him for nearly two years. And he already knew just what her presence could do to him. All his calculated moves and sacrifices would be for nothing if he lost control now.

His mother's voice pierced the fog of his improper thoughts. "Lady Northam, I'm so pleased you've arrived. Was your journey from London bearable?"

Meredith nodded. "I was lucky enough to find dry, good roads the entire way. Though I did encounter a few rough moments when one of my horses threw a shoe. Still, it was fixed quickly enough and without any trouble. It is the cause for my delay, though. I hope I haven't held up your party."

Tristan's mother shook her head. "No, my dear. You are the last to arrive, but only on the very heels of the others. You didn't cause us any trouble at all, did she, Tristan?"

Tristan shook his head. He'd been so focused on watching Meredith's lush mouth form words that he hadn't been fully aware of himself. Now he was being included in a conversation he had barely attended to. What had they been saying? Oh yes, Meredith's late arrival.

"No, Mother. No trouble." He glanced at Meredith, to find her staring back at him. For a moment he thought he saw strong emotions buried in the dark blue of her eyes. Emotions that had no place in such a casual acquaintance or conversation. Anger, fear . . . desire. Deep and dangerous desire that called forth an answering response in his blood.

He looked away. His mother lamented the fact, but this was exactly why he had been alone for so long. These needs, these wants, they were a distraction he could ill afford.

Meredith cocked her head. "Is everything well, my lord? You are very pale."

His mother's gaze snapped to his face at that remark and the lines around her mouth deepened with concern. A blast of guilt rushed through his blood as he straightened up.

"I believe you are mistaken, Lady Northam," he

forced out through clenched teeth. "I am in perfect health."

"Hmm."

She looked less than convinced. By the way her eyes slipped up and down his form, he had the unpleasant sensation that he was being interrogated. Of course that was ridiculous. She was merely making an observation.

"I am glad to be wrong, my lord," she said with a shrug. "For I've heard this party promises to be quite the event."

He nodded wordlessly. God, yes, the annual soiree was nothing but spectacular. Only this year there was a deeper purpose to it. He glanced at his mother, who was beaming back and forth at the two of them. It was so hard to see her so hopeful for something he couldn't deliver, no matter how much it called to him with a siren's undeniable song.

With a short bow, he interrupted the remainder of Meredith's comments. "I'm sorry, my lady, but as you say, this party is quite the event, and there are many details to be attended to. Now that you've arrived, I am sure my mother will ensure you're settled comfortably. I shall see you tonight at supper."

His mother's mouth dropped open at his flagrant disregard for manners. Meredith's eyebrows shot up and she stared at him as he backed away with only a final nod.

As he hurried down the hallway, he shook his head. It was difficult to be in polite company when he had such an ugly secret festering inside him. To pretend to be a gentleman was growing more tiresome by the day. He could only hope to end the charade quickly. It was the only way he could reclaim the life he once knew. The life taken at the same moment as his brother's final breath.

Meredith stared at the place where Tristan stood not a moment before. Her heart pounded. His eyes had such a wild desperation to them. The same flit of guilt and struggle she had seen at the party in London a few days before. It was evident he was battling inner demons, but was it the terrible betrayal she had been sent to prove that caused his eyes to be so empty? Or something else?

She didn't know. She didn't know anything except that she longed to chase after his retreating form and beg him to take her into his confidence. She wanted to comfort him. Help him.

The last thing she wanted to do was destroy him. Even though that was the inevitable if the accusations against him were proven true.

"I am sorry."

She started when Lady Carmichael laid a gentle hand on her forearm. "I beg your pardon?"

Lady Carmichael smiled sadly. "My son's behavior was impolite. I'm sorry he could not stay with us until you were ready to retire to your rooms."

Meredith shook her head, and her kindness was not contrived as she placed her own hand over Lady Carmichael's trembling one. No matter what, this woman had no idea of the potential heartache Meredith was there to uncover. Lady Carmichael only wanted her son to be happy, like any good mother would. Meredith was stung as she examined the other woman's face and thought of her own mother, long dead and unable to protect and console her. She hadn't experienced much maternal love since then. Even now she hardly saw her aunt and uncle, and was rarely included in their family gathering, despite having lived with them for nearly ten years.

"You needn't worry yourself, my lady," Meredith reassured her gently. "I'm sure Lord Carmichael has much on his mind with the country party and . . . and other things. Certainly I don't require his presence if he isn't able to share it."

Lady Carmichael's face relaxed as she gave Meredith's arm a squeeze. "Thank you. The other guests are in their rooms, but perhaps you'd like a moment to stretch your legs after the long journey. Would you take a turn with me around the garden?"

Meredith drew back. Her ladyship was making a special effort to befriend her, with no agenda except perhaps her blatantly obvious matchmaking attempts. To take the offer would give her the chance to probe deeper into Tristan's activities, as well as garner information about the estate and any other guests who could play into her inquiry.

Under normal circumstances, she would have jumped at the opportunity this gave her. But looking into Lady Carmichael's gentle green eyes, the same ones her son had inherited, a pang of guilty conscience made her hesitate.

"Unless, of course, you're too tired," Lady Carmichael said with a slight step away.

Meredith drew up straighter. This was ridiculous. She wasn't here to make lifelong friends or explore hidden desires. She was here to solve a case. She had to control these ridiculous emotions. She couldn't let anything interfere with her objectives.

"I would love a stroll with you, my lady. I have long heard stories about the exquisite gardens here."

With a smile, Lady Carmichael took her arm and led her through the house and out the garden doors. They made their way down a charming path, lined with well-trimmed shrubberies, until they reached a magnificent garden. Meredith momentarily forgot her plans as she gazed over the tended rows of greenery and bright, welcoming flowers.

"It's beautiful," she said on a sigh as she covered her heart with her hands.

Lady Carmichael beamed with pride. "Our family has always taken pride in the garden," she admitted. "It was first tamed into the general shape you see by Tristan's great-great-grandfather, and his sons and grandsons all took a hand in its development over the years."

Meredith paused in surprise. "Even Lord Carmichael, himself?"

Lady Carmichael nodded immediately. "Oh yes. Tristan ordered the planting of those lilacs that line the north wall there over a year ago." Her smile faded a little. "In memory of his brother, Edmund."

Meredith looked at the flowering bushes thoughtfully. Somehow she had never taken Tristan to be a lover of flowers. Everything she knew personally and everything in the files she'd read about him made him out to be a distant man. Certainly someone who loved his garden didn't fit that profile.

But then . . . very little did when she actually met him face-to-face.

"Your expression is very harsh," Lady Carmichael said with a furrowed brow. "I hope you aren't judging my son for his earlier behavior."

Meredith glanced at the other woman in surprise, but shook her head. She didn't add any comment to her silent denial. She had learned long ago that often it was better to let others do the talking. Without realizing it, they often gave away vital facts when met with silent attention.

Constance sighed. "Some say Tristan is arrogant. Proud, even. But that isn't true. The last few years have changed him."

Meredith drew in a short breath of anticipation. "I admit I have seen some changes in him myself," she said with hesitation. Garnering evidence was a fine art. It had to be undertaken slowly and with careful precision.

Lady Carmichael looked out over the garden with a faraway look that didn't take training to decipher. It was clear she was thinking about all the beloved men in her life who had tended this garden and were now gone. And about her one remaining son.

"I sometimes feel Tristan would have done better to be an irresponsible youth for a few years, as his brother took every opportunity to be. But life and his father didn't allow for that. My husband was a good man and loved all of our children deeply, but he had such high expectations for Tristan. And he demanded excellence and control from him his whole life."

Meredith nodded, drinking in the information she was being given.

"Sometimes I fear Tristan took his father's words too much to heart." Lady Carmichael sighed. "He was so young when my husband died. Tristan became Marquis over a large estate with many tenants who depended on him. And surrogate father for his two youngest siblings."

Meredith thought of what she knew about that part of Tristan's past. He had taken over his father's holdings and position when his youngest sister, Celeste, who had just been married very well the last Season, and his brother Edmund were still living at home. She could well imagine how difficult such a task must have been.

Was that why he'd become involved in such twisted dealings? To sow some kind of long wild oats?

No, that didn't make sense. If Tristan wanted to go wild, there were far better ways than to betray his country. Something else must have pushed him toward a life of criminal leanings.

With a glance for Lady Carmichael, she said, "Certainly the death of a parent would alter any man. Even harden him."

Constance sighed with a shake of her head. "No, not Tristan. Though I worried about his loss of youthful pastimes, he never seemed to mourn them. In fact, he thrived as Marquis. The deepest changes in him are more recent. Since the death of my youngest son." Her breath caught and she removed a lacy handkerchief from the pocket of her pelisse to dab at the tears that suddenly glimmered around the edges of her eyes.

Meredith nodded sympathetically while her mind searched for more missing facts. Edmund Archer was seven years Tristan's junior. He'd been killed in military service. If Constance was correct,

Tristan's involvement in dangerous activities might be related to his brother's death. She would need more information from London before she could move forward.

Meredith slipped a hand onto Lady Carmichael's arm and squeezed gently. "I'm so very sorry for your family's grief."

The other woman smiled, but the sadness stayed in her expression. "Thank you. The loss was difficult for us all, but Tristan took it hardest. His anger bubbled forward and he's never been the same." Her gaze slipped to Meredith. "I hope he'll settle down, take a wife. Perhaps that would give him his smile back."

At the pointed focus of the other woman's stare, hot blood rushed to Meredith's cheeks. She had become so accustomed to a covert world, such directness was uncomfortable now.

Lady Carmichael glanced away, giving Meredith a welcome reprieve from the statement she didn't know how to properly address.

"It probably seems odd to you that I've told you so much about our family's trials."

Meredith shrugged one shoulder, even though she agreed with the assessment. She had hoped for, rather than expected, such candor.

"I only give you these details because I know you experienced the same kind of loss when your parents died." Lady Carmichael smiled. "You were once quite fond of my son, were you not?"

Meredith sucked in a harsh breath. "Y-Yes, my lady. I suppose you could call us childhood playmates."

Lady Carmichael nodded. "Perhaps a renewal of that friendship would do him some good." The lady patted her hand. "I'm sure you are tired and wish to rest before supper. Shall we go back inside?"

Meredith nodded weakly as relief rushed through her. Of course, the spy in her wanted to be disappointed that the conversation had ended. Lady Carmichael was a font of information about Tristan and had opened her eyes to several possible motives for his turning to underground criminals. But the woman in her had a different reaction. The conversation, with its topics of family loss and old feelings, long forgotten, awoke emotions in her she did not wish to face.

As they strolled toward the house, Meredith cast a side glance at Lady Carmichael. Her thoughts drifted to long ago summers when Constance patted her on the head or gave her a kind smile or word. As a lonely girl, she devoured those moments like sweets. Years later, Constance was still everything she remembered. A lovely, compassionate woman.

Guilt stabbed her. She was using the other woman's kindness against her and her beloved son. Even worse, she was keenly aware that this woman was considering her as a possible mate for Tristan.

All while she had no idea what a blackguard he might be.

The entire situation made Meredith's head ache.

Lady Carmichael smiled as they entered the house. "Simpson will show you to your room. Please don't hesitate to ring if you need anything at all." She squeezed Meredith's arm gently. "I'm very glad you're here, my dear. I shall see you at supper."

"Thank you, my lady," Meredith stammered. "I look forward to it."

But she didn't. As she followed the footman up the stairs and down a long hallway to her chamber, all she could focus on was the bloody task at hand. And how many lives it would destroy if she found the evidence she sought.

She nodded to the man as he bowed away, leaving her alone in a lavish room she hardly took the time to examine. As her lady's maid came forward to help her remove her pelisse and bonnet, she sighed. Back to work.

First, she had to write home and obtain more information about Edmund Archer's tragic death. Then she had to get a grasp on her senses and concentrate on her case, not the ramifications her investigation would have on this broken family . . . or the man who led it.

Chapter 5

$\underset{\sim}{\text{—O©—}}$

"Tristan, did you hear me?"

Tristan glanced up at his man of affairs, Philip Barclay, with a start. "What? Yes, of course."

His old friend quirked an eyebrow. "Really? Because I just told you we would be dyeing the sheep housed in the southern fields a vibrant blue and you agreed."

Tristan pursed his lips. "Very well, I was *not* attending. No blue sheep."

Philip chuckled as he closed his ledger, but when Tristan didn't join in the laughter, his friend's face lengthened with concern.

"The situation is weighing on you."

Philip's words were a statement, not a question. Tristan turned away. There were very few people in this world that he trusted completely, but the man in his office was one of them.

Philip was the youngest son of a wealthy baronet. The two boys had attended Cambridge together and become best of friends during their wild years of school pranks and polo matches. But Philip's fortunes changed when his father died. After Tristan inherited the title of Marquis, he hadn't hesitated to offer his old friend the position of his closest advisor and confidant.

Philip had never failed him. And he was the only one who knew the truth now.

"Perhaps it's the lovely Lady Northam who makes you so reflective?"

Tristan glanced at his friend. Philip stared back evenly, arms folded. "I don't know what you're talking about," Tristan lied.

Philip's eyes widened. "Hmmm, you mentioned her ladyship at least three times since your mother invited her to the party. For most men, that wouldn't seem out of the ordinary, but since you haven't mentioned any woman in your acquaintance *once* in the last two years, let alone three times, it stood out in my mind."

Tristan rose from his chair and paced away. There were few subjects he wouldn't broach with his friend. Surprisingly, he found Meredith was one of them. If he stated his attraction out loud, he might lose the wire-thin control he had over the desire that made itself known whenever she was within a touch's distance. Doing that could open a Pandora's box he might not be able to close.

"What does this conversation have to do with my business?" he asked quietly.

Philip shrugged. "Absolutely nothing, but then again, my ledger is closed. I'm not asking you as your man of affairs, I'm asking you as a friend."

Tristan gripped a fist at his side, but didn't answer.

"I don't have to tell you that involving yourself with a woman could be a dangerous distraction at present. Especially with Augustine Devlin here, watching your every move."

Tristan winced. "You think I'm not aware of that? Of course Meredith—" He broke off with a curse. He'd slipped and used her first name. That familiarity destroyed any chance he had of denying interest in her. "Of course Lady Northam could be a distraction. And if I were to pursue her, I'd risk putting her in danger, as well as threaten my plan. *I'm* the one with everything to lose. I don't require your interference or reminders on that score."

Immediately, Tristan wished he could take back the words and the emotions laced in them. Not only did they reveal too much, but they were unfair. Philip was only reminding him of facts he too often forgot when he caught the sensual whiff of Meredith's perfumed skin or felt the tingling pleasure that accompanied her laughter.

"My apologies," Philip said softly. "I didn't realize the subject was such a sensitive one. I know how difficult this is for you, but I wasn't trying to interfere."

Tristan winced as he waved away his friend's concern. The subject wasn't one he wanted to pursue. "Has Devlin arrived?"

Philip nodded once, and it seemed he was willing to let the subject of Meredith go . . . at least for the time being, though Tristan was aware his friend had marked the topic. He was sure it would come up a second time. He would have to be more prepared with answers when it did.

"Devlin arrived nearly an hour ago. I made sure he was situated in a room exceeding the demands of a man of his station. He was pleased by that." Philip frowned. "I worry about this, Carmichael."

With a sigh, Tristan paced to the sideboard to prepare himself a drink. He swirled the sherry in his tumbler. "So you've told me, numerous times. But I have no other choice. I need the information Devlin can provide and he desires the item I procured. This party is the best place to make an exchange without arousing suspicion like that we encountered in London." He took a sip of his drink. "My mother isn't aware of anything out of the ordinary, is she?"

Philip shook his head. "Devlin's name was quietly added to the roster of guests with the notation that he is a business associate. Lady Carmichael hasn't inquired about his presence."

Tristan let out a sigh of relief. "I doubt she'll ask anything if she hasn't done so already. Good. I don't want her involved in this beastly business."

He shuddered to think what her reaction would be if she discovered the truth. It would break her heart to know what lengths he'd gone to. She certainly wouldn't be pleased by what he'd done, even if she understood his reasons.

"Be careful of Devlin, Carmichael," Philip said with a frown. "He's a treacherous bastard in more ways than one. If you push him too far—"

Tristan shook his head to interrupt his friend. "I know. But if I want to end this, I must follow the path I laid out over a year ago. The only way to best Devlin is to let him believe he has the upper hand."

"There are always other ways, Tristan," Philip said as he quietly made for the door.

Tristan watched his friend's retreating back. When the door closed behind Philip, he sighed.

"Not this time."

Meredith's eyes darted around the table as she took in each person's face and memorized their every word and gesture for analysis later. It was part of her assignment, yes, but also a good way to ease her distraction whenever she glanced to her left. Tristan sat at the head of the large table, overseeing the first dinner party of the gathering with a less than pleased expression.

She turned away from the stunning appeal of his angular face and found herself locking eyes with Lady Carmichael. Constance tipped her glass slightly in acknowledgment and Meredith forced a smile. Under any other circumstances, she would have laughed at the lady's blatant designs to have her as a daughter-in-law, but her case kept her from enjoying Constance's sweet attempts. Having the lady's attention only made Meredith's job all the more difficult.

Not to mention that it made her feel like the worst heel in England.

"Augustine Devlin. I believe he has some business with Lord Carmichael."

A whispered comment from a gentleman to a lady at Meredith's right brought her from her reverie. With reluctance, she let her gaze fall on the man in question. Devlin was seated about halfway down the table on the opposite side. He was dressed impeccably, as usual. His blond hair and stunning gray eyes drew attention to him wherever he went. But his mere presence was damning evidence against Tristan.

The faction Devlin belonged to had long been suspected of weapons smuggling, passing pertinent information to enemies in France and in

America, as well as having some part in several attacks on high-ranking political figures. But no agency, neither hers nor the male equivalent in the War Department, had ever come close to proving those allegations. So the man walked free, allowed to continue whatever fiendish plots he was concocting at present.

She looked at Tristan again. Those plots might involve him. The idea gave her an unpleasant shiver.

Devlin glanced down the table toward her, then past her. He examined their host carefully before a small smile turned his lips. Triumphant and utterly foul, despite residing on one of the most handsome faces in England. Devlin's almost angelic good looks were part of his arsenal. He could disarm nearly anyone with a smile. Those who he couldn't, he found other ways to dispose of.

"Lady Northam, you have some sort of charity society, do you not?"

Meredith started. She'd been so focused on Devlin and her wandering thoughts about Tristan, she wasn't prepared for conversation. She blinked at the young lady seated across from her as she searched for a name to match the pretty, but not particularly friendly, face.

"Uh, yes, that's correct," she stammered.

Georgina Featherton, wasn't that it? A second-year debutante. And by the way she looked at Tristan, a second-year debutante with an eye toward becoming a marchioness. The thought made Meredith's stomach tighten even though she hadn't witnessed him make any special effort toward Georgina.

"Something about widows or orphans or some such thing?" the woman continued, saying each word as if it were dirty.

Meredith nodded. "Yes, The Sisters of the Heart Society for Widows and Orphans. It's a cause close to my heart, as I lost my parents when I was young and my husband just a few years ago."

As the members of <u>the party</u> who were within earshot murmured their sympathies, Georgina's eyes narrowed. "You do not look like you need the charity of others, my lady."

A woman three seats down, apparently Georgina's mother, if the matching blonde hair and widening blue eyes were any indication, gaped, but she couldn't force her daughter to meet her stare.

Meredith arched a brow. Was this young woman *challenging* her? She had all but forgotten the ridiculous pettiness sometimes associated with courting.

"The Society does not raise funds for women of my station, my dear," she said with just the lightest touch of condescension. "But for those far less fortunate who find themselves in such a tragic circumstance."

Again those within earshot nodded their approval, but the young lady didn't seem content to finish with her strange interrogation. "Certainly those less fortunate could find some comfort in the church poor boxes. Why in the world would a lady wish to lower herself so?"

Tristan's eyes flashed up. Meredith was surprised by how much fire lit within the normally cool green. She hadn't thought he was even listening to the conversation, yet now his jaw twitched and his gaze pierced Lady Georgina with a coldness Meredith never wished to see focused on herself.

"Lady Northam uses her position to host events the church could never dream to hold. Like the ball a fortnight ago. Certainly you do not disapprove of that, do you? You told me you enjoyed it, did you not?" he snapped, loud enough that several heads pivoted.

The young lady's cheeks flushed dark with color. "Y-Yes, I did," she finally managed to stammer. "I had forgotten."

Tristan stared at the girl for a long moment, then his gaze flitted to Meredith and held there. Her heart stirred with unexpected flutterings. He was defending her, in public. Over something important to her. Never mind that she hadn't required him to "save" her from Lady Georgina.

Lady Carmichael cleared her throat and rose with a smile. Her expression didn't reflect the uncomfortable silence that filled the room. "Perhaps the ladies would join me in the Rose Room for tea while the gentlemen retire for their port?"

The murmurs of the crowd returned as they rose from their seats and began to split apart. Tristan got to his feet more slowly than the rest, his gaze lingering on Meredith's face as the others faded away. Her stomach flipped as she realized he intended to escort her. Which meant touching him.

Which was very, very bad.

"I'm sorry," he said as he offered his arm. "I should not have been so harsh, I hope I didn't embarrass you."

She smiled as she slipped her hand into the crook of his elbow. At even this slight contact, her heart began to pound. His masculine scent, clean and spicy, filled her senses, and her knees went weak. Damn, but the man continued to affect her. She cursed herself as she fought for control.

"Embarrass me?" she managed to say lightly. "No. It was very gallant of you to ride to my rescue. Though you may have to apologize to the debutante. She looks as though she may never recover."

Tristan winced as he watched the younger woman walk down the hallway ahead of them. She was on the arm of a handsome army officer and looked anything but devastated. In fact, it seemed she'd forgotten all about the incident.

"It will only bolster my current reputation of

being a proud, arrogant bastard," he sighed. "No harm done to anyone."

She frowned. "I've never heard such rumors."

"Then you do not listen, my lady."

He smiled as he released her arm. Meredith knew she should walk away, but somehow she couldn't leave things as they were. She struggled for some way to chase the hardness from his eyes, to comfort him.

Bringing herself up sharp, she barely managed to hold back a gasp. *Comfort* him? What in God's name had come over her?

With a frown, she said, "Perhaps that is true. Until later, my lord."

"Until later, Meredith."

He turned and walked away. It was only when he was no longer in sight that she realized he had called her by her given name. And that the sound of it sent her heart pounding with more excitement than she had felt in an age.

Tristan hadn't sipped a drop of his port, though a few of his counterparts were already finishing their second snifter. He couldn't afford to lose himself in the warmth of an alcohol haze. Not with Augustine Devlin watching him from across the room, ever analyzing, ever judging whether Tristan met his standards. He had made all the correct moves over the last year. Now it was imperative to be very careful.

"Gentlemen, I believe it may be time to rejoin the ladies," he said without taking his eyes off Devlin.

The men in the room muttered their agreement, some more willingly than others. Slowly, they set down their glasses, put out their cigars, and moved toward the sitting room where the women were gathered. None of them seemed to notice that their host didn't stir to follow, nor did Devlin.

The two continued to stare at each other as the last man disappeared through the door. Tristan carefully regulated his breathing and didn't allow emotion to move to his face.

Finally, Devlin pushed away from the sideboard where he was leaning and started across the room. He opened his mouth, but before he could get any words past his lips, the sound of a woman clearing her throat from the door interrupted them.

Tristan broke eye contact with Devlin to refocus on the door. His heart lodged in his throat as Meredith took a few steps inside. She looked from one man to the other with concern and a brief flash of what he thought was fearful recognition when her gaze fell on Devlin. Then it was gone, but of course it never could have existed. She probably only knew the bastard in passing. A lady would have no idea of the wickedness that was central to Augustine Devlin's life.

Which meant Meredith had no idea of the dangerous lion's den she was entering.

"There you are," she said with a quick smile for Tristan. "The ladies were beginning to despair of your return."

For an all too brief moment Tristan forgot about Devlin and the perilous tightrope he was walking. All he could see was Meredith. She brought light into the room, glorious light. It was in her hair, under her skin, in her smile. He was warmed by it, and yet she was a room away. If he touched her . . .

"Why don't you introduce me to your charming friend?" Devlin shattered Tristan's pleasant daydream with just a few words. "I have seen her at several events, but never had the pleasure of meeting her properly."

Sudden, fierce protectiveness clenched Tristan's chest. As with his mother, he had no desire to bring Meredith into the dark hole he'd dug for himself. He didn't want Devlin to be aware of her at all. She was a variable he hadn't included in his strategy.

"Lady Northam, may I present Mr. Augustine Devlin," he said with uncontrollable stiffness in his voice. "He is an—an associate of mine."

Meredith's smile seemed to falter slightly, but then she stepped forward, hand outstretched. "It's very nice to make your acquaintance, Mr. Devlin."

Devlin stepped closer and took her hand. Raising it to his lips, he pressed a kiss against the top and gave her a dashing smile. "I'm very pleased to finally know the most popular lady in society."

She gave a little laugh that grated on Tristan's ears. Without thinking, he stepped between the two and offered his arm to her.

"Shall we join the others, then?" he asked.

Meredith did not take his arm as expected. Instead she backed toward the sidebar.

"Would you mind terribly if I had a little port first?" She glanced at Augustine with a smile. "It isn't quite ladylike, but since my husband's death, I've developed a liking for it. He left a good deal behind, and I took to having a glass after supper. Now it's a habit I cannot seem to break myself of."

Tristan gritted his teeth. Why was she being so damned friendly and charming? It didn't matter that those qualities were part of her personality, he didn't like her making herself so appealing to a man who could destroy her if he wished.

Devlin laughed. "I shall never reveal your unusual habit, I swear it on my life."

Meredith didn't wait for Tristan to agree or disagree with her request as she turned to the half-empty bottle of port and poured herself a small bit. She sipped it with an appraising look at the two men.

"You said you and Mr. Devlin were associates, did you not, my lord?"

Tristan's chest clenched. He wanted, no, he *needed* to remove Meredith from Devlin's presence. It was clear the other man was gaining interest in her, but he couldn't jeopardize the relationship he'd built with Devlin.

"My lord?" she repeated.

He jerked out a nod. "Y-Yes."

"What business do you share?"

He snapped his gaze to hers, and she seemed surprised by the suddenness of the act. She raised a hand to her breast. "I'm always looking for new opportunities to invest my inheritance."

Tristan glanced at Devlin, only to find him staring back with twinkling eyes and a quirked brow. Obviously the bastard found this situation amusing. Hatred burned in Tristan's chest, and the constant anger that boiled just below his purposefully cool exterior burned even hotter, stoked, yet again, by Meredith.

"His lordship and I share a few endeavors, my lady. Trade. Shipping." Devlin smiled thinly. "Art."

She nodded. "It all sounds very intriguing. Perhaps when we return to London you can call on my man of affairs and discuss some of these ventures with us."

Tristan took a step forward. "We should return to the others," he said, louder than he had intended. Both Meredith and Devlin stared at him in surprise. He tempered his tone. "I'm sure we're missed. Devlin, why don't you go ahead? Lady Northam can finish her port and I'll escort her back."

Devlin smiled broadly, ever amused, and gave

Meredith a low bow. "I look forward to speaking to you again, my lady."

"As do I," she said with a nod.

Tristan followed behind as Devlin left the room. He shut the door behind the other man, barely resisting the urge to slam it.

When he turned back, Meredith was staring at him with wide eyes. She set her port on the closest table and said, "My lord, the door. We should not—"

He ignored her protest to propriety and crossed the room in a few long paces. She seemed surprised by his sudden advance and took a step back, but the sideboard was directly behind her and he pinned her in. Her lips parted, but deep within her eyes, hidden behind the surprise, a flicker of desire lit there. Tristan nearly forgot himself as he watched that flicker flame higher.

"My lord," she whispered.

He shook his head. "Meredith, Augustine Devlin is not a man you want to involve yourself with."

Her brow wrinkled. "But you said he was an associate of yours. Surely if you trust him in business—"

"No!" He shook his head violently. "Believe me, you do not want him interested in you. You don't want him involved in your money or your life."

"I don't understand. If you believe him to be untrustworthy, why do you work with him?"

He hesitated. He had a sudden, powerful urge to explain everything to her. To tell her secrets he'd kept from everyone important to him for nearly two years.

He shook that desire off. It would only endanger her and expose his plans. It could be disastrous.

"Tristan," she whispered, and the sound of his given name from her mouth shocked and thrilled him. How he wanted to make her cry out his name. Scream his name. "Are you in some kind of trouble?"

He stared at her, face upturned and eyes filled with concern and hope. Hope for him. It had been so long since he felt hope himself, he almost didn't recognize it.

"I could help you." Her voice broke. "If you only tell me what troubles you."

She was so close he could feel the warmth of her body. His nostrils were filled with the gentle scent of her skin. Every sense was bombarded by her presence and the desire that assault created was overwhelming.

With a trembling hand, he cupped her cheek. She seemed as surprised by the action as he was, but did not pull away. She stared up at him, dewy eyes alive with the desire that had been a mere flicker a few moments earlier. Tristan could no longer deny himself. He dipped his head and claimed her mouth.

* * *

Meredith parted her lips and melted into Tristan's kiss. He pressed her so close that it almost seemed they were one body, one shared, throbbing heartbeat that echoed in her head. She could do nothing but clutch his arms, cling to him as she was bombarded by sensations.

He tasted faintly of port, with a hint of mint in the background. His mouth was so hot against her skin that she wouldn't have been surprised if she were branded by his touch. Her lips certainly felt burned as his tongue swiped over them, filled her and demanded that she respond to every stroke.

She obeyed his silent order more than willingly, no matter how hard her rational mind tried to rein her in, tried to remind her that kissing a suspect was against protocol and common sense. She couldn't hear that inner voice over the roar of desire coursing through her blood. Control spiraled away, lost in a sea of need.

Certainly, she had been kissed before, but never like this. This was possession, claiming, and she wanted nothing more than to surrender.

Surrender to a potential traitor.

That sharp, shocking thought drove her from him. She shrugged out of his embrace and stepped back as she raised one trembling hand to her swollen, hot mouth. With effort, she forced herself to look into his eyes. He stared back evenly, his gaze smoldering green fire. There was no doubt he wanted her back in his arms as much as she wanted to be there.

If she hadn't been investigating him, she would have given in to that desire. But she was.

She had no choice but to gather her quaking emotions. Forget how much she was affected by his touch and use his reactions against him. Use the kiss to get more information. Now was the perfect time to demand facts about his relationship with Augustine Devlin, to press him about the painting or his reasons for being involved in such questionable activities.

Instead, her only desire was to throw herself back into his arms. Worse yet, let him lead her even further. Past mere kisses, past his warm embrace, all the way to his bed. Consequences to her assignment and sanity be damned.

"Meredith," he whispered. Even at such close distance, his voice barely carried as he awaited her response.

One she seemed incapable of making when she was still shaking from his kiss. She could hardly force herself to remember her case, let alone press it at this opportune moment.

"I—I must go," she stammered as she turned her back to him and went for the door. "I find myself suddenly tired. Good evening, my lord."

Without waiting for an answer, she fled the room and up the backstairs to the guest chambers. Her unseeing eyes somehow led her to her room where she slammed the door and leaned back. Her breath came in heaving gasps and her body trembled as she relived that forbidden kiss over and over again.

Covering her face, she crossed the room to sit beside the roaring fire. Its heat was nothing compared to the one Tristan sparked low in her belly. That flame had nothing to do with her investigation either. The kiss had been purely personal.

Which was exactly why she could never let it happen again. No matter how useful a private relationship with her target could be. And no matter how much she longed for just one more stolen moment in his arms.

Chapter 6

Meredith smoothed her gown as she took one last glance in the mirror. She smiled at her lady's maid.

"Thank you, Rebecca, that's lovely."

The girl bobbed out a curtsey before she left Meredith with only her troubled thoughts. A night's distance from Tristan's shocking, searing kiss was hardly enough to forget, but it had helped considerably. It *couldn't* have been as fantastic as she remembered. Her reaction had been part girlish surrender to a man she once had a *tendre* for and part surprise that things had progressed so far.

At least, that was what she told herself during the long, sleepless night.

But today was a new day. The case she was investigating would be her only focus from now on. Not kissing and not guilt. Only the case.

She sighed with satisfaction. Already an encoded letter was on its way to Emily and Ana, filled with questions about Edmund Archer's death and inquiries on the specifics of any legitimate business Tristan had with Augustine Devlin. Her friends would also compose a field report on her behalf for Charlie and Lady M.

She frowned as she turned from her mirror and slowly made her way toward the dining room. The party would be having a late breakfast before the day's events. Her mind turned on Tristan's reaction to her conversation with Devlin. He'd warned her off the man who was behind so many dark and dangerous schemes, so he knew the threat Devlin posed. Yet he continued to work with, and perhaps *for* the man. Even if he took no pleasure in the association, there was a deeper connection than merely business.

And she couldn't ignore Devlin's wry comment about the two of them being involved in "art" together.

"Art theft, more likely," she muttered before she put on a false smile and strolled into the dining room.

"Ah, Lady Northam." One of the women motioned her over to the breakfast nook where the others were gathering steaming plates of food and milling about for morning gossip and flirtation.

Meredith's heart gave a queer ache. For them, it was so easy. There was nothing keeping any of these couples from doing whatever their hearts desired. For the first time in a long time, she regretted her duty.

"Good morning," she said weakly.

"Are you feeling better, my dear?" the woman who had called her over asked as she patted Meredith's arm. She was the mother of one of the debutantes. A kind contributor to Meredith's charitable works, she was one of the few "mamas" in the group who wasn't lobbying outright for Tristan to turn his attention to her daughter alone.

"Thank you, Lady Conville," Meredith said and forced a brighter smile. "It was nothing but a slight headache. I'm sure it was brought on by travel."

The woman searched her face. "Are you certain? You look very pale, without your usual spark."

Meredith started. Normally she was able to hide her emotions and put up a glittering facade no matter what her troubles. If Lady Conville saw her worries, it would rouse suspicion and questions in others. Too many would not do. She liked being the one to ask, not answer.

Straightening her spine, Meredith laughed.

"You're kind, but I feel very well today." She motioned across the room to a young lady sipping tea. "Your daughter looks lovely. How old is she now?"

Lady Conville's focus faded at the mention of her child. "Eighteen years just last month." She dabbed at the corner of her eyes with a handkerchief. "She's the last of my children. When I marry her away, I will have no one left, I'm afraid."

Meredith relaxed as she fell into comfortable habits. No troubling emotions were required for this exchange. "But then you'll soon have grandchildren and all will be right again."

Her ladyship's eyes lit up in delight and they fell into pleasant conversation as they ate their breakfast.

Meredith glanced around while she finished her last few bites. The only people missing were Tristan and his mother. The rest of the party was there, their talk growing louder as the plates emptied and were cleared away. Even Augustine Devlin was among the chattering crowd. He nodded to her in recognition as he talked to another man who looked far too stupid to be involved in any plots.

"I wonder what we could be doing today?" one young lady asked, loudly enough that the rest of the table was included in her conversation.

"A picnic," came a voice from the door.

Meredith froze as the comfort she had regained

fled. She knew that deep, sensuous voice anywhere. Tristan. Indeed, when she looked up, he
stood in the entryway, his mother on his arm. He
looked around the crowd, barely sparing her a
second glance.

"And then kite flying," he continued.

Meredith nodded in time with the other guests
and murmured, "How lovely."

It was lovely, but somehow she couldn't think
about that. She could only wonder what Tristan
thought as his gaze fell on her. He hardly acknowledged her, let alone behaved like a man
who had kissed her senseless less than twelve
hours before. But then, hadn't that always been
his way? After he saved her that night so long ago
in the pub, he had pushed her away, far away. She
winced at the pain that memory brought up. But it
proved that Tristan had always been hotter than
fire, then colder than ice when it came to her. It
made gauging him all the more difficult.

He smiled, but there was little warmth in the
expression. As always, it seemed he was simply
going through the motions of a host, not truly re-
lating to his guests.

"If we gather outside in half an hour, we can
begin our day."

Loud agreement echoed as the gathering began
to depart to their various chambers for final preparation. Meredith attempted to put herself in the
middle of the crowd to avoid contact with Tristan,

but in the shuffle she was pushed to the doorway beside him.

As she passed by, he looked at her. "Lady Northam?"

She held her breath. "Yes, my lord?"

"Perhaps you'll find a moment to speak with me today?" His calm, almost flat voice betrayed nothing of his feelings.

She swallowed past her suddenly dry throat. Despite the fact that she needed to keep up contact with Tristan for her investigation, the idea of spending time in his company made her quiver. And she *never* quivered.

"Y-Yes. Of course."

He nodded once as Meredith moved away, and she couldn't help but notice the broad smile on Lady Carmichael's face. Her legs felt unsteady as she trailed behind the others up the wide staircase to the guest quarters.

As she entered her chamber, she muttered, "Pull yourself together, girl."

Her lady's maid cocked her head as she came into Meredith's dressing room. "I beg your pardon, ma'am?"

"Nothing," she said with a wince.

But as the maid made the final preparations for her outing, Meredith couldn't help but think of all the possible outcomes of an afternoon with Tristan. One thing was certain: While there were many scenarios that were good for her case, none were good for her heart, which was increasingly demanding that she follow its desires.

Meredith stood at the end of the lake, staring up at the swaying branches of a tall willow tree. Her sketch pad clutched in her hand, it appeared she was innocently drawing while the others in the party mulled about.

Of course, she couldn't have cared less about the tree. It could have pulled its roots from the ground and skulked three paces to the left and she wouldn't have noticed. Her position gave her the perfect opportunity to watch Tristan.

He was sitting on one of the picnic blankets, savoring the last of a sumptuous luncheon with Violet Conville, Lady Conville's daughter. The same one her ladyship had lamented marrying off earlier in the day. Normally, Meredith found no fault with the young lady. Of all the debutantes of the current season, Violet was the least frivolous and irritating. In fact, she had a serious, intelligent air that made her very appealing.

Meredith had actually once mused she would make an excellent addition to The Society, if only she were a widow. An unmarried lady could never be expected to investigate the darkest underbelly of the Empire. She didn't have the freedom to move about without a watchful escort, for one. And there were certain things a woman didn't understand until she had experienced a wedding night.

At the moment, however, all Meredith's prior considerations for the young lady's attributes were gone. She could have scratched her eyes out and never thought twice about it. Her conversation with Tristan looked so comfortable. Violet was from a good family, exactly the kind of young lady who would make a perfect marchioness.

Meredith jumped as her sketching pencil snapped against the notepad in her hand, tearing a hole in the paper. Carefully, she unclenched her fist.

Jealous? Was she actually jealous that a man she suspected of *treason* was spending time with another woman? It was utterly ridiculous. They had shared one burning kiss. It was a mistake.

So why did it keep popping into her mind? When she closed her eyes, why could she feel the pressure of Tristan's lips against hers? Taste the heady flavor of his mouth as it moved so slowly, so sensuously, against her lips, awakening dark, forbidden desires she thought she'd buried . . .

With a start, she flipped her notepad closed and jammed it and her broken pencil into her pelisse pocket. She had to stop thinking about Tristan as a man and remember he was a suspect. These strange, powerful desires must be extinguished.

With a scowl, she tore her gaze away from Tristan and Violet and scanned the crowd. She found Augustine Devlin. Sitting away from the main group on a low hill overlooking the lake, he observed the scene with as much focused intent as she.

His gaze was currently pointed in the same direction hers had been. Tristan. Devlin watched their host's every move with an unreadable expression. What did he see when he looked at Tristan? An ally? A threat? When she interrupted them the night before, their conversation hadn't seemed particularly friendly.

Perhaps Tristan was actually a barrier to whatever plans Devlin was making. Her heart soared with that thought, then sank when she remembered all the evidence against Tristan. And how desperate he was every time she delved too closely into his affairs.

Devlin turned his head and caught her eye. She jolted. She'd been so preoccupied she had forgotten herself. Now Devlin saw her attention. Judging from the way he nodded in her direction, he marked her interest.

With a quick wave of recognition, Meredith broke their stare and headed toward the main group, but she felt Devlin's piercing eyes on her with every step.

"Lord Carmichael, did you say there would be kite flying today?" she asked with what she hoped was an airy tone that didn't reflect her turbulent emotions.

Tristan had gotten to his feet while she was distracted by Devlin and turned toward her with a smile just as false as her own. For a brief moment she wondered what it would be like if they removed their public masks and simply stood before each other as who they truly were.

"Yes, Lady Northam, that's correct."

He nodded toward the footmen who had been attending to the group, and the men brought forth a few large chests. Once opened, they revealed kites made from all variety of colorful fabric, bright ribbons trailed from their tails and balls of string had already been attached.

"The weather is perfect for this, Tristan!" Lady Carmichael beamed as she watched the younger women and men take their pick of the kites. "What a grand idea it was to fly them."

Meredith glanced at Tristan with surprise. She never would have guessed he picked this activity to share with his guests. Yet the smallest hint of a real smile tilted the corner of his lips when a few of the more eager guests launched their kites into the sky and filled the breezy air with soaring, swooping fabric and dangling tails.

She drew one of the remaining kites from the rapidly emptying trunks and smoothed its blue ribbon carefully. "Will you join us, my lord?"

Tristan stiffened at the sound of her voice. "No, I prefer watching. But do enjoy yourself."

Their eyes met and Meredith found herself pulled in, but then he glanced away. Without another word, she backed into the open area and lifted her kite to the breeze. After a bit of finagling, it caught on an updraft and swooped into the sky.

She watched the child's toy soar and a rare sense of peace engulfed her. Her lifestyle didn't allow many quiet moments, but there was something about watching the effortless grace of the kite that let her forget, if only for a moment, the strange emotions this case evoked.

"Perfect."

Tristan's voice pushed that calming sensation away. Her body came to immediate attention. She felt him move closer, was aware of every breath he drew, the heat of his body. Aware of *him*, in every way.

"I haven't flown kites since I was a girl." She struggled with each word to keep her tone light and casual. "Probably since those summers you came to visit my cousins."

He didn't answer, just stared at the soaring toy as she released more string and let it fly higher. She couldn't help but notice the faraway look in his eye, as if he envied the freedom he saw above.

"Do you still keep in contact with my cousin Henry?"

"No," he said quietly, his gaze flitting to her.

She shrugged. Cutting himself off from his friends was sometimes a first sign that a man of society had become involved in something dangerous or sinister, but in this case she wasn't sure. Henry had never been unkind to her, but she'd found him to be quite stupid. Since his marriage, he had grown enormously fat and lazy as well.

She couldn't imagine that Tristan, with his intelligent, quiet manner, would have anything in common with his old friend.

Still, it was worth pursuing, if only to see his reaction.

"That's unfortunate." She tugged the kite string and let it turn in the air. "You were very close, if I recall. I hope there was no falling out."

Tristan shifted uncomfortably. "No falling out, I simply—"

He stopped and her intuition tingled. She stopped fiddling with the kite and looked at him. His eyes were dark with clearly pained emotions. He looked trapped, and an urge to help him filled her, just as it had last night.

"You can tell me," she whispered.

He opened his mouth as if he wanted to do just that, but before he said a word, the tension in her kite string vanished and she took a step back to right herself. She turned in time to see her kite blowing away on the wind as the string that had once been attached to it fluttered to the ground.

"Bollocks," she muttered under her breath.

Tristan's eyes went wide. "I beg your pardon?"

With blood heating her cheeks, Meredith turned away. She *never* did anything so unladylike as curse in front of people she wasn't utterly comfortable with. Which meant only Emily and Anastasia had ever heard her say such a thing.

"Nothing," she lied. "I'd best go search for it."

Without looking back, she hurried toward a thickly wooded area where her kite lost altitude. At least her investigative skills would come in handy finding the lost toy.

Because she certainly wasn't putting them to good use when it came to Tristan.

Chapter 7

Too shocked to do anything else, Tristan watched Meredith walk away. Though she denied it, he was sure he had heard her mutter a rather salty curse when her kite broke free. Certainly not a word any lady in his acquaintance normally said. But instead of being offended, he found himself wanting to laugh. *Really* laugh. Something he hadn't indulged in for a long time.

"What are you waiting for?"

He turned with a start to find his mother staring at him, arms folded. She cocked her head.

"Go help the lady, for heaven's sake."

"Of course," he said, remembering his manners.

Something about Meredith made him forget . . . well, forget just about everything but her.

He hurried toward the spot he'd last seen her, disappearing into the copse of trees on the other side of the lake.

"Lady Northam?" he called out. There was no reply as he moved farther into the grove. "My lady?"

Silence continued to greet him until, in the distance, he heard a distinct grunt and what could have been another muttered curse. With a smile he couldn't control, Tristan called out, "Meredith?"

"I'm right . . . here," came the strained reply.

He followed her voice, trailing around tangled brush and wide tree trunks. He found her standing on a wide log that had fallen some time ago, reaching up, up, up toward a branch of another tree where her kite was caught amidst the leafy limbs. She was on her tiptoes in the most precarious position, yet somehow maintained her balance.

"Good Lord, Meredith," he snapped, rushing toward her. "You'll kill yourself. Come down from there and let me fetch it!"

She shook her head. "No, thank you, I've almost got—" She strained up to catch the tail of the kite. A triumphant grin lit her face. "—it!" she crowed as she gave the kite a yank.

The toy fluttered free. Unfortunately, her sharp tug and the attempt to dodge the falling kite threw Meredith off balance. She flailed her arms to right herself, but it was too late. She pitched off the rotting log.

Tristan's life moved in horrible slow motion as he bounded forward and she keeled back. He held out his arms to catch her. She hit his chest as he wrapped his arms around her waist. Her fragrance filled his nostrils, and her warmth coursed through him as he stumbled and ended up flat on his back in an open spot amidst the brambles and felled tree branches.

For a moment, the woods around them were totally silent. Meredith lay perfectly still on top of him. With the air knocked from his lungs, he wasn't capable of doing anything but lying there, as well.

And then she began to tremble. Quiver. Before Tristan could sit up to ascertain how badly she'd been hurt, a giggle escaped her lips. She covered her mouth, but couldn't contain her laughter.

It took him a moment to realize he was laughing with her. It felt odd and wonderful at the same time.

With a grunt, she rolled off his chest onto the grassy area beside him. Where she had lain, he now felt cold.

"Well, that was ridiculous," she giggled. "Are you injured?"

He drew in a few panting breaths. Nothing felt broken. In fact, he felt better than he had for a while. "Only my pride. I wasn't much of a knight in shining armor, was I?"

"Well, you did catch me," she pointed out with a laugh.

Her eyes were bright and her cheeks flushed from mirth, and his stomach clenched. They were treading into dangerous waters. Ones he had vowed never to enter again with this woman who twisted his emotions so easily. But he desperately wanted to kiss her. Worse, she was staring at his lips as if she remembered the feel of them against her own.

"Are you hurt?" he asked, laughter gone from his voice.

She slowly shook her head though her gaze never left his. "No."

He smiled as he noticed a twig stuck in her tangled hair. Without thinking, he reached out to slide it away. Her breath hitched when the back of his hand brushed her cheek.

"Tristan . . ." she began softly.

There was his name again, coming from her lips to arouse him. Just that whisper made him forget his position, both in society and his current situation. Nothing mattered except touching his lips to hers. So he did.

Her reply was a little groan. Her lips parted, and he took what she offered, plundering her mouth, tasting her sweet breath as their tongues collided. His desire threatened to overflow with each touch, and the passion she returned was so pure, so right, he could hardly recall what it was like to resist this temptation.

He hauled her closer, dragging her across his chest, cupping the nape of her neck with one hand, as he cradled the small of her back with the other. She gripped his shoulders, kneading his jacket absently as she kissed him with the same desperate abandon that churned inside him.

Tristan had been forced to become a man of utter control and propriety at a young age. He'd missed out on the carefree irresponsibility he saw many of his contemporaries pursue in their twenties. He had never found a temptation worth throwing caution to the wind to pursue. In fact, he'd avoided such things.

Until now.

Almost as if his body was out of his control, he slowly cupped Meredith's backside and brought her closer, rocking her against his already straining erection. She shivered, but never broke contact from his lips. If anything, her kisses grew deeper. Suddenly the airy woods were hot and close.

He was going to surrender to the desire that heated his blood. It was inevitable. Like a moth to the flame, he couldn't resist Meredith. And he didn't want to. Not now. Later, he was sure he would lament his choice, but not now.

"My lord?" There was a distinct clearing of a throat before the voice that intruded into Tristan's erotic haze came a second time. "My lord? Are you here?"

Awareness returned with stunning, guilt-ridden clarity, jolting him. Meredith rolled away as he struggled to a seated, upright position. Looking around, he saw Philip standing a few feet away, examining an old oak tree as if it were the most interesting thing he'd ever seen. Though he was pretending not to see them, it was plain he did.

Tristan's gaze flitted to Meredith. She, too, was now seated, rearranging her wrinkled gown and running her hands over her hair in an attempt to repair the damage done by his seeking fingers. There wasn't a hint of a blush on her cheeks. He wouldn't have known she was embarrassed by their discovery if not for the slight trembling of her hands.

"I—" he stammered, trying to meet her eyes with no success. She kept her stare pointedly away from his. "I'm sorry."

" 'Twas nothing," she murmured. "A slip for us both, one we should forget."

A sudden, sharp sting worked through Tristan's body. Was it that easy for her to forget such an intense, unexpected encounter? He certainly wouldn't for a long time.

"Of course," he lied, reaching over to remove yet another twig from her hair.

She pulled back from his touch, and this time her gaze locked with his. "This is how we started, Tristan."

For a moment she couldn't hide her emotions. Tension. Fear. Anger . . . At herself or at him? Confusion. The same things boiling in his chest.

"You'd best attend to your friend," she whispered. "He's being polite enough to pretend he doesn't see, but he can only keep up the charade a few moments longer."

Tristan nodded wordlessly as he clamored to his feet. Turning toward Philip, he called out, "Here!"

His friend feigned surprise and took a few steps in his direction. "Ah, there you are. Your mother said there was an incident with a wayward kite and that you went this way."

Tristan nodded, trying to keep his face as free of emotions as Meredith seemed to be able to do. Difficult when he wanted to punch his best friend squarely in the nose. As wrong as it was, he wished Philip hadn't found them. If he hadn't . . .

He erased the heated thoughts from his mind and forced himself to focus. What he *wanted* was not important.

"Yes, luckily we found it." He half turned to help Meredith to her feet, but found she was already standing. She looked remarkably unruffled, considering. He might not have guessed she'd been thoroughly kissed if her mouth wasn't swollen. "Have you met Lady Northam?"

Philip arched a brow, but shook his head. "No, I haven't had the pleasure."

Tristan nodded. "Lady Northam, may I present Mr. Philip Barclay, my man of affairs and an old friend."

Without a hint of embarrassment, Meredith stepped forward, hand extended. As Philip took it, she said, "Actually, we have met, Mr. Barclay. At a ball before your father's death."

Philip drew back, and Tristan couldn't help but do the same. His friend hadn't been in society for many years. Most people wouldn't recall his former position, especially after hearing of his present vocation as man of affairs.

Philip nodded. "Yes, my lady. You have a good memory. That was a long time ago."

She smiled, her expression open and genuine, and it hit Tristan in the gut. That light she carried with her made him so much more aware of the darkness that had slowly surrounded him over the years. How he wished he could shed it and let himself be free to . . . Well, he wasn't sure what. But it involved Meredith, satin sheets, and no interruptions.

Clearing his throat uncomfortably, Tristan croaked, "Was there something you needed, Philip?"

His friend shook his head as if he, too, had been under Meredith's spell. "Yes, I'm sorry. That message you were awaiting has arrived, my lord."

Any remnants of desire were washed away as if he'd been doused by icy water. He'd been waiting for word from an investigator in London about the trail some money he provided to Devlin had taken.

"In my private office?" he asked as tension coursed through his body, filled his every word.

Philip nodded once. "Yes. I'd be pleased to escort Lady Northam back to the party and make your explanations. I believe the group is almost ready to return to the house."

Tristan shot a glance in Meredith's direction. She was watching him from the corner of her eye, taking in every expression, listening to every word.

"Would you mind?" he asked.

Her eyebrow arched, but she shook her head. "Of course not." She stooped to collect the long forgotten kite. "If you have business to attend to, I wouldn't keep you from it."

With a short bow, Tristan turned and headed for the shortest route back to the house. But as he walked away, he felt Meredith's eyes on his retreating back. The heat of her unseen stare warmed his blood and made the answers he sought seem less important than the chance to take her in his arms again.

Even though that wasn't possible.

"My lady?"

Meredith forced her stare away from Tristan's flexing shoulder muscles as he walked toward the house and . . . what? A cryptic message of some kind, but did it involve her case?

Her case. The same one she couldn't seem to concentrate on for more than five minutes at a stretch. Not when Tristan touched her.

She focused on the man standing a few feet away, and quickly reviewed what she knew about him. Philip Barclay had been Tristan's schoolmate, one of the few he kept in his confidence after his brother's death. Philip fell on hard times after his father's passing, but had taken to the position of man of affairs with great success, evidenced by how well the Carmichael holdings did each year.

"Shall we return to the others?" he asked with a smile. He offered her an arm to guide her out of the tangled forest, which she took for appearance's sake. Her extensive training in physical combat had given her perfect balance. She winced as she recalled how she had pitched off the rotted tree stump earlier.

Nearly perfect balance.

"Yes, of course, thank you." She watched him as he guided her through the woods. "Actually, I'm pleased we have a chance to speak privately, Mr. Barclay."

"You are? What can I assist you with, my lady?"

She smiled. "Last night, Lord Carmichael and I were speaking with Mr. Devlin—"

"With Mr. Devlin." His tone was flat and noncommittal, but his face tightened at the name. Plainly, the man beside her knew about Devlin's reputation and didn't like him any more than Tristan did.

"Yes. I was inquiring about the nature of their business together, as I'm always looking for new ventures in which to invest my inheritance," she pressed on, marking every expression that crossed Barclay's face. For now, it was frustratingly blank.

He nodded. "I see."

"Mr. Devlin mentioned he and Lord Carmichael are involved in some kind of art venture together. I wasn't able to garner much more information from his lordship—" She hesitated as she remembered why her interrogation had come to an end. The same reason why her mouth was hot right now. "—but I hoped you could tell me more. I'm very interested in the arts, you see."

Barclay's gaze slid to her with unexpected sharpness. "Devlin and Carmichael mentioned their association when it came to art?"

She nodded, her intuition pricking with the flash of anger in her companion's eyes. "Yes, very briefly."

His lips pursed as he looked straight ahead. "I'm surprised to hear that."

"Why?"

He released her arm as they exited the brambled woods and set their feet on even ground.

"Because Tristan rarely speaks about his connection to the . . . arts." His mouth tightened. "Can you make your way back to the party?"

She nodded, eyes all innocence even as her heart throbbed with the excitement of the chase. "Of course. The group is only a few steps away. You're going back to the house, then?"

He nodded. "Yes. Good afternoon, my lady."

Without another word, Barclay spun on his heel and headed for the house. Meredith watched him until he vanished over a hill, then she headed toward the guests.

The pieces of her case were slowly clicking into place one by one. First Devlin's sardonic mention of art, then Tristan's strong reaction to her interest in his dealings with Devlin. Now his man of affairs had reacted just as strongly to the same type of query. These things pointed to Tristan's involvement in the missing painting all the more.

She glanced over her shoulder, but Philip Barclay was long gone. He'd been *angry* when she spoke to him. An unexpected reaction. Why?

Her heart fluttered. What if *Barclay* was really the man behind the missing painting?

She stopped as wild hope blossomed in her chest. That made so much more sense. After his father's death, Philip lost his fortune. Certainly, he would profit more from an affiliation with a rich traitor like Devlin than Tristan could.

Her smile felt like it would crack her cheeks as

she walked the last few steps to rejoin the party. Her heart felt lighter than it had since she first heard of Tristan's involvement in this plot.

Still, a nagging voice in her head pulled at her. Told her she was searching for ways to prove Tristan's innocence. Searching for reasons to ignore the evidence already collected against him.

She shook her head, squelching the voice with violence. Yes, Tristan still acted suspiciously, but that could easily be explained away. Barclay and Devlin could be blackmailing him or threatening his family. There were hundreds of explanations far better than that he was involved in something so dark and sinister, it tore a hole in her soul.

"There you are, my dear," Lady Carmichael said as she approached. "Are Tristan and Mr. Barclay not with you?"

Meredith shook her head, taking the lady's arm with a smile she couldn't suppress. "No, they were called to business of some kind, but I'm sure we shall see them at the house."

Lady Carmichael tilted her head with a questioning glance. "It's nice to see you smile, my dear. Has something happened?"

Meredith squeezed Constance's arm and barely held back the urge to bounce with glee. "It's just a beautiful day, my lady."

As they walked back to the estate, Meredith steadied her nerves. She had to rein in her emotions. She could be wrong about Philip Barclay.

But the possibility gave her hope. Hope that Tristan wasn't the villain she feared he'd become. Hope that she didn't feel such powerful longings for a treacherous criminal.

Now she only had to support those hopes with evidence. Evidence Augustine Devlin could provide.

Chapter 8

Tristan watched the party from the balcony above the ballroom, yet he hardly saw the gaiety in his midst. Disappointment wracked him. The evidence he hoped to obtain had been snatched from his reach yet again. He had tried to create a money trail, but Devlin's shrewdness kept him from his objective: discovering the man Devlin reported to.

In addition, Philip had informed him that Meredith continued to press about Tristan's connection to Devlin and the "art" the bastard had alluded to the night before. Without even knowing it, she was putting herself in terrible danger. The kind that could lead to injury . . . even death.

Tristan fisted his hands. No. He wouldn't allow that to happen. He would not lose one more person he cared for.

The thought startled him. Care for Meredith? He desired her, yes. He was more than willing to admit that. Pushing his shoulders back, he slowly released his fists. He had denied himself before, he would need to do so again. Men in his position couldn't afford to lose control, give in to temptation. Meredith was temptation embodied, but until this was over, he couldn't touch her. Not if it meant endangering her. Not if it meant he was distracted from his goals.

"What a lovely view."

His fingers clenched again at the grating sound of Augustine Devlin's voice over his shoulder. Wiping emotion from his expression, Tristan turned to face his "partner" . . . his enemy.

"Thank you," he managed through clenched teeth. It was becoming increasingly difficult to mask the burning hatred this man inspired in him. "I'm surprised you aren't enjoying the festivities."

Devlin stepped up beside him, looking over the railing to the dancing party below. "Hmm, I bore of these things after a bit. Most of the ladies aren't willing to entertain the idea of anything more than conversation." He glanced at Tristan. "I'm sure you must feel the same frustration when you are out of London and the pleasures found there."

Tristan ground his teeth. "I suppose."

Devlin's smile was wide and lewd. "But then, it seems you are having more luck with a particular lady than I."

"I don't know what you mean." Tristan forced calm, clenching the terrace railing until he feared the wood would splinter in his hands.

Devlin's eyebrow arched with amusement. "Are you not involving yourself with Lady Northam? I thought I sensed a spark there last night, and then today at the picnic you slipped away together."

Tristan counted to ten in his head. He needed the pause to appear nonplussed by Devlin's observation.

"I'm sure I have no idea what you're talking about. Lady Northam and I have no special relationship. We knew each other as children, yes. And today when her kite was lost, I helped her retrieve it." He shrugged as he scanned the party below.

He found Meredith instantly. She was standing along the perimeter of the dance floor talking to a fat earl who was well-known for his boring monologues on current politics. Yet she smiled as if he were the most charming man she'd ever encountered. She wore a striking icy blue gown. Pearls were draped around her neck and a diamond headpiece sparkled in her chestnut hair. She looked like a princess from a fairy tale, only he couldn't seem to muster the chaste thoughts of a prince sent to awaken her from eternal slumber.

No, his thoughts were of a sinful nature.

Devlin cleared his throat, and Tristan moved his gaze away from Meredith. "You, of all people, are aware I have no time for anything but work, Devlin. Certainly her ladyship is a beautiful young woman, but as you said, women of my class are rarely interested in anything less than a lifetime of commitment."

Devlin glanced down. "I don't know. Lady Northam seems different to me. There is a fire beneath her exterior that I find quite intriguing. If you're not pursuing her, then I am free to do so."

A red curtain of pure rage slid in front of Tristan's vision. For the first time in a long time, he lost control of the anger that constantly bubbled beneath the surface of his emotions. He wanted to tear Devlin apart, dangle him over the balcony until he squealed like the pig he truly was. He wanted to destroy him.

"Carmichael?" Devlin cocked his head.

Tristan carefully shoved the anger down deep, back to the dark place where he normally kept it, along with his grief, his wants, his love . . . anything that could distract him from matters that required his attention. He breathed as he collected himself. This was another test, that was all.

"You wish to pursue Lady Northam?"

"You don't approve of that idea." Devlin's mouth twitched with a grin. "I thought you said you had no interest in her."

"I don't," Tristan said quickly.

"Good." Devlin was watching him with every word. "You see, my lord, I *want* to trust you. I *want* to give you access to the man who leads our organization, but I cannot do that if you're going to be unreasonable."

"Unreasonable?" Tristan barked, louder than he'd intended. He controlled his tone. "I have done everything you asked. I put myself at risk because you required it. How can you call me unreasonable now?"

The snakelike smile on Devlin's face twitched. "You say you have no relationship to this woman, yet you obviously do not want me near her. Don't you trust me, Carmichael?"

The smug tone of the other man's voice hit Tristan in his chest. There was no way out of the trap Devlin had laid for him. Either he had to allow Devlin to pursue Meredith—and he had a feeling the other man wouldn't take no for an answer if he truly desired her—or he had to admit wanting her for his own. Having her by his side would endanger her by the mere fact that *he* was always in danger now. If she was his, she would be walking in a field of hidden steel traps and not even know it.

But which was the lesser of the two dangers?

Tristan looked evenly at Devlin, into eyes that were as cold as any impenetrable block of ice. He had seen what this man could do to those who crossed him. He could only imagine what he did to the women in his life, what he would do to Meredith if she resisted . . . or even if she acquiesced.

His mouth thinned into a harsh line. "All right, Devlin, you've found me out. I do desire Meredith Sinclair. My resistance to you pursuing her has nothing to do with a lack of trust. I have certainly shown loyalty in the past year. You cannot deny that."

Devlin's face relaxed, though his smirk remained as smug and unpleasant as ever. "No, I cannot deny you have done everything I've asked. And I promise you that your loyalty will be rewarded soon." He turned to the entryway that led to the staircase. "I'll respect your claim on Lady Northam, but I do hope you'll bed her as soon as possible." His mouth twitched. "I would sorely like to know how she tastes, but I'm willing to live vicariously through you."

Tristan barely kept himself from lunging for Devlin. Once the other man had gone, he let loose with a string of curses to echo in the air around him.

This was exactly what he had feared. By letting emotion in, he'd ceded some control to Devlin. Now he was forced to alter his plans. In order to protect Meredith from threats she didn't even perceive, he had to get closer to her. And that opened them both up to a world of other dangers.

Physical . . . and those of the heart, which sometimes cut deeper.

Meredith cast a last glance over her shoulder as
she slipped away from the party and down the
long, dim hallway leading to the servant backstairs. Her steps were careful, silent, as she crept
through the labyrinth that took her to the guest
quarters.

From a seemingly innocent talk with the young
lady who brought her tea that afternoon, she had
devised a spotty blueprint of which guest was in
which room, as well as where certain servants
were housed. Now it was just a matter of searching the correct chambers.

She'd already started Ana and Emily on research with a hastily penned, encoded note that
went out the moment she was alone long enough
to scribble it. Within a day of hard riding, her
partners would be using Charlie's resources to
look into the affairs of Mr. Philip Barclay. She only
prayed her instinct would be proven correct, that
he was the one truly responsible for the robbery of
the painting, not Tristan.

She froze at the thought. That wasn't the way
she'd been taught to perform an investigation. The
truth had no bias, no desire for one person to be
guilty or innocent over another. If she were per-
forming her duties properly, personal feelings
would not be an issue.

"But I can't this time," she whispered, raising a hand to her lips as she remembered Tristan's kiss. "I don't want him to be guilty."

Shaking her head, Meredith moved to the door she'd been searching for. With another careful glance around, she turned the knob. Locked. Scowling, she lifted a hand to her hair and pulled out one of the long, diamond-encrusted pins that held her complicated style in place. She depressed a hidden button on the underside of the diamond decoration. There was a click, and she was able to pull away the outer covering of the pin to reveal a sharpened, slender lock pick hidden beneath.

"Thank you, Ana," she muttered as she slipped the pick into place and snapped the lock open with little effort. With a grin, she replaced the pin sheath and returned it to her hair.

Shutting the door behind her, she locked it again, both to ensure that she would rouse no suspicion and to give her time for escape if the occupant of the room returned.

The chamber was dim. The fire had been allowed to burn low while the party was in full swing. She stirred the embers until the fire leapt and filled the room with brighter light. Carefully, she lit a candle from the mantel to carry with her and looked around, taking in every detail.

"Very well, Augustine Devlin," she muttered as she stepped to a large cherrywood armoire. She set her flickering candle on top and opened it. "Let's see what secrets you're hiding."

Methodically, she skimmed over coat pockets and waistcoat lining, searching for any hidden weapon, note, or other evidence. Nothing. She ran a hand over the back of the armoire, looking for secret hiding places, then carefully moved the clothing back to its original position.

Next, she went to a little table beside the window. Papers were scattered across the surface, but none were of interest. Just sketches of the garden view Devlin had out his window.

"Bastard is talented too," she muttered as she rearranged the drawings back to their original chaotic piles and made a note of his designs as an artist. Perhaps that was why his organization was transferring sensitive information via a painting. If nothing else, it was one more fact to add to The Society's ever growing list of Devlin's attributes.

She turned to face the bed along the back wall of the room, beside the door that led to Devlin's private dressing room. On either side were two bedside tables. She went to the one closest to the window and opened it. Nothing of interest aside from a few sketch pencils.

Coming around the bed, she tried the other drawer. Locked. Her intuition pricked. She pulled the pin from her hair a second time, then stared at the table. This was delicate business. The last thing she wanted was to arouse Devlin's suspicions by leaving evidence of her presence behind. If he realized someone was spying on him, he might alter his behavior, and then she wouldn't be able to determine his purpose or accomplices.

Tucking a loose curl behind her ear, Meredith crouched in front of the locked drawer to give her a better view of her work. The pick slipped into place with a rattle, but the lock was old and didn't budge immediately. She felt the catch loosen with each twist, but couldn't force it open.

"Just a bit more," she murmured. "Come on."

The sound of footsteps in the hall brought her to full attention. Were they passing by? No. She drew in a sharp breath. They stopped outside the door and she could hear two voices as a key was slipped into the lock.

She immediately went into the routine her training laid out for her. She blew the candle out with a puff of breath and pulled at her hairpin to remove it from the lock. To her horror, it didn't budge. She pulled again, twisting as calmly as she could even as she listened to the rattle of the door handle. She was out of time. There was no choice.

Abandoning the lock pick, she set the candle on Devlin's nightstand and dove under the bed just as the door came open and two men entered. Meredith held her breath as they walked closer, talking about the party. She could only see the men's boots, but she recognized one voice as Devlin's.

The other she didn't know. Disappointment filled her. If only it were Philip Barclay. Then her hopes could be proven and she would no longer have to suspect Tristan.

"Good God, Elsworth why is this room so blasted hot?" Devlin snapped.

Meredith watched as the less expensive pair of boots hurried around to the other side of the room.

"I'm sorry, sir," the man said. "I thought the fire would have burned down by now."

"It hasn't. Open a window, man." Devlin sounded in ill humor. Why?

They headed for the door that led to Devlin's dressing room, and Meredith held her breath. They would pass by the table with her hairpin sticking from its lock. She could only pray they would be too distracted to notice.

The door opened and the two men went into the adjoining room. Immediately, Meredith slid out from under the bed and grabbed the lock pick. With a yank, she forced it free and looked to the door. To get there she would be forced to pass the other room. Since she couldn't see inside, she would have no way of surmising if Devlin or his servant were turned in her direction. It was too big a risk.

The window. Scrambling over the bed, she made for the open window. But just as she was about to put her leg outside, Devlin's voice came from the other room.

"Tristan Archer—" came his broken statement.

She froze, heart lurching. She strained to hear their words as the men approached the door leading back to the bedroom.

"—send the message tomorrow. Either his lordship will be a great help to us"—She could hear Devlin's smug sneer—"or I'll be forced to kill him. Either way, he'll serve a purpose."

"Yes, sir," the servant said. "I'll do so right away."

Meredith started as the man began to reenter the room. With a swish of her icy blue skirt, she stepped out the window onto a very narrow ledge. Holding her breath, she waited, hoping to hear more from the men inside, but the room was silent except for the shutting door as Devlin's servant left.

Meredith centered her balance as she had been taught during training. Using smooth, slow motions she shifted her weight and peered into the room. Devlin stood just feet away, glancing over the sketches on the table to the left of the window. She yanked herself out of his line of vision and began to move away from the room. So much for going out the way she'd come in.

She glanced around. A few tall trees were nearby, but too far for her to jump and hope to shimmy down their branches without getting herself killed. Aside from which, if someone saw her afterward, it would be obvious she'd been involved in arborial activities. As it was, she was covered with dust from beneath the bed, which would be difficult to explain.

She slid along the narrow ledge around the house's guest windows. Each step was a balancing act, with the potential to send her crashing to the ground far below, where she would definitely be hurt, even killed.

"Don't think about that," she ordered herself through gritted teeth.

She wished she wasn't wearing such pretty slippers. They did nothing to help her maintain balance or grip the ledge. Carefully, she shifted to one foot and slid one shoe off, then repeated the action with the other foot.

She watched as the dainty footwear fell, the diamonds on the buckles glinting in the moonlight before they hit the shrubbery below. She would have to retrieve them as soon as possible to keep suspicion from being roused.

Meredith gripped the ledge with her stockinged toes and glided toward the next window.

"Please be open," she whispered as she pressed her back against the stucco wall and reached over to shove the glass. When it creaked open, she barely held back a sigh of utter relief.

Taking her time, she listened for any evidence of an occupant in the room. When it remained quiet, she pushed over until her backside rested on the windowsill, then slung one damp foot into the room. She had never been so happy to feel hardwood floors beneath her toes.

She swung her other foot over the ledge and closed the open window with a quiet click. The room was pitch-black, as the low fire provided almost no light at all. She managed to find her way to the door by feel and exit.

Normally, after such a great escape, excitement thrilled through her system, but tonight it was all she could do not to collapse onto the hallway floor and sob.

Her theory about Philip Barclay being the only guilty party had been damaged by Devlin's comments. Only Tristan's name had come up in the conversation with his servant. Her heart sank.

It sank even further as she thought of Devlin's comment that Tristan would help him . . . or Devlin would kill him. Her blood chilled. Did Tristan even know how much danger he was in by involving himself in Devlin's schemes? How close he was to falling from a precipice more dangerous than the one she had just escaped if he continued to align himself with the blackguard?

She didn't know the answers to those questions, but she did know one thing: She wanted to protect Tristan. From Devlin's murderous intent . . . and from her own investigation.

But how could she protect the prime suspect of her case? How could she manage to keep collecting evidence while she sheltered Tristan from the storm that threatened on the horizon?

Her mind turned to its natural tendency to make plans in the face of troubling uncertainty.

"Somehow I must obtain the note Devlin spoke of to his servant tonight," she murmured as she walked toward her room for a new pair of slippers. "I *must* intercept it before the danger toward Tristan grows even greater."

Chapter 9

The letter. She had to get the letter. The letter was all that mattered.

Meredith slipped down the main staircase into the foyer and looked around. She *should* have retrieved it last night. She would have, too, except for a multitude of interruptions. There were benefits to being a popular lady of the *ton*, but there were also serious disadvantages.

First, it had been the handsome lieutenant who insisted she dance with him. Then it was one of the ladies close to her age who had wanted to share some silly piece of gossip about another in their set. Then Lady Carmichael had set her sights on her. By the time she managed to slip away, she had no idea where Devlin's servant had gone. Now she could only hope she would intercept him before his message left the house. She even had a folded sheet of blank paper in her pelisse pocket in case she had a chance to make a switch.

Which was the reason she was awake so blasted early after being up half the night dancing. She stifled a yawn and moved down the hallway. And then, as if conjured by her very imagination, the library door opened and Augustine Devlin stepped into the hallway just a few feet in front of her.

"Why, Lady Northam," he said with that signature smile that could melt hearts or freeze her very blood. "What a pleasant surprise. I wasn't aware any other guest was awake at such an early hour."

Immediately she fell into investigation mode.

"Ah, good morning, Mr. Devlin." She gave him her best smile. "We are both early risers, I see."

She was relieved how easily the friendly words and smile came to her. After all her struggles covering her emotions with Tristan, she had begun to fear she'd lost her touch. But it seemed only one man could make her forget herself.

"Yes. But if I could have plucked one other person from the group here to find roaming the halls, it would have been you, my lady."

He smiled again, and she fought the urge to shake her head in wonder. The man did have charm. She gave him that.

"And what woke you so early?" she asked, tilting her head.

His smile shifted ever so subtly from flirtation to smug satisfaction, and Meredith's entire being snapped to alertness. "Perhaps you did not notice I slipped away from the party early last night. I had business to attend to. Business I plan to finish this morning."

"I admit, I did notice your absence. You were sorely missed by quite a few ladies." Stupid, stupid women who had no idea what kind of blackguard they desired just because he had the face an ancient god would covet.

He leaned in a touch closer. "And were you among them, Lady Northam?"

She resisted the urge to allow her expression to reflect her disgust. "Now, Mr. Devlin, you know a lady does not reveal such secret little thoughts."

He let out a chuckle and gave a shrug. "A man can always hope."

"But you say you'll finish your business today?" she pressed, steering the conversation back to the topic she needed to pursue.

Devlin hesitated. "Ah, well, not all of it, but I will have a very important part completed once my man arrives to deliver a message to London."

Meredith froze as she watched Devlin lift a hand to his breast pocket and tap gently. The letter. The letter about Tristan's fate was right there. She could reach out and snatch it with no trouble.

She had no doubt she could take Devlin down to the floor with a few of her best moves of defense. He wouldn't expect them from her. The letter would be hers.

The case would be destroyed, so of course she couldn't do so. But the thought of putting the flat of her palm to the man's nose and watching him scream with pain did give her a small moment's pleasure.

But if she stayed, she might be able to quickly slip the letter away from the servant when he wasn't paying attention. If she did it correctly, he might not notice its absence until it was too late. Excitement thrilled through her.

"Would you mind if I—" she began.

"Lady Northam!"

She spun to see Tristan coming down the hallway like a bull beckoned by a red cape. His eyes flashed fire. What the hell was he doing up? He had retired much later than she had.

He came up short in front of the two of them.

"Good morning, Carmichael," Devlin drawled.

Tristan's gaze flitted to her companion, and Meredith saw an intense rage in his stare. The same anger she'd seen the night he saved her life. She shivered as she recalled what lengths he had gone to when it came to her protection. If he attacked Devlin, she wasn't sure she could keep him from killing the man.

"Devlin," he said through clenched teeth. He

turned on her, and she was surprise that the intense anger had been masked. "I must have a word with you."

He reached out and grasped her elbow in a grip of steel. The sudden action surprised her, as did the heat that sparked between them at his touch.

"My lord?" She tried to shake free of him.

He held fast. "Truly, Meredith, it is vitally important I have a word with you."

In a heartbeat's time she considered her options. If she refused his demand to go with him, she risked losing the tenuous link they shared. If he no longer spoke to her, her investigation could be limited.

She stopped pulling against him and said, "Very well."

She glanced at Devlin and opened her mouth to murmur something polite, but Tristan didn't allow it. He hauled her away to the closest sitting room, slamming the door behind them.

They were alone, but still he didn't release her. He stood in the middle of the parlor, drawing in deep breaths as if to calm himself. She stared at him, mesmerized by the intensity of the emotion in his eyes and in the heat of his touch.

Tristan shook his head and looked down at her, as if he had almost forgotten she was there. Their gazes locked and the fascination Meredith felt turned to something deeper. Something she had to deny. With a yank, she pulled her elbow free and backed away.

"What in the world is wrong with you, Tristan?" She searched his face for answers, explanations, even as she fought to rein in her wild emotions.

"I told you that man is dangerous!" He turned away, raking a hand through his hair. His desperation was clear with every motion, every word.

And she longed to take that desperation away. To soothe him. As foolish as that desire was, she found herself reaching for him. Her fingers curled around his bicep as if someone else controlled them. He jolted at the contact and turned his head to face her.

"If that is true, why do you do business with him?" she whispered. "Why do you invite him to your home? Tristan, please, if there is something wrong . . . some trouble you have found yourself a part of, let me—"

Before she could finish, the door opened behind them. Both of them started and spun on the intruder, ready to see Devlin's face greeting them. Instead, Tristan's mother stood in the doorway. When she saw how close Meredith was to her son, her eyebrows went up in surprise. But then a tiny smile tilted the corners of her lips.

Meredith backed a long step away as Tristan rolled his eyes. Evidently he recognized the matchmaking glimmer in Lady Carmichael's eyes as much as she did.

"Oh," Constance said, putting a hand to her chest in mock surprise. "I'm so sorry, I didn't know you were here."

Tristan's nostrils flared in disbelief at her statement. His voice was taut as he asked, "Did you require something, Mother?"

"Oh no, my darling." His mother's smile was filled with the joy of playing Cupid. Meredith's heart ached. How hurt Lady Carmichael would be when she discovered the truth. About Tristan. About her. "But we're all awake so early. Most of the others won't rise for hours now. Wouldn't it be nice if we took a ride together? It's such a nice morning."

Tristan's eyes fluttered shut, and Meredith thought he muttered something under his breath about not being able to put her off. Then he opened them again and glanced her way. She felt his appraisal, his mind turning on whether riding with her was an acceptable risk.

She wondered that herself. Going out with him would allow her to push her case a little more. But the presence of Lady Carmichael would certainly prevent any intense exchanges like the one they had just been having. Or any more kisses that melted her resolve and turned her knees to jelly.

She smiled at Lady Carmichael. "I would be pleased to ride with you, my lady. I've wished to see more of this lovely estate since my arrival."

Tristan opened his mouth, but his mother waved

off his words. "Grand! Change into your habit and we'll meet at the stables in half an hour."

With effort, Meredith nodded and slowly crossed to the door. But before she left, she dared a glance over her shoulder. Tristan was watching her, and though his stare did not contain the desperation she had seen in it earlier, the desire that was always evident was still there. Burning. Waiting for the right moment to destroy her resolve.

Meredith adjusted her bonnet as she stepped into the stable. She drew in a sharp breath at the sight that greeted her. Tristan stood in the middle of the large room, brushing a massive black stallion as he murmured quiet endearments to the nickering beast. He didn't notice her entry. It was one of the few times he hadn't been totally aware of her when they were together, and she took the opportunity to study his face.

His chiseled features were handsome in the morning light that streamed through the stable door and windows. But the light revealed something else as well. Though he was calmer than he had been earlier, there was a sadness in his eyes she'd noticed many times before.

She sighed. She *couldn't* empathize with him. There was no room for sympathy in an investigation. Or desire, though that powerful emotion coursed through her still. She was conscious of how she tingled with heated awareness. Of how

her fingers trembled as she shoved loose curls behind her ears.

He looked up and smiled. Not the tight, forced
expression she so often saw, but something honest. Like he was truly happy to see her. Guilt
stabbed, but she pushed it aside. There was no
place for that in her investigation either.

"You look lovely," he said, taking in her appearance from head to toe. The sweep of his gaze was
like a caress, and she was suddenly happy she'd
worn her best riding habit.

The heat of blood rushed to her face at his compliment. How long had it been since a man's attentions actually made her blush? But like a
schoolgirl, she covered her hot cheeks.

"Thank you," she said softly. The intensity of
the connection between them was too much, so
she focused her attentions on his stallion. "He's a
beautiful animal."

In response, the melancholy returned to Tristan's
expression. "Thank you. He is magnificent."

"How long have you had him?"

"One year, eight months, fifteen days," he said
softly.

She cocked her head. "He must mean a great
deal to you if you know the very day he came into
your possession."

"He was my brother's horse. He became mine
when Edmund was killed."

The pain that bubbled just below the surface of his face tore through her.

"I'm sorry," she said, but the sentiment sounded unsatisfactory. Like she was offering a small binding to cover a gaping wound.

He shook his head. "No, I'm sorry. I shouldn't have brought him up." He motioned to a nearby stable hand who came forward leading a spirited, honey-colored mare. "Here is your horse for the day. Lily."

She smiled as the stable hands helped her into her seat. "I suppose we have only to wait for your mother, then."

One of the men stepped forward. "Lady Carmichael sent word that she was taken by a sudden headache, but she asked that the two of you take your ride without her."

Meredith's mouth twitched as Tristan ducked his head and muttered something under his breath. Lady Carmichael would make a marvelous agent. She had a brilliant way of turning any situation exactly to her liking.

"Thank you, Chester," Tristan said with a sigh. "Please send word to her ladyship that I hope her headache has passed by the time we return." As he nudged his stallion into motion, he added, "Not that I have any doubt she'll be right as rain in no time."

They rode in silence as they moved down a road

that led through the areas of the estate closest to the house. When they broke away from the path and the manicured lawns and magnificent gardens, Tristan shot a brief glance in her direction.

"I want to apologize for my mother. She is a bit . . . overzealous in her not-so-veiled attempts at matchmaking."

Meredith smiled as she thought of her ladyship. She liked Constance, probably a good deal more than she should, considering. Her smile fell. "I don't mind. She loves you. Who could blame her?"

She heard the statement leave her lips, but it was too late to call it back. "I mean—"

Tristan chuckled. "I know what you meant."

A second blush heated her cheeks, and Meredith rolled her eyes. What in the world was causing these missish reactions? Very well, she knew *what*. Being close to Tristan, smelling the spicy, masculine hint of his skin, having him touch her . . . those things brought out long forgotten feelings and urges she hadn't been able to name as a girl. Now she knew what they were. Need. Desire. Passion.

But to actually allow herself to be swept away by such things, to show her reactions when her motivations weren't purely related to her case, that was unacceptable. Yet she couldn't stop herself. Not when Tristan looked at her and his gaze drew her in so deep she feared she would drown.

No, she had to drag herself to the surface. What

he said about his brother in the stable and the exchange they just had . . . both were perfect opportunities for reconnaissance.

Clearing her throat, she said, "You never told me what the horse's name was."

Tristan reached down and absently stroked the animal's mane. "Winterborne."

She glanced at the magnificent animal. "It must have been difficult to lose your brother. He died in the war, did he not?"

The tendons in Tristan's neck tightened and his posture changed. This subject was a source of high emotion for him. The pain in his face she understood completely. But the anger buried in his eyes and in the tension of his muscles, she didn't. Was it purely anger that his brother had been taken too young? Or was there some other reason for his rage?

His jaw slowly relaxed as if he were forcing calm. "You understand feelings of loss. After all, your parents were taken from you."

Meredith was jolted by his observation. Her status as an orphan was common knowledge, but few people understood the pain and emptiness that loss had caused her. Tristan did. He'd witnessed it firsthand. For the first time in years she felt vulnerable.

"I—" she stammered. "I was very young then."

He slowed his horse as they left a wooded path and emerged onto an open, hilly area. She hardly noticed its green beauty and was not calmed by its serene warmth.

"But I think experiencing death so early must be worse. Especially since you were forced to go to your aunt and uncle's estate. I was little more than a boy, but I recognized how unhappy you were there."

Her lip quivered and she fought to remain in control by keeping her gaze straight ahead. "They took care of me."

He shrugged, but she felt him watching her. Why was he scrutinizing her reaction? "I remember you as very . . . sober. Lonely."

She sucked in her breath. With a few observations Tristan had drawn her back to a time she'd buried long ago. When she was an outsider in the only remaining family she had. When she ached for affection, longed for love.

She shook her head. This conversation would go no further into topics best left unexplored. She didn't speak of the pains of her past. Not to anyone. Even Emily and Ana only knew the most skeletal details. She certainly wasn't about to bear her soul to this man, this potential traitor.

With a brittle laugh she urged Lily to quicken her pace over the gently rolling hills and long stretches of open meadow. "I hardly remember that time, my lord. I'm surprised your recollections are so clear."

He nudged Winterborne and easily matched

Lily's canter. "Your aunt and uncle showed you little warmth. My mother often commented on that fact. And you do not seem to have contact with them now."

Meredith winced. It was as if she was being stripped down, laid bare to memory. "We are not close," she admitted, trying to remember the last time her aunt had sent her a message of any kind. "But I don't blame them. I wasn't their child. Indeed I was thrust upon them by the deaths of my mother and father. My aunt was only my mother's stepsister, you know."

Why was she talking? Why was she explaining this? But she couldn't stop.

"They weren't ever close. Who could blame her for not seeing me as flesh and blood? Yet, despite that, she and my uncle provided me with a roof, food, a Season—"

Tristan's lips pursed. "Yes. A successful Season, for you found a husband." He paused, as if considering that. "But then he died as well. In reality, you've experienced far more tragedy in your life than I."

A bitter laugh bubbled from her lips as she allowed Lily to walk. "The difference is, you loved your brother."

Again, it was as if some other woman had spoken those words and she only heard them. Except they were in her voice. They were her private thoughts.

Pulling Lily to a halt, she clamored down and paced away from Tristan. She walked up a hill and stood on its peak, gazing down over the little valley below as she cursed her stupidity.

Why had she confided in him?

The gentle touch of his hand on her elbow startled her, and she realized just how completely she had abandoned her training yet again. Never turn away from a suspect. What a laugh. She was constantly turning from Tristan, from the heat he caused in her and the emotions he excavated.

With a sigh, she looked at him. He said nothing, just watched. Waited.

She licked her dry lips. "I . . . It wasn't as if I hated Daniel," she said, though she didn't know why. This wasn't the purpose of their ride, yet she somehow felt compelled to explain herself. Explain why she felt no love for her husband. Say things she had never said before.

Tristan didn't answer, but continued to watch with an intense focus that shocked her from her comfort zone and pulled her into places she couldn't go. Was he judging her? And why did she care?

"It was not a love match," she continued. "We had very little in common, just like many other couples. But when I produced no children, the distance increased."

"And when he died . . ."

"I didn't feel much loss." She shrugged. "You

must think very little of me for admitting such a thing."

Smiling, he trailed his fingers up and brushed her cheek. Lightning flashed from the point of contact, sending shivers of awareness and feeling to every sensitive part of her body.

"No. Actually, I'm cursing myself for not seeking you out before you married instead of after."

The heated lightning flashes were replaced by colder shock as his confession sunk in. "Y-You sought me out?" she croaked.

For a moment Tristan only stared at her, then he seemed to realize the utter impropriety of the situation. Yanking his fingers from her cheek, he took a step back.

Without meeting her stare, he said, "You were married by then."

Meredith's breath came in sharp bursts as she pondered his statement. She had always believed he had forgotten about her entirely after the night he saved her. His coldness toward her, his avoidance, had stolen away any warm emotions she held in her heart when it came to him. But to hear now, all these years later, that he had sought her out . . .

How different would things have been if he had, indeed, approached her before she married Daniel Sinclair? If he pursued her before she was the woman she was today. Before he was the man he was now.

The thoughts, unwanted, unasked for, shocked her already shaken system. "Remember your duty," she muttered under her breath before she turned to Tristan with a false smile. "I think your mother's ailment is catching."

"Your head?" he asked in a strangely monotone voice.

She nodded.

"Perhaps we should return to the house."

With a sigh, Meredith headed back to Lily. But when Tristan helped her into her seat, she couldn't help but notice how his hands lingered on her waist a moment too long and how her body reacted too powerfully to that touch, no matter how much she reminded herself that Tristan, the man she had secretly wanted, was now one man she could never have.

Chapter 10

Meredith stared out her chamber window, watching the breeze flutter through the tree leaves, but her thoughts weren't on nature. Instead, they drifted, turning always to Tristan, to the way she was betraying the fragile bond they were forming. To the way he might be betraying their country, their King.

"Why am I tormenting myself?" she muttered as she snapped the window shut.

Her excuse of a headache had served her well the previous afternoon when her ride with Tristan turned too personal. Today it served her again, as she used it to escape going with the rest of the party to the annual bazaar being held in

Carmichael's main village a few miles away. Now she had only the servants to contend with as she searched for more evidence.

So why hadn't she started that search?

She sighed. Because with every piece of proof, every observation that led her to believe Tristan was a traitor willing to barter military secrets, some emotion in her interfered. Her intuition insisted he wasn't capable of such treachery, and she had come to trust her instincts as much as she trusted the facts. But the two had never been at odds before. Until now her heart hadn't included itself in debates over guilt and innocence.

"My lady?"

With a start, she turned to see a housemaid standing at the door. She motioned the girl in and took the letter she carried on a silver tray. Immediately, she recognized Ana's steady hand, and her excitement grew. Perhaps her friend had deciphered something from the evidence she'd already collected. Something to clear Tristan.

"Will there be anything else?" the girl asked.

Meredith barely spared her a glance. "No, thank you. I'll be lying down once I read my letter, so please tell the staff that I don't wish to be disturbed."

The girl bobbed out a curtsey, then left. No sooner had the door closed, then Meredith tore into the missive from her friend. It was encoded, of course, but after so many years of exposure to

Ana's ingenious system, Meredith read it like it was written plainly.

She frowned as she sank into the nearest chair. No evidence had been found to implicate Philip Barclay. In fact, Barclay's only dealings with Devlin coincided with meetings the man took with Tristan. There were many more times the two met when Barclay wasn't present at all.

Disappointment raced through her. She had so hoped Barclay was the key to absolving Tristan. But he wasn't. And her lack of impartiality slapped her in the face.

Her mouth thinned as she moved to the section regarding Edmund Archer. Tristan's younger brother joined the military against Tristan's wishes, but that wasn't so very uncommon. Most men of position or rank could buy their way out of military service, but some felt it their duty to defend their country. In Edmund's case, he had paid the ultimate price.

Her eyes widened as she read the final paragraphs. Edmund Archer had been killed in an attack thought to have been caused when secret information fell into the hands of enemy soldiers.

She let the letter drop at her side. If Tristan's beloved brother was killed because of traitorous activities, why would he involve himself with a group responsible for the same thing?

Her thoughts drifted to the anger in his eyes, the rage that pulsed beneath the surface, especially when the subject of Edmund's death arose. Could he have turned that anger toward the government?

She shivered at the thought before she glanced at the note one final time. To her surprise, Ana had scribbled a message, unencoded, at the bottom of the letter. "Are you well? We are worried."

Meredith pursed her lips as she tossed the letter into the fire. Her turmoil had been plain, even in her hastily jotted notes asking for information from home. She had to work harder to mask it or she might find Emily and Ana on the doorstep offering to help with her case.

Or worse, she might not be able to keep others from seeing her heart. Like Devlin. Like Tristan.

Thrusting her shoulders back with determination, she slipped into the hallway. Quietly, she crept through the house, hiding in doorways and ducking behind furniture to avoid the occasional bustling servant.

With little difficulty, she reached Tristan's private office. She entered and shut the door behind her, leaning back as she let out her breath in relief. Even after years of training in the fine art of stealth, she hadn't rid herself of the absolute terror that she would be caught while sneaking into a place she didn't belong.

She didn't have much time. She might be interrupted by a servant at any moment, or Tristan could return home. She would be forced to hurry.

Men under suspicion often hid the evidence of their crimes in plain sight. Some even flaunted their deeds by putting them in the open where only a trained eye would detect what they meant. She glanced around the room in one sweep, taking care to examine each portrait on the walls, as well as the various knickknacks and books on Tristan's shelves.

Her attention was drawn to the far wall above the mantel, and a large portrait of a young man in military dress. She guessed he was Edmund Archer by the setting and style of the piece and her memories of the boy as a child.

Edmund had his brother's dark hair and sensual mouth, but his eyes were different. Instead of the haunting, dark green, they were a rich brown. He had been a handsome young man, and she momentarily mourned the loss this family had endured.

Searching her memory, she tried to remember what he'd been like the few times he joined his mother and Tristan on their visits to her aunt and uncle's estate. Wild, she recalled, but friendly. In trouble more often than not. Meredith could only imagine that the mischievous boy had been more troublesome as a willful young man who refused to accept his elder brother's new role as father figure.

Turning away from the portrait, she refocused her attention on her search for clues. Tristan's desk attracted her eye. For a man so cool and collected, it appeared quite messy. Papers were strewn across the top with no clear order. That could be because Tristan had been busy lately with his guests . . . or it might be a tactic to keep servants from stumbling upon incriminating information. If his desk was sloppy, his house staff wouldn't move his papers, fearing they would disturb the order.

She tapped her fingers along the desktop. Some of the items related to Tristan's business on the estate. Ledgers regarding his tenants, notes on improving the agriculture of the area, and a maintenance list for the grounds caught her eye.

Taking care to note the basic arrangement of the papers, she moved a few aside to view what was beneath. The blood drained from her face.

Letters. Written from Augustine Devlin and others of his ilk who had long been suspects in various crimes.

She picked one up and pulled the missive from the envelope.

"Damn," she muttered. Like Ana's letter to her, the note was encoded. Her heart clenched. If Tristan was trusted enough to have been taught Devlin's code for delicate information, that meant he was more involved with the other man's organization than she hoped.

She scanned each word. The code didn't seem complex, but it was Ana who was the genius when it came to that part of their duties. She was sure her friend would be able to break it with little trouble, but Meredith knew there was no way she could remove a letter without risking Tristan's notice. With a sigh, she read the note a few times. She could only hope her memory would serve her well, at least until she could transcribe what she'd seen.

She put the correspondence back in its original position and slipped around the other side of the desk to open the top drawer. There, right in front, where she could not pretend not to notice, was an advertisement from the Genevieve Art House, describing in detail the auction that was approaching when the painting was stolen.

Her breath left her in a gust and she sank into Tristan's chair. Tears stung her eyes as she glanced over the descriptions and found the one for the painting at the center of her case. Her only consolation was that it hadn't been marked in any way to indicate Tristan's interest.

"Still," she murmured, unable to take her eyes from the page, "why would he have it here, so far from London? Even if it was brought here by accident, wouldn't he simply discard it rather than put it in his desk drawer for safekeeping?

She had no answers to those questions. At least none she wished to entertain at present. She covered her eyes and forced tears not to fall. She wasn't going to cry over a suspect.

As she dropped her hands, she heard footsteps

in the hallway. When they passed, she got to her feet. She'd stayed too long, distracted by emotions. It was time to go.

Moving to the doorway, she placed her ear against the solid wood and listened for sounds outside. She heard none. Creaking the door open slowly, she peered around. The hallway was empty. She took a few steps out, shut the door behind her, and was three paces down the hall when she heard another door open. Without pausing to look at who was behind her, she ducked into the first room where she could easily explain her presence.

The library.

Inside, she rushed to one of the bookcases and grabbed the first tome in easy reach. The door opened before she could look at the title.

She turned with what she hoped was a friendly smile and found herself meeting the stare of Philip Barclay.

"Hello," she said, pulling the book she had torn from the shelf against her breast.

Suspicion lit in Barclay's stare. "Good afternoon, my lady." He folded his arms as he glanced around the room. "I did not realize you were up and about. I was told you'd taken ill and were lying down while the others explored the bazaar."

She shrugged. "My ailment was merely a headache that happily passed. I thought I'd find a book to read until the others return." She smiled sweetly. "I hope you don't think me too terribly rude."

To her surprise, Philip didn't automatically respond in the negative as would be polite. Instead, he glanced at the book she held in her arms.

"Well, at least you'll find more interesting choices here."

She cocked her head. "Yes?"

"As opposed to Tristan's office." He met her stare with an arched brow.

She held back a curse. She had been seen. Well, there was nothing to do about it now but try to come up with a good lie. "You know how it is at these events, Mr. Barclay. It's so easy to get lost in someone else's home."

For a moment they only stared, sizing each other up. She did her best to keep her gaze innocent, but when he looked at her with such unguarded doubt, it was hard not to return the favor.

"Well, I have now found an interesting diversion." She held up the book in her hand and prayed it wasn't some tome on agriculture or worse. "And I think I shall return to my room."

As she moved past him toward the open door, Barclay's voice called her back.

"My lady?"

She turned with her best blank smile. Passive, empty. Totally against character. "Yes?"

"Do you know if any ladies in the party have lost a dancing slipper?" He looked at her evenly.

Her heart sank. After her narrow escape from Devlin's quarters, Meredith had returned to the garden in the wee hours of the morning to find her slippers, but had only been able to find one. She intended to search again when she had more light and time. Now it was clear she was too late.

"A dancing slipper? Like in the fairy tale?" she said with a laugh.

He didn't join her. "Yes. I made a check of the estate after the ball and discovered a lady's slipper tangled in a bush."

"What a mystery." She clenched the book in a sweaty palm. "I wonder how it ever came to be there?"

"I really don't know."

"Perhaps some of Lord Carmichael's guests became—" She forced a blush. "—amorous during the ball. Certainly a lady could lose a slipper during such an activity."

Barclay's nostrils flared. "Perhaps. I only ask because the shoe put me to mind of your very lovely gown that evening and the beautiful diamonds you had in your hair."

Blast! Her slippers *did* have little costume diamonds sewn along the top. She blinked. "My, how nice of you to compliment my attire. It is a favorite gown of mine, I admit."

He folded his arms. "But the slipper is not yours."

With a shake of her head, she placed a hand on her breast. "Oh my, no."

His lips thinned. "Well, if you hear from any of the ladies that they lost the item, they can send their maid to fetch it from our housekeeper, Mrs. Landon. She has it in safekeeping."

Meredith barely held back a snort. Obviously, Barclay suspected the owner of the shoe of some kind of nefarious doings. Anyone who fetched the item would be watched.

"I will do so, of course," she said. "Now, if you'll excuse me, I'll return to my chambers. Good afternoon."

He nodded as she left. Heading down the hall, Meredith scowled.

"And I really loved those slippers too."

Tristan smiled blankly at the young woman he was assisting from one of the many carriages that lined the drive. Somewhere in the back of his mind he knew her name, but for the life of him he couldn't recall it, even when she turned her pretty face up and blinked long, thick lashes at him.

His distraction wasn't a new affliction. Actually, it had dogged him all afternoon, ever since he was informed that Meredith wouldn't accompany the group to the village.

He had not been close to her in nearly twenty-four hours. Not since their awkward parting after their ride the morning before. Oh, she had been at luncheon and supper. He'd been but a stone's throw from her side all evening as his guests played whist, gossiped about society, and even entertained each other by playing the pianoforte. He had been aware of her every breath, her every smile, her every side glance.

But he hadn't spoken to her. Hadn't been close enough to breathe the intoxicating scent that hung so dark and sensual around her. He hadn't touched her since he helped her take her seat on her mount when they rode together.

He missed her.

The forgotten young woman at his side slipped a hand into the crook of his arm as he led her back into the foyer, but he barely felt the touch. He could not keep his mind from straying to altogether inappropriate thoughts of Meredith.

He told Devlin he was pursuing her, and his mother's matchmaking attempts certainly forced him to act the part. But he had hoped to keep reality separate from his attempts to shelter Meredith.

Instead, he found himself thinking of her at the most inopportune moments of the day. And at night? Well, his dreams had become most pleasurable. He was starting to despair waking from them.

"My lord?"

He started as he came back to the present. The young lady he had escorted into the house was tugging at his arm. He released her and she all but stumbled back. Her brow wrinkled in irritation.

"Thank you, my lord. It was a most pleasurable day."

He nodded absently as Meredith's face appeared before his eyes. Smiling. Laughing. Daring him to forget his troubles, if only for a brief time.

The war within him had been lost. He had to see her.

Turning on his heel, he started for the stairs when Philip's voice stopped him.

"Tristan?"

Startled, he turned to see his friend staring at him. "Yes?"

"Did you not hear me say your name?"

Tristan drew a breath. This was exactly the problem. When he thought of Meredith, his mind blocked all else. He was so close to ending the madness his life had become. To let anything divert him so thoroughly was a dangerous mistake.

"No." He gave his friend an apologetic shrug as he crossed to him. "I'm sorry. Obviously I was . . . distracted."

"Obviously." His friend's tone was worried as he searched Tristan's gaze. "May we have a moment?"

Tristan cast a glance up the staircase. Like a siren to a helpless sailor, the lure of seeing Meredith called him. "Could it wait? I was hoping to look in on Meredith—" He held back a curse. "To look in on Lady Northam. She's been unwell two days now."

Philip's mouth thinned. "I believe Lady Northam has fully recovered from whatever 'ailment' troubled her. I saw her this afternoon."

"You did? Very good."

"She was leaving your office, Tristan."

That statement yanked him from his haze. All his attention swerved to Philip as he ran over a long list of items in his private office that he would never want Meredith or anyone else he cared for to see. He motioned to the parlor behind his friend.

After he'd shut the door behind them and checked to ensure that no guest or servant was in the room, Tristan said, "Tell me."

Philip sighed, as if he regretted what he had to share. Tristan's heart sank.

"I believe her ladyship may have been searching your office."

Tristan stumbled into a nearby settee. Shock coursed through him as he digested this claim. "What do you mean? Why would she do that?"

Philip shrugged one shoulder. "I wish I knew."

"Why do you accuse her of such a thing, then?" His voice level notched up, but he could do nothing to prevent it.

His friend's eyes widened at the sudden anger in Tristan's tone, but he did not respond in kind. "There was something in her manner and expression when I questioned her that told me she was not truthful."

A little sprout of hope germinated in Tristan's heart. "And what was her response to your questioning?"

Philip shook his head. "She told me she was looking for a novel to read after her headache passed, but that she had gotten lost on her way to the library."

The hope bloomed. "And *that* is why you have decided she was searching my office? Dear God, Philip, you made me believe this was serious. Her explanation is totally understandable. Obviously the strain of our deceptions has made you unreasonable."

Philip's eyes widened. "I am not unreasonable. Meredith Sinclair is hiding something."

Anger rose in Tristan, the kind he had never felt toward his friend before. But he'd never before had to defend a woman he cared for against his friend's callous accusations. "What could she be hiding?"

"I don't know." The words were ground past Philip's teeth. "But I confronted her about the slipper I found in the garden after the ball, and she seemed uncomfortable with that line of conversation as well."

For a moment, Tristan didn't even know what Philip was talking about and then he recalled a passing comment after the ball. Something about a woman's slipper found in the bushes near the house.

"Well, it's a ridiculous topic."

Philip was silent, then said, "May I say something as your friend, not your man of affairs?"

Tristan shrugged, though he wasn't sure he wanted to hear whatever his 'friend' was going to say.

"I've known you a long time. I have been a part of your boyish pranks, seen you change after your father's death, and been a party to—" Philip broke off. "Well, I've helped you in every way I could because we're friends. But you are blinded by Meredith Sinclair's charm and beauty. And she knows that."

"Enough." Tristan took a menacing step toward Philip, and his friend took a corresponding step away, his eyes lighting with sudden . . . fear. The expression was enough to check Tristan's anger. "What reason would she have to deceive me?"

"Augustine Devlin has been testing you for nearly a year." Philip glanced at him briefly before his gaze flitted away. "He has been trying to determine if you're trustworthy enough to enter the inner circles of his group. If you are to be granted access to the leader of his organization."

Tristan scowled. He wanted that more than anything. "Yes."

"What if—" Philip's hesitation grated. "What if Meredith is a part of the tests?"

Tristan's fists clenched on reflex. "What do you mean?"

Philip dipped his chin. "What if Meredith is

working with Devlin? It's clear she has an effect on you like no other woman I've ever seen. What if *she* is another test? Has she asked you to take her into your confidence?"

Tristan stormed to the poorboy and splashed scotch into a tumbler. He downed it in one swig as he thought about the many times Meredith had asked about his most secret desires and pains. He had believed it was because of their prior connection, and the new attraction between them. But now . . .

"That is ridiculous!" he said, with less certainty than he wished he had.

"Think about it before you dismiss it," Philip insisted. "You haven't had any contact with this woman for years. Yet she approached you and obtained an invitation to your country soiree on the same night . . . the *last* night you would be in London."

Tristan wanted to block the words, but they seeped in. Along with memories of conversations with Devlin. His interest in Meredith. His questions about Tristan's loyalty. If she was a test, certainly Devlin had played his hand perfectly, forcing Tristan to stake a claim and spend time with her in order to "protect" her. If Philip was right, her inquiries might have more to do with Devlin's desire to determine his loyalty when someone he cared for examined him than her own interest or concern.

But then his mind slipped to both times she surrendered to his kiss. Her reaction to even the graze of his touch. Her honesty about family pains when they rode together. Those things were real. He knew that as surely as he knew his own name.

"You doubt me," Philip said softly.

Tristan looked up. "No. What you say could well be true. But I feel . . ." He trailed off.

Philip nodded. "I know. Just be wary. And know I'm watching her, as closely as I watch Devlin."

Frowning, Tristan stared out the window behind his friend with unseeing eyes. "Yes. Very good."

With a sigh, Philip left him to his thoughts. As the door closed, Tristan scrubbed a hand over his face. He was watching Meredith too. In fact, he couldn't keep his eyes off her.

He only hoped he wasn't being blinded by the feelings she inspired.

Chapter 11

"There is no word regarding Augustine Devlin's letter." Meredith read the last, most hated line from Emily's latest encoded message out loud. She tossed the missive on the table with disgust and paced the room. "Damnation."

She had worked so hard to intercept the letter Devlin penned the night she was nearly caught in his bedroom. If Tristan hadn't interrupted her, she would have had it to Anastasia for decoding right now. She wouldn't have to fear for Tristan's life each time Devlin wasn't accounted for, and she might even have more evidence to end this case.

But because Tristan decided to act like her unwanted protector, the message was missing.

Vanished like a petal on the wind. Even The Society's best contacts within the post hadn't been able to uncover its destination.

She strummed her fingertips along the mantel. Not knowing where that potentially deadly letter had gone was an element out of her control. She did not like that, especially in this volatile situation.

Her very emotions were wild, and the inner turmoil was not something to which she was accustomed. For years she had worked hard to measure her reactions.

When she arrived at her aunt and uncle's home after the death of her parents, it was made abundantly clear that she would receive no special attention from the family, and so she closed her feelings off in order to protect herself.

The next time she'd allowed her emotions to come into play was with Tristan. Her girlish crush had led nowhere, though. When he pushed her away, it broke her heart, so she had allowed her aunt and uncle to arrange a marriage for her with a man she didn't care for.

Daniel did not seem to want her love, and she never made an effort to connect with him beyond polite tolerance and conversation. Their marriage was proper, passionless. She had been fine with that. But lonely.

Tristan had reminded her of just how lonely when he revealed that he had come looking for her, only to discover she was already married.

Now, she dashed that thought from her mind as she stomped to her chamber door and into the hallway. She had no idea where she was going. No idea where she could hide from the new feelings Tristan inspired in her. But she wanted to hide. *Needed* to hide.

"Oh, there you are, Lady Northam."

Tensing, Meredith shut her eyes. It was Lady Carmichael's voice drifting down the hallway behind her.

Plastering a false smile on her lips, she turned. "Good afternoon, my lady."

"Won't you join me?"

Constance stepped back and motioned toward her private rooms. Meredith searched for a way to escape this invitation, but found none.

"Of course." She came down the hall and stepped inside.

The sitting room in the Lady Carmichael's bedroom suite was as lovely as any she'd seen. Soft floral colors decorated the walls and furniture. The floor was polished to a high shine, and a wonderful Persian rug covered the area where a small tea service had been set.

"What a marvelous room," Meredith breathed even as a sense of discomfort filled her. As always, being alone with the kind woman filled her with guilt. Here Constance was trying to arrange a marriage for her son, and Meredith was just as busy trying to prove he was a traitor and preparing his neck for a noose. Tristan's actions forced this course of action, but she didn't like lying to Lady Carmichael just the same.

"I hope you'll have tea."

Again she sought an escape, but before she could come up with one, Constance stepped forward and placed a hand on her forearm. A spark of that dreaded emotion she tried to rein in shot through her.

How long had it been since she felt a motherly touch? So many years. Memories of her mother flooded back, soft with the passage of time.

"Please, stay and talk with me," Constance coaxed as she motioned to the settee by the fire.

Meredith had battled traitors and criminals of all kinds, yet now found herself utterly helpless. She was led, mute and without protest, to the settee and found herself being handed a cup of hot tea, prepared just as she liked it, though she didn't recall telling Constance what her preferences were. Apparently, her ladyship had done some investigating of her own.

"May we speak plainly, my dear?" Constance asked, her sharp green eyes observing all over the edge of her teacup.

Meredith considered that question. No, she could not speak plainly. Ever. But she shrugged one shoulder. "Of course."

Constance placed her teacup back in its saucer. "I know you had a—well, it was a painful past."

Meredith flinched. "Not so, my lady, I assure you."

Her face softened. "My dear, I was a frequent visitor at your aunt and uncle's home. There was no cruelty, but little love. I often spoke to your aunt about it. 'Hilde,' I said, 'that is no way to treat a child.' "

Blood rushed to Meredith's cheeks. She hadn't been aware Constance had intervened on her behalf. The idea gave her a warmth she had not felt in ages. Replaced immediately by more of that stabbing remorse.

"I'm sorry." Constance sighed. "I didn't mean to remind you of painful things. I only meant to say that you have experienced some powerful hurts in your young life . . . and so has my son."

Meredith swallowed as she dared to peek at Lady Carmichael. Her eyes had grown distant and clouded with unshed tears.

"Tristan's father may have been severe with him, but when Tristan lost him, it took away any carefree enjoyment he may have found in life. Then Edmund died not long after. He knows what it is like to lose. As do you." Her eyes refocused on Meredith with an undeniable intent. "Perhaps together you can find a balm for those pains. I have watched you when you are in each other's company. It's done my heart good."

"My lady—" Meredith began as she struggled for breath.

Constance raised a hand. "I realize it is truly none of my affair. And normally, I attempt to be far more subtle in my matchmaking attempts."

Despite her shock at Lady Carmichael's forward statements, Meredith couldn't help a small smile.

"I see you laughing to yourself," Constance teased.

Meredith's grin grew wider. "You love your son very much."

Constance's smile fell. "I do. And I see you two making some kind of tenuous connection, yet you each maintain a distance."

Meredith scrambled to her feet and paced away. Her hands trembled, her heart throbbed. Constance Archer could have trained in interrogation techniques, given the way she made Meredith feel. Helpless. Unable to resist.

"Certainly, I do—I do care for your son, as I always have. But if you see anything more than friendship between us, it is your imagination playing tricks on you."

Lady Carmichael rose. "No, it is not. I know Tristan. Since his brother died, he's been haunted. Nothing could tempt him from the darkness he has inhabited."

Meredith wanted to close her ears, force herself not to hear Constance's freely given admissions as evidence. For the first time ever, she wished she could listen without the filter of her training, without the suspicion natural to her vocation.

Constance continued, oblivious to the war raging inside Meredith's heart. "Since he saw you in London, there has been a light in Tristan's eyes. One I've missed seeing for so very long. That light I see is not imagined, it's real. And I think if you allow yourself, you might discover a lifetime of happiness with him."

Meredith slowly turned to face Lady Carmichael. Everything in the kindly woman's demeanor said true hope, absolute honesty. Constance wanted to believe there would be a fairy-tale ending for her son.

Yet, with each passing day, Meredith collected more evidence to prevent that. With her. With any woman. She felt a powerful desire to warn Constance of the pain that could come shortly.

Truth be told, she sometimes wanted to do the same for Tristan. Warn him. Betray her organization to keep him safe.

"I so appreciate your thinking of me and my happiness," she stammered. "Your kindness touches me more than you'll ever understand, but—"

Lady Carmichael held up a hand. "It is none of my affair, I know. I only wanted to say my thoughts, but I won't interfere again. You and my son must work out whatever is between you alone." Her face softened as she reached out to stroke the back of her hand across Meredith's cheek. "You were such a sweet child. And you've become a lovely young woman."

"Thank you, my lady," she choked out with difficulty.

Constance pulled away, and the spell she seemed to weave faded. Now that Meredith was able to draw breath, she looked at her companion. As much as she wanted to bolt from the room and the emotions Constance inspired, she couldn't.

"I wonder how much you know about Mr. Devlin?" she ventured, treading lightly as she struggled to bring her tremulous feelings under control.

Lady Carmichael cocked her head. "Not much, I'm afraid. Tristan has many friends in London whom I do not know." A shadow moved over her face. "More now than ever before, actually. Mr. Devlin is one of those people. He seems amiable enough."

Meredith searched her companion's face. Though she said proper and polite things, Constance's eyes had changed and her mouth tightened when she spoke of Devlin. Still, there was no deception in her demeanor. She didn't doubt that Constance knew nothing about the true nature of Devlin's dealings. If there was dislike from Lady Carmichael for the man, it was born from intuition, nothing deeper.

"I ask because it has been mentioned they are involved in business together, and I'm always looking for new avenues in that area."

Constance beamed. "My son has a good head

for business," she said. "Look at how well the Carmichael holdings have fared since he took over as Marquis. If you have interest in his investments, he can definitely be of assistance."

"Is there no one else whom he entrusts his dealings to?" she asked.

"Not that I'm aware of. Philip Barclay is his man of affairs, but Tristan has taken great pride in being personally involved in all aspects of his estates and other dealings. If it has to do with Carmichael or the Archer name, Tristan has a hand in it."

Nausea churned Meredith's stomach, though Constance was only confirming facts she already knew. There was no hidden person pulling strings in the background or taking advantage of Tristan's trust.

Masking her disappointment, Meredith got to her feet. "I should excuse myself. I have a few things to take care of before I ready myself for supper and the masquerade ball tonight."

Lady Carmichael nodded. "Of course. Thank you for joining me and indulging an old woman in her musings."

With a smile, Meredith slipped from the room. The second she shut the door, however, she collapsed against the wall, her breath coming in pants. Pain exploded in her chest as she relived the conversation, but she knew that was nothing compared to the heartache she would cause with the evidence she was collecting.

It would destroy this family. Constance would be broken. The Archer name would never recover. Tristan would be transported to Australia at best . . . and at worst . . . She shivered and refused to finish the thought.

But as she stumbled down the hallway, she knew there was one more person who would be affected and harmed by her investigation.

Herself.

Her emotions had become involved with everyone in this family. There was no escaping the disappointment and pain at the thought of destroying Tristan.

"Tonight at the masquerade," she whispered as she headed for the stairway that would take her outside to the fresh air.

While the other partygoers enjoyed their drinks and wondered what dashing gentleman was spinning around the floor with which lovely lady, she would conduct the search she had been avoiding.

A search of the place she most feared to tread.

The ball spun around Tristan like an ever-turning child's toy. It was a mass of blurred color and mysterious masks. The annual masquerade was a longtime tradition of his family, stretching back to his great-grandfather's era. His mother had kept it up, even during the years his father and brother died.

"It is our duty and our expectation," she had said through her tears.

"Duty and expectation," he murmured. His father had pounded both concepts into his mind, but he never dreamed he would become so intimately acquainted with them. Or with lies and betrayals. Yet here he was.

Suddenly, his mind was pulled away from those dark musings. From the corner of his eye he caught a glimpse of a pale pink gown with a dark rose overskirt. Its wearer also bore a dusty pink mask with petals attached. A flower amongst thistles.

Meredith.

Tristan tracked her movements around the dance floor. At least she wasn't in the arms of any of the young bucks who had come to Carmichael for the ball. It was an older man who guided her through the somewhat complicated steps of the country dance. He was glad of that. Seeing her with some handsome rake would have bothered him. Another fact he hated to admit, but couldn't deny any more than he could deny himself breath. He didn't want Meredith in anyone's arms but his own.

She gave a little hop as they made the next turn, and her skirt flared, giving Tristan a glimpse of a trim ankle and the beginnings of a slender calf, both clothed in pale pink stockings stitched with little rosebuds. Hot blood burst through his system at just that hint of flesh, and his mind exploded with fantasies of stripping those stockings off, along with that pretty gown.

"She is lovely."

Tristan started. Without his being aware, Augustine Devlin had slipped up beside him. Devlin's mask, a dandified contraption of feathers, hid most of his features. Only his hard mouth and cold, gray stare were visible.

The mouth was turned up in a wretched, cocky smirk. The eyes regarded Meredith with predatory interest. Tristan fisted his hands and counted to ten in his head before he answered.

"All the ladies here tonight are lovely," he said with forced disinterest. "The masks make them all the more alluring."

"Hmm. So you claim you do not know exactly which woman is yours?" Devlin's eyes crinkled with disbelieving humor. "I saw you watching the one in the rose mask. You know who she is."

Tristan's mouth thinned as he let his gaze slip to Meredith a second time. "Meredith is difficult to overlook."

Devlin barked out a triumphant chuckle. "You are correct on that score." He paused. "I'm surprised you have not made your affections more known if you truly have a claim on the lady."

Tristan's scowl deepened as Meredith bowed to her partner with a light laugh and pushed a strand of hair that had pulled out of her elaborate style away from her eyes. He didn't make his "claim" on her more apparent because if he touched her once more, he wouldn't stop. Because every moment he was near her, he walked a fine line between all the dangers he could expose her to with his presence.

Devlin continued, "You have walked together and you rode out a few mornings ago . . . but only briefly."

Tristan's gaze shot to Devlin. So, he had been collecting information on Tristan's activities. Briefly, he thought of Philip's warning that Meredith might be a test created by Devlin. No. It couldn't be true.

"If your affection for the lady has waned, I would be happy to—"

"No!" A few people nearby swiveled their heads at his loud voice. Tempering his tone, he said, "No. In fact, I am dancing the next with her."

He watched the other man carefully. Normally, his every move toward Devlin was carefully calculated. When it came to Meredith, though, he had to act on his feet. Devlin's smirk broadened.

Bastard.

"A shame," he sighed. "But I told you I'd stand clear of the lady while you were involved. It is my token of trust." Now the smug enjoyment left his tone and his stare was more focused. "What will you give me in return?"

Clenching his fists tighter, Tristan spun on his heel and started across the ballroom. Anger tingled in every nerve ending, fed each blood vessel and vein. It coursed through him, bubbled at the surface. Only years of practiced control kept the emotion from overflowing.

Control and the sight of Meredith. Her latest dance partner had left her side. For the moment, she was alone, looking around, her blue eyes soaking up every part of the scene as if she were storing them in her memory for later.

He glanced over his shoulder. Devlin was watching, arms folded, his smug expression visible even from a distance. Without a word, Tristan clasped Meredith's elbow. She gasped at the contact, and he had to hold back his own breath of surprise when electric heat snapped between them. Just this slight touch set his body at the ready. He could only imagine what the slide of her naked skin against his while he made love to her would incite.

He dragged her onto the dance floor and pulled her into his embrace just as the orchestra played the first lilting strains of the waltz.

Though she couldn't see his face clearly behind the dark mask, Meredith had no doubt that the person who hauled her to the dance floor as if she were his to command was Tristan. She felt it in the spark that flickered between them. In the way her body swayed toward his, even though she should have resisted his brute demands. In the heat of his body, which seemed to suffuse her pores.

Without a word, he caught her hand in his larger one. The fingers of his other hand spanned her hip, possessive as they spread and pressed against her body. She was branded by the burning heat of his touch, even through so many layers of silk and satin.

Catching her breath, she gathered her composure. She could not make a scene, but she had to regain some control over herself. For propriety if nothing else. By the curious glances in their direction, it was clear others had noticed the powerful way Tristan claimed her . . . and the way she did nothing to resist.

"Wh-What are you doing?" she gasped.

The heat of his breath stirred her cheek as the music began and he glided her into motion. Why did this dance have to be a waltz? At least in a country jig she would have space from him, not this tantalizing grazing of bodies with each and every step.

"You're dancing the next with me," he said in an even, matter-of-fact monotone. His voice said he didn't really care. His eyes told a different story. Beneath the protection of his mask, desire flamed in the green of his stare. Could he see her answering need as clearly?

"I—" she began, intent on scolding him. On reminding him that he had not asked for such liberties and she was not his to claim whenever he had the urge.

"Shhh." A smile tilted his lips beneath the mask edge. Something she so rarely saw that it halted her protests. "Dance with me. Don't argue or analyze or bargain. Just dance."

Her lips parted, but she stopped herself from retorting. This might very well be her last chance to be so close to him. To feel his touch.

If he was proven a traitor, he would be put away, or worse. Even if he wasn't . . . even if all her hopes and desires came true and it was proven he had nothing to do with the painting's disappearance, she wouldn't find herself living the happily ever after existence of a fairy tale. She would know she'd lied to this man. She would know she used his family, suspected and investigated him and his friends.

That was too big a secret, too big a lie to keep between them. Not to mention the fact that she was an active spy. And she wanted to remain active. There was no way that would happen if she entangled herself with this man.

So this dance could very well be a dance of farewell.

She glanced up into his eyes and shivered beneath the burning focus of his scrutiny.

"Are you cold?" he whispered.

She shook her head, eye contact never breaking. "No."

The music around them faded and the crowd on the dance floor began to thin. But Tristan stayed where he was, staring down at her in the middle of the floor, seemingly oblivious to the scene they were creating.

"Tristan?" she whispered, and her voice cracked with the feelings she was being forced to crush down. The hopes she couldn't dare have for this man and her future.

He glided his hand to her face and his fingertips slipped beneath the edge of her mask to stroke her cheek. The touch was so intimate, so pleasurable, that she shut her eyes for a brief moment and held back a moan.

Before her shuttered lids floated images of everything she knew. The carriage with Tristan's crest driving away from the scene of the robbery, his refusal to cooperate with an investigation, the encoded letters from Augustine Devlin and his suspicious private conversations with the man, the flyer from the auction house . . . they converged in her mind as one giant arrow pointing toward Tristan's guilt.

Her eyes flew open and she pulled back from his embrace. "Thank you, my lord. Good evening."

Turning, she bolted from the ballroom onto the

terrace outside. As the night air cooled her hot skin, she glanced up at Tristan's bedroom window. She could not avoid her duty any longer. Not if it helped her distance her heart from the man and the damage he could do if she let herself care for him any more than she already did.

Chapter 12

〜〜◯◯〜〜

Tristan's door was unlocked. Meredith's heart swelled with irrational joy at that fact. An unlocked door could mean he was a man with nothing to hide.

"Or," she muttered as she closed the door behind her and pushed the mask she'd worn during the ball away from her face. She slipped it up to perch on the crown of her head. "It could mean he's so sure of his cleverness, he feels no need to hide his misdeeds."

With a sigh, she looked around. The sight of Tristan's chamber gave her a shock. It was so *him*. Dark green paint graced the walls, a color not dissimilar from its owner's eyes when they darkened with desire. Certainly, she'd seen that desire a great many times since her arrival. And she ached for it, even though it was to her detriment.

Firelight flickered off the beautiful cherrywood furniture and drew her attention to the big bed that was the centerpiece of the room. With high pillars and a draping canopy above, it wasn't something anyone could ignore. It was difficult not to imagine Tristan sprawled across the sheets with an inviting look in his eyes.

Or better yet, imagine them together on that bed with nothing between them. Lies. Investigations. Clothing.

She shivered. Those thoughts wouldn't help her. She had to banish them from her errant mind. Now that she had made a cursory sweep of the chamber, it was time to deepen the search.

She moved to the chest of drawers, trying to ignore the reflection of that distracting bed in the mirror above the piece. Along the top were a collection of miniatures in gilded frames. She recognized the one of his mother first, done recently, judging from the style of her hair and gown. Next to it was another of a man she guessed was Tristan's father. She had only met the man once very long ago, but she saw Tristan in his face.

There were three more young ladies represented in the little pictures. Tristan's sisters. Each was wearing the white gown of a debutante, though she knew them all to be married now. They were a handsome family. The only one missing was—

From the corner of her eye she caught sight of a little elevated platform on the corner of the chest of drawers. Edmund's miniature was there, set off from the rest. She lifted the picture and examined the image more closely.

Unlike the portrait in Tristan's office, Edmund wasn't wearing regimentals. He seemed younger. This miniature was done in an earlier time, a happier time.

She set the picture back in place, but couldn't tear her eyes away. What did Tristan see when he looked at his brother? A life taken too soon? Or one stolen by the government? Did he feel only regret, or a drive for revenge?

With a shake of her head, she turned away. No manner of investigation would ever tell her those things. They were matters of Tristan's heart, his soul. Hidden in places she couldn't touch . . . no matter how much she wanted to.

Her gaze flitted back to the bed. Her troubled thoughts faded as she moved toward it, trying to convince herself it was only to determine if any evidence was hidden there. But that was a lie.

She glided her fingertips from the foot of the mattress to the head of the bed, memorizing the feel of the soft silken coverlet that matched the green walls. When she came even with the pillow, she found herself reaching for it as if she no longer had control over her limbs.

Slowly, she lifted it and breathed deeply. It smelled of Tristan. Clean and masculine, a mixture of potent male and fresh springwater. The combination made her knees go weak.

"What are you doing to me?" she whispered as she rested her forehead on the pillow in her hands.

The sound of the door opening behind her made her spin. Tristan stood in the doorway, his big, strong body framed by the brighter lights of the hallway lamps and candles. His hair was slightly disheveled, as if he'd been running his fingers through it, and his mask dangled from his hand. He stared at her, eyes wide and wary. And wanting.

The pillow in her hand swished to the floor as their gazes locked. His lips parted and his eyes widened. And then they darkened, not just with surprise, but with that same desire that she feared beyond all measure. Especially now when she was standing in his chamber, touching his bed.

And she had no good explanation for why she was here.

"Meredith?"

The word was a question, but it was also a caress. The rough sound of his whisper reverberated down her spine, making every nerve tingle. She clenched her fists as if she could bodily fight the need he inspired.

When she didn't answer, he took a slow step toward her. He left the door behind him open, the light from the hallway brightening the room and also offering her safety. As long as the door remained open, nothing could get too far out of hand.

"Why—" He cocked his head. "Why are you here?"

She swallowed hard as her mind went wild trying to find an answer to that question. What could she say? That she'd come to search his room for incriminating evidence but she'd be going now? Oh yes, that would be just perfect.

And there was no use pretending to be lost either. The family quarters were not housed in the same wing of the residence as the guest rooms. She would have to be a complete idiot to roam aimlessly into the wrong place and happen to stumble into his private chamber.

Aside from which, it wouldn't explain why he had caught her with his pillow in her hand.

She sighed. There was only one reason she could give that would ring true. And it was the most dangerous explanation of all because it would force her to call upon the honest truth.

"There is something between us, Tristan."

Her voice trembled, a reaction that was anything but forced. Saying those words out loud terrified her. And she hated herself for using the real, pure attraction she felt for him against him for the sake of her investigation. It cheapened the feelings in her heart. It cheapened *her* in a way she never thought she would do for her country.

He stared, his face unreadable. Her heart pounded.

"Please tell me I'm not alone in feeling it," she whispered, and this time her words had nothing to do with her case. She couldn't bear it if she had misread his intentions, his kiss. Couldn't bear it if he pushed her away as he had all those years ago.

"You are not alone," he whispered. His voice was rough and husky with need.

Her relief at his words made her knees weak. She hated herself for it. For giving this potential traitor, this suspect, this man, so much power over her.

She took a deep breath. What she was going to say next was the most dangerous confession of all. She only hoped that when she said it, she could control what would happen afterward.

"I—I'm here because of that. I came because I can't deny that attraction any longer. I don't *want* to deny it any longer. Tristan—" She hesitated. "I want you."

A breath, silent, dark, and deep passed between them as Tristan allowed Meredith's shocking statement to sink in. Then a thousand thoughts assailed him. There were too many reasons why he should gently refuse her offer and send her to her room.

Instead, he reached behind him and placed a palm on the door. Without looking, he pushed it shut with a loud, echoing bang. Thoughts and reason faded, replaced by a clarity he hadn't experienced since long before his brother's death. For the first time in a long time he knew exactly what he wanted. Not what he needed. Not what circumstances or plans dictated he do. Just what he wanted.

Meredith. He wanted her to help him remember. To help him forget. Mostly he just wanted to lose himself in her touch, her scent, her taste.

Moving toward her, he drank in every detail. The way her eyes widened, the way her breath hitched as he stopped in front of her and tossed the mask in his hand toward the table beside the fire. He missed and didn't care.

Slowly, he reached down to thread his fingers through the silk of her chestnut hair. Her own mask, which was perched so charmingly on her head, as well as a few hairpins that held her elaborate style in place, slipped away as he cupped her scalp and tilted her face up.

His last breath was a shuddering sigh as he let his lips meet hers. Her taste was familiar, warm. He nibbled her mouth, tugging her lower lip until she gasped with pleasure and deepened the kiss. He forced himself to take his time, matching his breath to hers as their tongues tangled and dueled. Her hands, which had been clenched at her sides, relaxed as she lifted them and wrapped her arms around his neck. She rose to her tiptoes, taking the kiss even further and putting a sizable chink in the armor of his control.

"Slow," he whispered against her mouth.

It was as much a warning for himself as a promise to her. He couldn't remember the last woman he had in his bed. He certainly couldn't remember a time when he desired one more. Perhaps because he had never wanted a woman like this. To the point where he would throw everything away for the solace she offered in her arms. Once he had feared that. Truth be told, he still did. But he couldn't deny himself. He'd done so too long.

She smiled against his mouth and the urgency faded, though it still throbbed in the background like an ever-present heartbeat keeping time. Eventually he wouldn't be able to ignore it and it would take over.

But not yet.

He gathered her closer, resting one hand in the curved small of her back while the other slid lower. Caressing, massaging as he cupped her hip, then around to stroke her backside through the maddening layers of her ball gown.

Meredith groaned low in her throat as he brought her hips flush to his own and let her feel the power of the desire burning in his chest. It was a feral, intense sound that seemed to vibrate through his entire being and send hot blood pulsing even harder to the erection that now nudged her stomach.

Her fingers bunched in his hair as her kiss grew wilder. Tristan reached for the buttons and ties that held her dress together in the back. One by one he released the little rose-shaped buttons, feeling her skin heat as his hands stroked down. Finally her dress sagged and he peeled it forward until it dropped in a pool around her feet.

He sucked in a breath at the sight of her. He'd spent an inordinate amount of time imagining what Meredith would look like in this state, but the reality was even better than his most scandalous dreams.

Her chemise was the same pale pink of her gown's underskirt, but it was nearly sheer, revealing the dark peaks of her nipples and hiding no curve of her body. When he reached for her, pure silk covering heated skin greeted his rough hands.

Meredith arched, lifting her breasts in mute offering. An offering he didn't refuse. Meeting her bold stare, he gently cupped one breast, massaging the already taut nipple as her head dipped back and her body tensed with pleasure.

"Tristan," she groaned, clenching his jacket as he lowered his lips to capture one thrusting nipple.

Meredith uttered a helpless cry as Tristan suckled her breast. Sensations she had all but forgotten roared through her, weakening her knees and sending hot desire to pool low in her belly, between her thighs, at every sensitive nerve ending and in every heated part of her.

This was what she had feared. That her explanation that she wanted to give in to their mutual desire would spiral out of control before she could pull back. But it was also what she'd secretly hoped for. She recognized that now as his tongue did wicked things to her nipple and made her hips rock helplessly.

"Please," she heard her voice whisper, but it seemed distant, foreign in its huskiness, its desperation. "Please."

He drew back from her aching breasts to meet her eyes. The look he gave her was one of pure possession. A promise of pleasure. A pledge of fulfillment she had never truly experienced.

Dropping his mouth to hers, he guided her to his bed in stumbling steps. Then she was off her feet as he lifted her onto the mattress. Without arguing, she settled back on the pillows and watched him.

Through her hooded gaze she took in every moment. Tristan shrugged from his jacket and made swift work of the cravat knot at his throat. In an instant he stripped away his shirt, and her heart stopped.

She was no blushing virgin. She had seen a naked man before. But never had she looked at one and marveled at the beauty of his body. His shoulders seemed impossibly broad, strong and muscled, as were his arms. His entire upper body put ancient statues of Rome and Greece to shame. None could live up to the specimen before her.

"I take it that stare is a compliment?" he asked with a low chuckle as he took a spot on the bed beside her and gently shut her gaping mouth by placing a finger beneath her chin.

"Touch me and see," she whispered.

Tristan smiled, and just before he took her in his arms, she saw the flicker of a long forgotten rake in his eyes. Demanding. Powerful. Full of sexual need and energy.

And all hers.

His arms came around her, his mouth came down, and she melted. Every feminine part of her wept with anticipation, ached with a need that would be finally fulfilled. She hadn't known she wanted to have a man hold her so badly, but when Tristan brought her close and she felt his heart pound against his chest, she realized she *had* missed this. The warmth and intimacy of a man's embrace.

She explored, running her fingers through the fine dusting of hair on his chest. She smoothed her palms against the flat muscles there and smiled when his nipples hardened and he groaned into her mouth.

"Careful," he whispered, catching her earlobe with his teeth and giving a gentle nip that made lightning bolts of pleasure burst before her eyes. "I might take that as a challenge."

"This?" she asked, wicked as she grazed a thumb over his nipple again.

Before she could tease him further, Tristan pulled her into a seated position, grabbed the edging of her flimsy, pink chemise and pulled it over her head. She was bared to him. Naked as she hadn't been for a long time.

And she loved it. Surrendering the careful control she had mastered over the years was terrifying and exhilarating at once. Especially when Tristan's green eyes devoured her nude form as if he were a hungry man being presented with a never-ending feast.

"My God." His voice was husky, dark. "You are magnificent."

She blushed, but didn't have a chance to reply as he bent to press a hot kiss against her collarbone. He let his mouth move lower, sucking and kissing her throat, then dipping between the valley of her breasts.

Sensations so powerful and focused they almost hurt exploded inside her, stealing her breath and any remnants of reason that remained. She couldn't help the wanton arching of her back or the way she clutched at his hair when he returned his mouth to her tingling nipple. This time there was no scrap of silk to separate his hot tongue from laving her skin, and the sensation was more focused and powerful.

His hands, which she had forgotten about thanks to the seductive play of his skilled tongue, now drew her attention. He stroked down the apex of her body in feather-light torture. Lower and lower until he grasped one bare thigh. She found her legs opening of their own accord in a shameless offering of her feminine core.

She was surprised when he didn't immediately take that offering. Instead, his fingers teased, tracing the outside line of her hip and down, stroking across the top of her trembling knee, then making the opposite journey up her inner thigh, all the while suckling her nipples as she writhed in blissful agony.

His fingers moved up and up, and she lifted her hips as he came closer and closer to the center of her heat. The burning point of origin of her desire. But he stopped just as his hands promised relief.

He drew back to look at her, searching her face with intensity.

"Please," she found herself murmuring, begging. "Touch me."

"I want to touch you. By God, I want to touch you. But if I do . . ." He trailed off, and she saw the internal battle reflected on his tense face. "Meredith, if I touch you now, I won't want to stop. I may not be able to stop until I've taken you, claimed you. If you want to change your mind about sharing my bed, giving me your body, now is the time to say so."

His words sank into her haze and forced her to remember the duty she'd all but forgotten in the heat of passion. She had fully intended to pull away before things went too far . . . as far as they already had and as far as they would surely go if she didn't take his offer. But with every touch, Tristan stole those rational plans, made her forget her purpose in being in his home, his room . . . his life.

She stared at him, his face so close to hers. His eyes filled with desire and passion and promise. And she let herself forget again. Tomorrow would be soon enough to remember duty.

She let her trembling hand slip to his and lifted it. Gently, she pressed his fingers to the heated juncture of her thighs.

"Touch me," she demanded in a harsh whisper.

Not a breath passed before his mouth came back to hers, harder and with more purpose. She groaned as his fingers clenched, gently massaging as powerful pleasure began to pulsate rhythmically in every nerve ending.

Tristan smoothed the damp curls aside. Her heat, her wetness greeted his fingertips, letting him know just how ready she was. But he hesitated to simply take her. No, he wanted to savor these shared pleasures. When morning light broke, he knew it might not be a night they repeated.

She let out a broken sob as he slipped one finger across her, then inside. Slowly, he stroked, watching her face as her pleasure mounted. Surely she was never more beautiful than at this moment, her face flushed, her eyes partly closed as she gripped his shoulders. Little moans broke from her lips, signaling an impending loss of control. When her body trembled and clenched around his finger, he let his thumb find the little pearl of her pleasure and pressed down.

Immediately, Meredith let out a cry, her heels digging into the mattress, her back arching as she quivered around his fingers in powerful release. Pride swelled within him, matching his desire, perhaps even surpassing it. *He* had given her that pleasure. *He* had made her cheeks and chest flush with release. And he could make it happen again and again.

In fact, he intended to do just that.

Rising, he slipped out of his boots and the trousers that confined his throbbing erection. Though Meredith's lids were hooded, he knew she took in every movement. A fact proven when he freed his member and straightened up.

No training in the world could have held back Meredith's gasp when she saw Tristan in all his naked glory. And it *was* glorious. With firelight framing him, he looked even more like the gods she had compared him to earlier.

Her stare was blatant. She knew it. She didn't

care. She needed to burn the moment into her memory because she might not . . . well, she didn't want the desperation that accompanied that thought, so she pushed it far from her mind.

His trim hips and powerful thighs were strong enough. Certainly Tristan Archer was not a man who would ever need padding to fill the tight breeches that were currently in fashion. But it was the thrusting erection she couldn't take her eyes from.

Even as he climbed on the bed beside her, she stared. Only when he cupped her cheek and turned her face toward his did she stop.

"I'll be gentle," he whispered, smoothing tangled curls from her cheeks.

"I never feared you'd hurt me." She smiled. "I am not some missish debutante. But it has been . . ." She trailed off with a blush. "It's been a long time."

There was a brief expression of triumph that brought the rake back to his face. A possessive gleam in his eyes told her how pleased he was that he would be the first man since her husband to fill her, to claim her and give her pleasure.

"Then I will make it worth the wait," he said, low and close to her ear as he slipped her beneath him.

"I know."

He met her eyes, never breaking his gaze as he positioned himself between her legs. The hard tip of him nudged her weeping entrance, and then he was gliding inside, filling her, awakening pleasure and rekindling desire long extinguished and never so intense.

She clutched his shoulders, digging her nails in as he took her inch by inch. When he filled her to the hilt, he shut his eyes with a low groan that told her just how long he'd denied himself this pleasure as well. And, like him, she felt triumph that she was the one woman he couldn't resist.

His mouth came down and the passion in his kiss belied the utter control of his body. She melted into him, wrapping her arms around his neck. Then his hips rocked. He took her with slow, sure thrusts, coaxing her to move with him, to climb higher and higher with each grinding movement.

She heard cries echoing in the room each time he filled her. It took a moment to realize they were her own. She wanted more. She wanted everything.

He seemed to read that desire, to understand it even though she hadn't spoken her request. He broke their kiss, watching her as he slid his hand down her body. He massaged her aching breasts, his hands warmed her bare sides, then he slipped his fingers between their surging bodies. He found the same pleasure bud he had stroked before, but this time she had the added pleasure of his body filling hers. His weight claiming her. His mouth taking hers with the same slow cadence of his hips.

When he stroked her, the tingles of release focused. The next stroke made them spread and intensify. The third sent her over the edge. She exploded with a sensation more powerful than anything she'd ever known. Her hips jolted wildly, her legs wrapped around him as her cries were lost in his mouth.

He stiffened, his head dipping back, and he clutched her closer as she stole his last vestiges of control and he filled her. Meredith sighed with utter contentment as Tristan relaxed on top of her. She held him tighter, smoothing her hands along his back and pretending the moment would never end.

But the hateful little voice far in the back of her mind told her over and over that it *would* end. And then she would soon face the consequences of sleeping with the enemy.

Chapter 13

Meredith was awake, but didn't have the energy to open her eyes. She felt too languid. Her body too heavy. Warmth suffused her skin and sated pleasure made her lazy.

She felt . . . *good.* And she realized she hadn't felt that way for a long time. Certainly, she'd been happy. She'd laughed and danced and been thrilled by her work. She thought she'd been satisfied by those experiences, but now she knew that wasn't so. Until this moment, she hadn't known the meaning of satisfaction or pleasure.

It was a terrifying realization, and she opened her eyes with shock. But what she looked upon brought her no less shock or pleasure.

Tristan lay on his side next to her. Like her, he wasn't asleep. But he was watching her. Not touching her, but simply *watching*, eyes soft with emotions she couldn't place. White sheets rode low on his hips, making his skin look tanned in the dying firelight. And accentuating each curve of every beautiful muscle on his body.

Without thinking, she lifted her hand to touch his shoulder. She traced the line of his arm, smoothing her hand along his skin and awakening her desire with every stroke of her trembling fingertips.

He smiled at the touch, and when she reached his hand, he caught hers and brought her fingers to his lips for a kiss. Seeing his mouth brush her skin gave her a shiver of anticipation, but she resisted that sensation.

She had to leave.

Surrendering to the emotion that crackled between them was something she refused to regret, but it was a fantasy, nothing more. Pulling away was the only way to keep herself sane and finish this investigation. Pretending she never found release and passion in Tristan's arms was the only way she could force herself to keep compiling evidence of his guilt.

But doing that was so hard when he rubbed a stubbly cheek against her palm.

"I—I can't stay," she whispered, but the statement was too quiet and weak to be believed.

His eyes darkened and he held fast to her hand. "Don't go."

She shut her eyes. It was so hard to resist him. Especially when he slipped a hand around her waist and dragged her across the short distance that separated them to hold her against his chest. Their naked skin brushed, and her body reacted of its own accord, just as she felt his body respond to hers.

"Tristan," she said, fighting to recall her intentions, her duties. "This was . . . a moment in time. One I shall never forget, but it cannot go further . . . can it?"

He looked down at her, his eyes nearly black in the dying light. His lips thinned and his brow furrowed, as if he remembered something about the truth of her words. But what? His guilt? His misdeeds?

Her chest tightened, but she couldn't make herself pull away from his embrace.

"Perhaps you're right," he said.

Disappointment flowered inside her, even though he was only making things easier. Gently, she pulled back, but his grip on her waist only tightened, imprisoning her.

"Perhaps we cannot go any further than what we've already shared," he continued. "Certainly, I'm unable to make promises of a future. It isn't fair to you. My every gentlemanly instinct tells me I should let you leave this bed. We should pretend we never shared tonight, but I—I want—"

Her heart throbbed, the rush of her blood drowning out everything but Tristan.

"What do you want?" she whispered, praying, though she wasn't sure what answer would give her what she desired. Hell, she wasn't sure *what* she desired.

He cupped her cheek and pressed one kiss next to her eye. "I want tonight. I want what I found in your arms, here in my bed." He pressed another kiss against her cheekbone, and her heart fluttered. "I didn't believe anything so good, so right, could exist for me again after—"

He shook his head as he cut himself off. "I need that, Meredith. I need you."

Her breath caught as swells of emotion threatened to overtake her. "But you're not able to offer a future? Only this?"

"No." His voice was so low she strained to hear the response. "Not now."

"Why?" she asked, unable to silence the spy in her completely.

Tristan leaned away. For a moment he only stared at her, and she thought he might confess whatever ill deeds he was involved in. Explain the things that so obviously tormented him. She held her breath, praying he would. If only he could trust her enough to share the truth, there had to be a way to save him. To repair whatever he'd done.

But then he shook his head again. "My future is uncertain."

"No one knows their future. Why is yours more uncertain than anyone else's?" she asked, wanting to pound her fists against his chest and demand he tell her the truth.

He shrugged one shoulder. "Too many reasons to explain. But since I cannot see my own future, I can't, in fairness, offer one to you."

Tears stung behind her eyes, and she shut them so he wouldn't see the torture in her soul. His words brought reality crashing around her. When he spoke of the uncertainty of his future, she knew what he meant. The lies. The evidence sitting in an ever-growing pile in her chamber.

But when she composed herself, she also knew, just as strongly, that she couldn't deny she wanted a part in his foggy future. Despite everything.

It was wrong. It went against her very character. But she couldn't change it, no matter how she tried to fight the feeling, pretend it didn't exist. It was there and grew more powerful each moment she spent with Tristan. These stolen hours only proved that point.

"But you still desire me, even if you cannot promise me anything more than the moment we're in?"

He dropped his mouth to hers and kissed her with all the passion and emotion they had already shared. With everything in him that hadn't been tainted. She felt him give her all that he had. It wasn't enough.

She didn't care. She had denied she was a woman for so long, a woman with needs, a heart ... and hopes that Tristan seemed to fulfill.

"I want you more than anything. But if you cannot live by those terms, I understand. I won't torture you or myself by forcing you to give more than you're able." He waited, as if holding his breath, for her reply.

Feeling dueled with duty. But passion won, as it hadn't for so many years. Slowly, she threaded her fingers into his hair and brought herself closer.

"I'll take whatever you can give, for as long as you are able to give it," she whispered. "It is a devil's bargain, I know, but I can't refuse."

Relief was palpable in the room. It hung in the air, it was clear on his face, she felt it in his touch. Tristan slipped her beneath him and she surrendered to his hands, to his mouth, to the moments she could take.

Outside of this bed, she would continue her investigation. But here with him, she vowed to be a woman, Tristan's woman.

Not a spy.

Tristan strummed his fingers along the waist-high stone wall of the terrace overlooking the garden below. His mind wandered as the partygoers drank tea and chatted. It was one of the last events of the fortnight-long soiree. He could hardly believe the party was coming to an end.

He scanned the group and found Meredith. He was mesmerized by the way she stood, the way her face lit when she smiled or laughed at something her companions said, the way she lifted a hand to push a wayward strand of hair away from the corner of her delectable mouth.

When the gathering was over, he wondered if their attachment would end as well. He had confessed he could give her no future, but perhaps once he finished his business, something that would occur in the next two days, that would change. Once his duty was fulfilled, didn't he deserve some happiness? Even his father couldn't have denied him that.

For now, he comforted himself with thoughts of a less distant future. Tonight, in his bed with Meredith. The smile that had been tilting his lips more and more of late did so again. The smile Meredith had returned to him.

"You look different."

Tristan started at the sound of Philip's voice at his elbow. He wiped the surprise from his face as he turned to his friend. "Different? You're absurd. There is nothing different about me."

Philip tilted his head. "There is. I hadn't noticed it until now. You seem more at ease."

Tristan frowned. He'd been trying to keep the changes in his soul seperate from his behavior, especially around Philip, since his friend had continuing doubts about Meredith.

"If I am, it's because this business with Devlin will be over soon. That is all you sense."

"No. It's more than relief." Philip shook his head. "You look—happy. I haven't seen you this way for a long time."

Tristan hesitated as he watched Meredith's posture change. She had sensed him watching her. Slowly, she turned toward him. From the distance, he saw her smile.

"It's *her*." Philip drew back a step. "It's Meredith Sinclair."

"No, you're being foolish." Tristan folded his arms and tried to keep all reaction from his face. "I've told you before, any connection I have with Meredith is merely for show, to divert Devlin's interest."

Philip's eyebrow arched. "You're lying." Tristan opened his mouth, but his friend held up a hand to interrupt. "Do not threaten all you have done, all you've sacrificed, for a woman! Especially one we are not sure isn't affiliated with Devlin herself!"

Tristan clenched his fists and did his best to measure his response. "*I* know she's not in league with Devlin, Philip. *You* are the only one unsure."

Philip motioned below with one hand. "She is about to engage the bastard at this very moment."

Tristan pivoted to see Meredith approach Devlin. Her smile appeared genuine, and then she began speaking to Devlin as if he were a normal partygoer, not the devil himself in disguise. Bile rose in his throat. How little she knew of the danger she created with her actions.

Except . . . Tristan had told her at least twice not to put herself in Devlin's path. True, he hadn't explained his reasons, but why couldn't she listen? It was almost as if she was flouting him.

That thought sank into his consciousness. That was exactly what Philip was saying, wasn't it? That Meredith knew far more about Devlin than he wanted to admit. She had no fear of him because she was in league with him.

"No," he murmured as he pushed the doubt away. He didn't want this one good thing in his life to be tainted.

"You can't shut your eyes to the possibility just because you're falling in love," Philip insisted.

Tristan's muscles clenched. He hadn't labeled the emotions he felt for Meredith, and he didn't intend to start doing so now. It was a foolhardy exercise when he didn't know what would happen tomorrow. It was best to leave their relationship as it was: a diversion neither was able to give up at present.

Still, the idea that he loved her didn't seem so very foreign now that the words had been said.

He didn't spare Philip a glance as he continued to watch Meredith converse with Devlin. "I understand what you're saying, Philip, and I appreciate your concerns. Trust that I'm taking them seriously, although I cannot believe Meredith would be in league with a man like Augustine Devlin."

"Then why—" Philip began, but stopped when Tristan raised a hand to silence him.

"In a few days our business with Devlin will be completed. Hopefully, I will garner the access I've been looking for and I can end this madness. Once I have, everything will become apparent." He scowled as Meredith laughed below. "My future, whatever it may be, will finally be clear."

She didn't want to do this.

That Meredith was standing an arm's length from Devlin, carefully navigating the waters of polite conversation should have thrilled and excited her. Instead, she was terrified. What if Devlin revealed something incriminating about Tristan? What if he confirmed her deepest fears?

She pursed her lips at the thought. That was exactly what she was here to determine, yet she dreaded it. How far she'd fallen from her training. How disappointed Charles and Lady M and her friends would be if they could see her now, so unsure, ready to run if Devlin began to confess anything to implicate Tristan.

"Is something amiss, dear lady?" Devlin asked in that lazy drawl that indicated he was bored by life in general. A popular affectation among the men of the *ton*. One she despised all the more in this man who had caused so much pain.

"Of course not, Mr. Devlin," she answered with what she hoped resembled a bright smile. Emily was the master of disguise, not she, and she now longed for her friend's talent at covering her true identity, as well as her true emotions.

He smiled, and she was again taken aback by how handsome the man was. It proved one couldn't judge a villain by his outward appearance. If Devlin's golden good looks were the only thing to recommend him, he would be considered a saint, not a demon.

But she knew better.

"I am glad. Your expression seemed to reflect some kind of upset or anger."

She cursed herself. "Oh, not at all, Mr. Devlin. I could be nothing but pleased on a day like today." She motioned around the beautiful garden with a wide smile. "The sun is warm and bright, the gardens are delightful, as is the company. How could I be upset or angered?"

"I thought perhaps you might have had a misunderstanding with our host."

Meredith froze at Devlin's secret smile, at the icy tone of his voice.

"With our host?" she repeated, blinking vapidly. "Why in the world would you think that? His lordship and I have no special bond."

Devlin watched her with suddenly sharp eyes. The affectation of ennui was gone, replaced by an amused interest that told Meredith he knew something.

"Is that true?" he drawled, folding his arms with a sly smirk. "Perhaps my dear friend Tristan has been playing a cruel trick on me."

She stiffened. Was he toying with her?

"His lordship, play a trick that involves me? Well, sir, you certainly have my attention."

He watched her without answering for a moment, like a man considering his next move in a complex game of chess. "You are aware Lord Carmichael and I are involved in business."

She nodded.

Devlin continued, "When men work together on projects of secrecy and delicacy like his lordship and I have done, it sometimes brings them together as friends."

Meredith covered a wince. How she hated the implications of Devlin's seemingly innocuous statement. Projects of secrecy and delicacy. Like treachery against the Crown? And the idea of Tristan calling this man *friend* turned her stomach.

"I can see how that would happen," she said carefully. "But I don't understand how it involves me."

"Men talk, my lady. And Lord Carmichael told me long ago that your hand had already been claimed. By him." Devlin watched her, and she fought to keep a reaction from her face. "I think everyone here has seen the two of you grow closer since our arrival in Carmichael, but just because two people find common interests does not mean there is a true bond between them. So tell me, my lady, is my *friend* using a lie to discourage me from pressing my own suit, or are you merely being coy about your intentions?"

Meredith fought to draw breath. Telling Devlin there was no union of any kind between herself and Tristan would allow her to gauge his reaction to Tristan's lie. It could enlighten her to just how close the men were, how deeply they were entangled. And giving Devlin hope that she might one day welcome his vile attentions could also open doors in this and future investigations.

Her thoughts drifted to the letter she had not been able to intercept. To the threats Devlin made the night she hid in his chambers. Revealing Tristan as a liar would surely put him in greater danger.

She blushed as she turned her face. "My, you are very forward, Mr. Devlin."

"I am sorry, my dear. Normally I wouldn't speak so boldly, but I do have both a personal and business stake in whether or not Carmichael is lying to me."

She allowed him a shy glance. "I was merely surprised by your knowledge. I did not know Tristan spoke of our . . . relationship, even to his closest friends. It has been a secret shared between only us until now. But he has not lied to you, Mr. Devlin."

Devlin's eyebrow arched. "I cannot pretend not to be disappointed that my own hopes for a chance at such a fine lady's heart would be dashed."

She forced a playful laugh even as bile burned her throat at the mere thought of such a thing. "I doubt you'll mourn the loss for long. Certainly there are many ladies here and in London who would happily fill the void."

Devlin caught her hand. Her pulse quickened with momentary fear as he lifted it to drop a brief kiss on top. Though she wore gloves, she could have sworn she felt the chill of his lips even through the kid. It seemed to seep through to her very bones, and she fought the urge to yank her hand away.

"I appreciate that, my lady," he said with a wink.

She opened her mouth to reply, hoping to press for information now that he was more comfortable with her, but before she could, she felt a hand grasp her wrist.

She turned as Tristan pulled her away from Devlin for a second time in a few short days and tucked her hand into the crook of his arm. He glared at Devlin with a look that reminded Meredith just how dangerous he could be. His touch reminded her of other things too.

Desire.

"Meredith," he ground out through clenched teeth, though he hardly looked at her. "I would dearly love to steal you away for a moment, if you can bear to be parted from Mr. Devlin."

With a glance from the corner of her eye for Devlin, she said, "Of course. Good afternoon, Mister—"

But Tristan was already dragging her along the garden path toward the house and whatever awaited her there. Judging from the anger evident in his sparkling gaze and tight lips, it would not be pleasant.

Chapter 14

Tristan slammed the parlor door and spun on Meredith. Before he could say anything, she yanked her arm free and stomped across the room.

"I grow tired of these antics, Tristan. You cannot simply demand my presence whenever you desire it. And you certainly have no right to drag me off like I'm a puppet to be controlled!"

Tristan drew in a few deep breaths as he watched her pace in front of the fire. Her eyes flashed brighter than the flames, and he was drawn to her heat. Yet, he couldn't help but picture her with Devlin. Her hand had been in his. She hadn't seemed to be trying to withdraw it.

Could Philip be right? *Was* she a part of the elaborate tests Devlin delighted in putting him through to prove his allegiance? And if she was, could he trust anything she said and did, whether in his parlor or his bed?

He squeezed his eyes shut to block out the image of Devlin and Meredith together, and the lies she might be telling. When she touched him, he felt her sincerity, her desire, her need in every part of his soul, and he would have to trust that feeling a little while longer.

"I was having a private discussion, Tristan," Meredith continued.

Her statement snapped his attention back. "With a dangerous man. I have told you of Augustine Devlin's character too many times to count!" He drew in a breath to calm himself. "Please, Meredith, believe I'm only trying to protect you."

Her lips thinned and she searched his face with eyes that saw too deeply into his soul. He longed to turn away, but she had already snared him, there was no escape now.

"Is that why you told the man we were involved in some kind of affair before that was true?"

Shock tightened Tristan's throat. Meredith's expression begged an explanation, but there was anger along with the hope. Dear God, what had Devlin told her?

Carefully, he cleared the emotions from his

face. It was best not to jump too quickly to tell her any information.

"What I told him or did not tell him is not at issue, Meredith," he insisted. She gave a gasp of exasperation. "The point is that Devlin is a villain. I don't want you to involve yourself with him in any way."

"If he is such a villain, then why in the name of all that is holy have you aligned yourself with him?" She shook her head. "You've told me again and again that he is treacherous, yet you continue to do business with him. You invited him into your home. You have brought him close to your family, Tristan! A man who could and would destroy—"

She broke the sentence off and turned away suddenly. Tristan cocked his head. Her passionate plea went further than he expected. Almost as if she truly understood how desperate and dangerous a man Devlin was.

Yet, despite his growing doubts, Tristan found himself longing to explain. Not give another excuse for why he continued to work with Devlin, not lie as he had been lying for so long.

He wanted to tell her the truth. To tell her everything that had brought him from where he started to this dark and lonely place. Perhaps she would understand what drove him to such lengths. Perhaps he would find the forgiveness he constantly sought in her arms.

She turned back, blue eyes sparkling with un-shed tears. He couldn't tell her. Doing so would endanger her. And beyond that, if he admitted the truth, she might turn away in horror. He didn't want to lose her. Even if she wasn't really his.

"There are things I am unable to explain," he whispered. "Complications."

She let out a disappointed sigh as her head dipped. Her frustration was clear in the way her shoulders slumped, her fists curled at her sides, the way she kept her gaze focused away from him. It was almost as if she already knew his lies.

But no. That was his own conscience pulling at him.

She continued to stare at the floor. "Very well, you cannot tell me why you continue to affiliate with Devlin. But you *must* explain why you chose to share information about me—about us—with him. I have a right to know."

Tristan searched her face. What portion of the truth would ease her concerns without opening more confusion?

Drawing in a breath, he said, "Devlin came to me the second day of this soiree, expressing an interest in you. He hoped I would have some insight into how to pursue you since we had a previous relationship."

She folded her arms as she gave a little nod of encouragement. "And?"

"With his reputation, I recognized he wasn't the

kind of man who would take no for an answer."
He hesitated. "If you refused his suit, he might
take revenge. If you encouraged it, you would expose yourself to his less savory qualities. Either
way, allowing him to believe he had a chance to
woo you put you in danger."

Her arms remained folded like a shield in front
of her chest. Tristan frowned. He hated to see her
so guarded, especially when she protected herself
against him. After the pleasure and passion they
had shared, he hated losing the light of desire in
her eyes, and hated even more that it was replaced
with wariness.

She thought about his statement for a moment.
"So you staked a false claim on me in order to
what? Protect me? You believed Devlin wouldn't
pursue me if he thought you already had a place
in my heart?"

He nodded. "If Devlin believed pursuing you
would disrupt our business, he wouldn't take the
risk."

Hurt momentarily flickered in her eyes before
she turned her face. "And is that why you pursued me? To maintain that facade? Is that why
you took me to your bed? To complete some charade?"

Tristan didn't hesitate. In three long steps, he
crossed the distance between them and caught
her elbow, breaking the shield she'd put up with
her arms and forcing her to look into his eyes.

The hurt was still on her face, though she fought to cover it. He had to take it away.

"No," he said firmly. "Even when I told myself I was only pursuing you for your own protection, that was a lie. I turned to you, I pursued you, because I wanted you. I wanted the falsehood I told Devlin to become the truth."

Her lips parted with surprise.

"Each time I kissed you it was because I could no longer deny myself the pleasure of your touch," he continued. The room around them was rapidly shrinking, growing hotter as he pulled her close. "And when you came to my room and offered yourself to me, I did not make love to you for any other reason than I wished to claim you."

"Tristan," she whispered.

"Whatever is between us is real. It has nothing to do with Augustine Devlin."

He realized just how close he had drawn her. Her breath stirred his throat and every trembling movement of her body rocked through him.

He also realized if he touched her now there was nothing in this world to stop him. He wanted to taste her, touch her, make her his.

He cupped the nape of her neck and her mouth parted, eyes widened.

"Tristan," she began. Her voice trembled. "But I—"

He cut her off before she could deny him, dropping his mouth to hers. If she'd been planning to protest, the words were lost, as was the sentiment. Almost immediately, her fingers threaded through his hair and she returned the kiss with as much heat and need as he gave.

He moved her, step by step, until her back touched the wall. She murmured an endearment, but it was lost against his lips. Her hips tilted, colliding with his and sending powerful sparks of pleasure and awareness through his body. He moaned, control fading as the balm of her kiss drove out any harsh thought or fears that tormented him.

He lost himself in her, stroking his tongue along the roof of her mouth, tasting the warm honeyed sweetness of her lips. As it was every time they kissed, he longed to memorize her taste, along with the little mewling sounds of pleasure that came from her throat. He wanted to remember every moment just in case it was the last they shared.

She seemed as desperate to imprint his body on hers. As if she, too, recognized the ending to these stolen hours could be around the next bend. He wondered, faintly, why. Was it because he had told her there was no promise for a future? Or something more?

And then it didn't matter as her fingers slipped to his shirt buttons and she began to glide them open. All that mattered then was the way her fingernails gently raked his skin in her haste, the echo of her panting breath as she broke the kiss to look at her work.

She yanked at the buttons, finally tearing enough open to bare his chest. Her mouth surged up as her fingers dove inside to touch the flesh she revealed.

Meredith couldn't hold back her little sigh of pleasure as her fingers touched Tristan's hot skin. He felt so good, and she wanted more. She couldn't get enough, even though she'd spent the past three nights in his bed. Touching him now was just like the first time, filled with electric excitement.

He wasn't immune to the wracking desire either. That was clear by his growl when she slid a hand over his chest, by the way he rocked his hips against her. She let her eyes flutter shut and savored every sensation. Wet heat flooded her, readying her for the inevitable.

Tristan would make her his. She would surrender willingly—again. She would forget for a few moments why she had been sent to Carmichael, and those few moments would be the happiest of her recollection.

After . . . well, she didn't have to think about that. Not when Tristan was moving against her, working at the little buttons that held the front of her own gown in place. She arched toward his fingers, gasping when they slipped in their work and brushed her aching breasts.

Finally, he managed to free the last remaining button that separated her from heaven and pushed her gown away from her shoulders. As it drooped at her waist, he caught her for another deep, promise-filled kiss.

Wickedness filled her at the pleasure of his touch, and she couldn't help but surrender to it. Slowly, she brushed her breasts back and forth against his chest. The beads of her nipples tightened beneath her chemise at the friction of silk against skin.

Tristan groaned even as he cupped her backside and lifted her, rubbing the apex of her thighs against his impressive erection. She dipped her head back with a little cry as he kissed her throat.

Somewhere in the distance, she thought she heard a sound, but desire clouded her senses. Her whole world was Tristan, there was no room for anything but his musky male scent, the brush of his skin, the heat of his mouth. Nothing else mattered.

Except the damn noise that was so insistent. The fog around her drifted away and the world came into clearer focus. The noise was a voice. The voice was a woman's. The woman was Lady Constance Carmichael.

Meredith's heart, which had been pounding with the force of her desire, now threatened to come to a complete stop as she turned her head. Lady Carmichael stood in the entryway to the parlor, cheeks flushed with high color as she said her son's name once again.

"Tristan," Meredith hissed, tapping his shoulder and trying to forget how good his mouth felt trailing down her throat to where her pulse throbbed. "Tristan!"

He lifted his head, and before he could say the sinful things she guessed were in his mind, he saw her expression. He followed it behind him to where Constance now tried to cover her eyes.

Immediately, he released Meredith, steadying her before he turned and used his body as a shield while she fumbled to yank her dress back up over her shoulders and rebutton what he had taken so much pleasure in removing.

"Mother!" he gasped, his cheeks filling with blood. Dear God, was he *blushing*? It was an untenable situation.

"I—I'm sorry," his mother stammered, refusing to meet his gaze. He wasn't sure if that was for her sake or his own, or because Meredith was still struggling to dress. "Lord Farthingworth was asking about your new mare. When I couldn't find you, I was told you were seen going into the house, so I followed."

Tristan glanced down to see that his own shirt was still unbuttoned, yanked from his trousers.

He went about refastening it as he tried to find a way to explain himself.

"Ah," was all he could come up with as a reply.

"I'm terribly sorry," his mother said, peeking at him from the corner of her eye.

She seemed relieved he had covered himself, and even more so when Meredith slipped out from behind him. Her gown was wrinkled and slightly crooked, but fastened nonetheless. She had even managed to salvage her hair, or at least repair it somewhat. Despite that, she still looked like a woman who was on her way to being well-pleasured. The fact that he had not completed that quest was a rousing disappointment.

"No, my lady," Meredith said, her voice little more than a husky whisper. Tristan turned on her in shock. He had never heard her like that before. Shamed. Awkward.

Worse, he had caused it. The situation he created with his out-of-control desire had caused it. Guilt tore at him.

"It is I who should apologize for—for—" Meredith motioned around her awkwardly. "I apologize. Excuse me."

Without a backward glance for either mother or son, she rushed to the door and into the hallway, leaving Tristan alone with his mother. He looked at her, watching her expression change now that they were alone. A little twinkle replaced the shock in her stare, and a smile began to twitch at the corners of her lips.

He was in trouble. The kind there was no getting out of.

Meredith covered her hot cheeks as she raced away from the parlor toward the main stair. She had to get to her room, away from the crowd, from Constance . . . from Tristan and the touch that seemed to mesmerize her and control her. No man had ever had that power over her.

But a potential traitor did! What was wrong with her?

His touch—no, her *need* for that touch—drove her to nearly make love to the man in the middle of the afternoon in a front parlor, for heaven's sake! Her training had no dictates for such activities, but it seemed even someone with just good common sense would have at least checked the door before they started tearing clothing off in surrender.

But her mind had been so addled, so clouded with lust, she hadn't even paused to consider the risks. *She*, who always analyzed each circumstance so carefully. *She*, who never forgot herself, even in the most emotional of situations.

One brush of Tristan's lips, and all that she was, all that she had to be, fled. Worse, she didn't care. When he touched her, she was more alive than she could remember. She was free and she loved it.

With a low sob of frustration, she stopped in the middle of the staircase and sank to a seated position. Covering her face with her hands, she attempted to pull herself together.

How far she'd fallen in just a few weeks. She had put herself in a situation where emotion warred with evidence. Where intuition led her to a suspect's bed, and allowed that same suspect into her heart piece by piece.

"Pardon me, my lady?"

She removed her head from her hands and found herself staring at a footman who was shifting uncomfortably as he tried to pretend she wasn't sitting on the stairs, or at least that the position was totally normal.

She scrambled to her feet. "No skills left at all."

"I'm sorry?" the young man asked.

"Nothing." She smoothed her wrecked gown and tried not to recall how Tristan's hands had put it in its current state . . . along with her. "Was there something you needed?"

He reached into his pocket and withdrew a thick letter. Holding it out, he said, "This was delivered a few moments ago."

Meredith froze as she saw the hand. Anastasia.

"Thank you," she whispered as she reluctantly took the message.

"Are you quite well, my lady?" he asked with a concerned expression at her suddenly pale face. She could feel the blood draining away, certain he could see the same. "Do you require anything?"

"No," she whispered as she turned and continued her journey to her room. "I'm fine."

"Should I send your lady's maid to attend you?"

She didn't even look over her shoulder. She couldn't tear her gaze from the missive. "I want to be alone. Thank you."

He must have answered, but she didn't hear his voice. She made her way to her room without seeing her surroundings. All she could do was stare at the envelope bearing Ana's meticulous handwriting.

Inside were answers. Meredith crossed her room and sat down in a chair beside the fire. Answers she had to know.

But if they incriminated Tristan, did she *want* to see them? No. She didn't. For the first time she accepted what had long been the truth: She didn't want to know if Tristan had done all he was accused of. She didn't want to know anything except that he moved her. That she wanted him, and he retuned that desire with a powerful version of his own.

She looked at the letter for another moment before her gaze slipped to the fire. It would be so easy to toss Ana's communication into the flames. Let them devour whatever hateful things were surely inside. She could go back to Tristan and pretend she didn't know the things she knew. That she hadn't seen the things she had.

Couldn't she?

Her hand trembled as she held the letter out. Heat from the fire warmed her skin as her hand moved closer and closer. Tears pricked her eyes, burned her as she watched her hand tremble near the flames.

"I can't," she whispered, pulling back with a sigh. "I am what I am. I cannot pretend I'm not simply because I wish I never received this assignment. I must finish it or I'll never have peace."

Turning the letter over, she broke the seal and pulled the pages out. Ana had broken the code in Devlin's letters to Tristan. Meredith had been able to remember nearly a page of text, and Ana had included it.

Her heart hurt with every word. Devlin wrote incessantly about "the item" they had spoken of and his desire for Tristan to obtain it. Apparently they'd talked about "the item" at an earlier time because Devlin did not describe it. He also spoke about finding a perfect place to turn over "the item" and how Tristan would receive what he wished if he could do this. Entrance into the inner circle of Devlin's group.

More tears stung, but she blinked them back violently as she read the last few words of praise for Tristan's work with Devlin so far.

"Your loyalty will be rewarded, Lord Carmichael. I assure you of that," she read aloud as bile rose to her throat.

The words were her every nightmare come true. They weren't enough proof to arrest Tristan, but clearly the painting was "the item" Devlin referred to. Tristan had done things for the bastard, had offered to do more. The painting was a last step, a final barrier between him and a position in the inner circle of one of the worst groups of traitors in the history of the country.

Heartbreak wracked her, but it was joined by anger. Why would Tristan do this? Why would he align himself with such treachery when he had no financial reason to do so? Even if he believed the government responsible for his brother's tragic death, why would he turn to a group that had caused even more deaths like Edmund's?

And more importantly . . . what was she going to do about it? Time was ticking down and there were decisions that had to be made. Ones about her case.

And ones about her heart.

Chapter 15

⌒◯◯⌒

Tristan shifted uncomfortably. The moment Meredith had hurried from the room in embarrassment, his mother's shocked expression faded to one of a cat who's found a vat of cream unattended. And now she was just . . . *staring* at him, which made him all the more aware of his disheveled appearance. And just how he had gotten that way.

Guilt washed over him as he thought of the position he found himself in now. And the position in which he had put his family, not just with this display of lust, but also with everything else he'd done in the last year.

Dipping his head, he muttered, "My apologies."

His mother seemed surprised by his statement. "Apologies?"

He nodded with a frown. "I've done my best to protect this family from any scandal of my creation, to live up to Father's expectations of how a marquis lives his life. Everything I have done has been to control that. But now I've failed."

She wrinkled her brow. "You think I am humiliated by this . . ." She waved her hand. "This little indiscretion?"

"I—"

She cut him off by coming across the room and laying a hand on his forearm. "I am not, Tristan."

Powerful and unexpected relief surged through him. Even though his mother didn't know even a fraction of the things he had done, the fact that she didn't despise him gave him hope.

She smiled, and the expression made her look far younger than her years. "My dearest, I have never made it a secret that I wish to see you settled, married with children."

"No, never a secret," he agreed with a wry smile before he went to the bar in the corner of the room. He held up a bottle of sherry in offering. His mother nodded and he poured two, barely resisting the urge to drain the remainder of the bottle.

She continued after a sip of her drink. "You have *obviously* made a connection with Meredith."

He jolted at the comment as his thoughts turned back to the one subject he'd been trying to avoid.

Once he started pondering Meredith, he had a hard time stopping. And he had to stop. For a wide variety of reasons, he couldn't allow this obsession to continue. It never should have come as far as it had, but he could no more resist her than he could stop breathing. Wanting her had become a part of him.

"I suppose it would be foolish to deny that after what you witnessed," he said with a sigh.

She smiled again. "In all honesty, I could not be more pleased. A swift engagement is in order, but that doesn't mean we cannot still plan a lovely family wedding."

Tristan backed away. "Engagement? Wedding?"

"Of course. You're my last child to marry. We'll have a few weeks, even a month or two, to enjoy the pleasures of an engagement." She hesitated and her cheeks darkened with a blush. "Unless Meredith is already with child?"

He reeled back even farther. The thought had been one he refused to consider, as foolish as that denial was. "No. I—I don't know. Mother, Meredith and I have no understanding of anything beyond—beyond—"

His mother's lips thinned as she locked gazes with him. He knew that expression. He'd seen it as a boy when he'd done something naughty.

She put her hands on her hips. "You are pursuing a—a—" Her voice dropped to a whisper.

"—physical relationship with a lady of society and you have no understanding?"

Hearing the words come from someone else's lips made them sound even worse. "It is complicated."

She shook her head furiously. "No, it is not. There are choices we make, Tristan, and consequences to those choices."

Pain ricocheted through him like a well-placed bullet. "You think I don't know that?" His voice was low as he once again considered all the actions he'd taken lately. And all the consequences to those actions.

She ignored his statement. "You have admitted you do not know if the lady could be carrying your child."

That powerful possibility moved through him a second time. Meredith, her belly large with his child. Holding his son or daughter. Creating a family with the woman who had filled his life in such a short time, a woman he'd wanted for so long but had denied himself.

"You *must* offer for her hand, Tristan."

Augustine Devlin's image invaded his pleasant musings and swept the future away, crushed it . . . and Meredith with it. Tristan flinched. "I cannot."

"You must." She grabbed his hand. The images in his mind fled and he looked down to see only his mother. Not his fantasies or his nightmares. "I know you have been troubled since Edmund's death. You've tortured yourself with all the things you think you should have done."

He turned his head in pain. "I failed him."

"You didn't!" she snapped as tears filled her eyes. "You have this image in your head of what you *should* do, *should* be, because of your father."

"He was the best of men," Tristan began with a frown.

She nodded. "Yes. He was. But he was also human! He had flaws. He wasn't perfect, and despite what you recall, he never expected you to be either." She sighed. "You did not fail your brother. But if you don't do what is right by Meredith, you will fail her. And yourself."

He pulled away. His mother was right, of course, though he hadn't considered it in that light before. He had put Meredith in a precarious position. It didn't matter if he'd been trying to protect her when he began, of if he felt like he was protecting her by keeping her at arm's length now.

His mother tilted her head, and there was a kindness, a gentleness in her eyes he wasn't sure he deserved. "You obviously care for the young lady. It's the right thing to do. And not only for the social reasons. But because the times you've spent with her are the first I have seen you smile in an age."

Tristan pondered that. It was true. Meredith

made him . . . *happy.* And he wagered she would keep him happy the rest of his days.

He could only endeavor to do the same for her.

Surrendering himself to his fate, Tristan gave his mother a brief hug. "Of course you're right. I'll speak to her tonight."

Meredith should have burned Ana's letter hours ago to protect her case. Even though it was encoded, there was no reason to keep it.

But she still held it in her hand. She read the words over and over, despite the fact they were branded in her mind. She doubted she would ever forget them or what they meant.

"Meredith?"

She rose to her feet when she heard Tristan's voice at her door. Turning, she shoved the letter that spelled another piece of his doom behind her back and forced a smile.

"Tristan, you startled me!"

He took a step into her room and her awareness doubled. It was ridiculous at such a distance, but she swore she could almost feel the wall of his body heat and smell the scent of masculine skin and a hint of lust.

The corner of the envelope in her hand dug into her palm, and she winced at both the sharp sting and the reminder of the truth.

"I'm sorry. I knocked, but there was no reply,"

he said, stopping as if suddenly aware he was moving toward her. "Is everything all right?"

She jumped. Was her upset so clear? Had he seen the letter in her hand? Slowly, she backed toward the fire. Once he wasn't looking, she could toss it in.

"Of course, why wouldn't I be fine?"

He cocked his head. "You seemed upset after my mother discovered us. And with good reason. I'm sorry my carelessness put you in such a position."

She paused, and for a moment everything else was forgotten except for heated memories of them in the parlor, tearing at each other's clothing and throwing caution to the wind. Her heart throbbed with the memory and her body tingled to attention.

"You needn't apologize," she said softly. "We were both carried away by—" She hesitated. By what? Desire? Emotion? "—by everything."

"I wanted to speak to you about that," he said. "Do you mind if I close the door? It's a private matter."

She nodded. When he turned his back, she tossed the letter into the fire and hurried to a chair in her sitting area. She motioned to the other and he took it.

For a moment only silence hung between them. She cocked her head. A thin sheen of sweat had broken out on Tristan's upper lip and he was pale.

Nervous. Her curiosity and worry grew in response.

"Tristan—" she began.

He cut her off by clearing his throat. "Yes. The point of why I'm here. I—I know I told you before that I could offer you no future, but today that changed. When we were caught in such a delicate situation, our choice to keep our affair quiet was taken."

She wrinkled her brow. "What do you mean?"

"I mean . . ." He took her hand. His thumb stroked across the top of it once, setting her skin on fire and turning her knees to mush. "Marry me, Meredith."

Her mouth dropped open as she snatched her hand from his. Rising, she backed away to the window and turned to stare outside.

She couldn't breathe. Her already jumbled thoughts exploded. Snippets of evidence collided with the memory of his kiss. Lies met with making love. Feeling met with intuition.

But one thing rose above the riot.

Meredith *wanted* to marry him. Despite her understanding that he was probably a traitor. That she would not be able to save him from the fate of such a criminal. That she ought not *want* to save him. She wanted to be his wife. To run away from her duty, from his activities, from the heartache that waited in the not too distant future. Her heart and soul screamed for her to turn around and accept the proposal without hesitation.

She spun on her heel and from the corner of her eye caught a glimpse of the letter from Ana. It was so thick that the flames were just now devouring the last of the packet. She could still see its shape in the cinders, and in her mind the words Augustine Devlin had written to Tristan rang clear.

She turned her head a little farther and saw a small pile of papers on the table nearby. Encoded bits of other evidence. Notes for Ana and Meredith and the beginnings of her final report for Charlie. They were bound to destroy this man. And the wheels of his destruction had already been set in motion. By her. By him.

She met his eyes. Everything in her soul roared at her to simply tell him the truth and demand the same of him. She opened her mouth, drew a breath to do just that, but her training stopped her.

If she broke her cover now, Tristan could shut down in an instant. He could use the knowledge that the government was following him to warn Devlin, to hide evidence. Everything she had worked for, sacrificed, would be for nothing.

"Tristan," she whispered, her heart breaking with a pain unlike any she'd ever felt before. "I cannot marry you."

Tristan's world slowed to a painful degree, and Meredith's words echoed in the suddenly quiet room. Then disappointment took seed in his chest, burrowing through his body, blooming until it was all he felt. He hadn't realized just how much he wanted this. Wanted her.

How much he loved her.

The idea that he loved Meredith didn't come as a shock. Perhaps because, when he considered it rationally, he realized he had loved her from the moment he'd gone into that pub so many years ago and discovered her being manhandled. When he rescued her, when he took her home, he'd fallen in love with the fragile strength that glittered in her terrified eyes.

At the time, he'd convinced himself that the reason he'd pushed her away was because he'd nearly killed a man defending her honor. That the rage he felt that night was too potent. But it wasn't the anger he feared. It was the love.

He'd believed he could forget it, but over the years her strength had only grown. Secretly, so had his feelings. Avoiding her hadn't helped, but by the time he'd sought her out, she'd been married. He'd shoved the pain of losing her aside and moved on, but hadn't he always been utterly aware of her?

In every ballroom, in every soiree over the long intervening years, he had found her. Never approached, but always watched and taken warmth from her light. He had loved her through the year of her grief, but by then he had too many responsibilities of his own to contemplate pursuing anyone.

But still he had loved her. Loved her even while his world was falling apart. When his brother ran away, and later when he died, Tristan still found himself looking for Meredith. When he found her, it was the one moment of light in an otherwise dark and guilt-filled existence.

But he never allowed himself to recognize his feelings, to acknowledge he searched for her, until she approached him in London. The power of his attraction and his feelings had been too hard to ignore, despite his best efforts.

So here he stood, in a room with the woman he'd loved for so long he hardly remembered a time when he did not love her, but she refused to be his wife. Refused to return his feelings.

"Tristan?" she whispered, not meeting his eyes but allowing herself a concerned glimpse.

He quietly gathered his emotions. "Why can't you be my wife?"

Perhaps it was foolish to demand she explain her rejection, but he wanted to know. Needed to know.

She hesitated, and he realized she, too, was fighting strong feelings. That gave him a little hope.

"The night we made love," she said, and finally met his eyes. A storm of emotions made them a dark and dangerous blue. "We lay in your bed together and you told me you couldn't offer me a future. That what was between us could only be temporary passion. Did something change?"

"We were caught, Meredith," he answered, though that was a lie. In truth, his mother's insistence had nothing to do with why he was asking for her hand. It had only been the last shove down what seemed to be a preordained path leading to her. "Propriety dictates—"

She frowned. "So this union would be one based on societal expectation? One based on the fact that when a gentleman takes a lady to his bed, he must in turn take her as his wife?"

He shifted. Now that she had refused him, he found it difficult to offer her any better explanation. Giving her too much of his heart could result in greater pain than already exploded inside him.

"You know there is more than that between us," he admitted as he reached for her. She let him take her hand, even as she shook her head.

"But whatever *more* there is, it was there before today. And the potential for being caught also existed. Still, you told me there was no promise of a future attached, and I expected none. So I must ask you again . . . has something changed, beyond your mother's interruption this afternoon?"

He shut his eyes. All that had changed was that he realized now how much he loved her. But perhaps it wasn't enough. There were the dangerous games he continued to play with Devlin. The lies, the secrets that hid in this house and in his heart.

Those had been his reason for keeping her at arm's length before.

"No," he said softly as he dropped her hand. "Nothing in my life has changed."

"I doubt your mother would harm my reputation or yours by telling the world about our indiscretion," she reasoned. "She wishes you to make a union, but not at the price of hurting you. Or me, I wager."

"So you are saying you have no interest in a future together?" he asked, and the steel came into his voice at her calm refusals.

She drew a harsh breath, and for the first time he saw raw emotions in her face. Pain and anger in equal measure. And other things he couldn't place. But they were emotions, they were real, and they proved she was as tied to him as he was to her.

Still, she shook her head. "I cannot marry you because I do not wish to ever be tied to another man's will again." Her voice trembled slightly. "Even yours."

"But you care for me," he said, taking the risks he'd avoided until now. "I see it in your eyes."

She seemed surprised he could see that feeling in her. Immediately she erased the emotion from her face and withdrew a step. "That is inconsequential, Tristan. You and I made an agreement. We wouldn't seek a future that could never be. I do care for you, but that future is no more possible now than it was that first night."

He followed her lead and took a bitter step away. Disappointment returned, laced with anger. Anger at himself for daring to hope. For forgetting the barriers that separated him from happiness. He'd allowed himself to indulge in a fantasy of more, but he had to forget that now. Forget he loved this woman and return his concentration to the important business at hand.

"I understand, my lady," he said with a stiff bow, using formality as a shield.

He headed for the door, but when he reached it, he found himself turning. Meredith stared at him, hands clenched at her sides, her body trembling. In the dying firelight he saw tears glimmer in her eyes.

"My offer stands if you change your mind."

He turned away before he saw her reaction to his final statement and closed the door behind him.

Meredith's candle had burned down until it was no more than a nub with a glowing, sparking wick, but she hardly noticed. She was too busy sitting on the floor before the fire with every piece of evidence she'd collected spread out before her. She had even gone so far as to write a detailed layout of her case. For hours she had pored over the items, looking for something, *anything,* to clear Tristan's name.

Something to allow her to take his offer of marriage.

She let out a sigh as she struggled to her feet. She stretched her back before she paced to the window. Darkness reigned outside, so only her own reflection greeted her in the glass. And a dismal sight it was. Her eyes were puffy from her efforts to hold back tears, her face drawn by disappointment and anger and longing.

Yes, longing. She admitted she felt it. Tristan's offer of marriage rang in her head like a Hallelujah chorus. It reminded her of the lightness of her heart when he held her. When he touched her, she could almost forget a life lived in loneliness.

But what a dangerous man to allow herself to feel that way with. He, who she knew for a fact would be taken from her when her case was presented. Who had involved himself in treachery and lies for reasons she couldn't fathom.

She turned away from her faint reflection and paced to the other side of the room. Glancing down, she looked at the mounting pile of evidence. There was nothing there to say Tristan hadn't done everything he was accused of.

Nothing except the voice in her head. Her heart told her he would not, *could* not, do these things. Not only because of the way Edmund died, but because of the noble heart she believed he possessed. That same voice told her he had to be offered a chance to explain and defend himself before she turned him over to those who would condemn him to transportation or worse.

"I must tell him." She swiped at sudden tears.

For the first time since her arrival in Carmichael, she felt sure of herself. This was the right decision. She had enough evidence that he could not avoid telling her the truth, or at least couldn't deny what she'd gathered so far.

Her hands shook as she walked to the door. The hallways were dark so late at night. No servants bustled doing their duties, and most of Tristan's houseguests had retired to their bedchambers. But she had a suspicion he would still be awake. She guessed he had not been sleeping much of late, and their discussion about marriage had obviously shaken him.

She crept down the stairs. Somehow she didn't think she would be able to confront him in his bedchamber. It would be far too easy to surrender to his touch there, so she prayed he would be in his private office or the library or anywhere else.

She came around a corner into a long, wide hallway where Carmichael family portraits hung on every side. There, in the middle of the walkway, stood Tristan. He hadn't heard her approach. He seemed too caught up in what he was doing.

He stood staring at a large portrait. She could not see who it depicted, but by his body language, it was clearly someone important to him. His expression was dark, his brow drawn down, his frown deep as he studied the picture.

On instinct, she drew into the hallway's shadows.

His demeanor and expression told her she was witnessing something important. Something key to the man, if not the case.

Perhaps both.

"I am trying, Father," he said, so low that she wouldn't have caught the words at all if it weren't for the echoing hall.

Then he stiffened, as if he sensed the presence of another. She flattened against the deepest shadow as he looked around. Her breath caught when she witnessed the torment on his face. All the emotion she sensed beneath the surface, all the feelings he hid so well were no longer masked by a veil of propriety. He looked . . . broken. And she longed to comfort him.

But before she could do something so foolhardy, he spun on his heel and started down the hallway at a fast clip. She had no choice but to follow. He passed parlors, the library, and came to a stop at his private office. There, he hesitated.

He leaned forward to rest his head against the door before he opened it and went inside.

Meredith moved forward with as much haste as she could and still mask her footsteps. She pressed her ear to the door but could hear little. Tristan moved around his office, but wasn't near the entrance. She bit her lip as she slowly began to turn the knob, taking care to keep her movements as silent as possible.

Finally, she was able to push the door open just

a fraction of an inch. She pressed her eye to the opening, but it revealed nothing of interest. Tristan's desk was only partly in view, as well as the left side of the room, which included a bookcase and reading chair. He wasn't in sight.

She pushed the door open farther, revealing more of the office. He wasn't sitting at his desk either. Finally, she took half a step inside and peeked around the door.

Tristan stood on the other side of the room. His back was to her and his distraction kept him from noticing her entrance. He stared up at the portrait of his brother she had noticed during her search of this room a few days ago.

She opened her mouth to alert him of her presence, to start her confession of investigation, to demand the truth about his betrayal, when he leaned forward and began to do something with the picture frame. She couldn't see what in the partial darkness of the room, but she heard an audible click and then, to her utter surprise, Edmund's portrait swung away.

Nausea threatened to overwhelm Meredith at what she saw, and she clung to the edge of the door to keep from going down on her knees in total horror. Behind the benign picture of his brother, the landscape that had been stolen from the Genevieve Art House not one month before was hidden. The painting she had been looking for. The one she prayed she would never find.

Her fingernails scraped the door frame and she struggled to hold back a moan. Somehow, despite the evidence, she had believed the voice in her head that said Tristan was incapable of such a crime.

Now she could no longer deny it.

"Two more days," Tristan said. His voice shocked her, and for a moment she actually thought he was speaking to her. "In two days you will be Devlin's and I shall never have to see you again. This will all be over."

She withdrew from the room before he turned and caught her spying, and managed to close the door soundlessly behind her. She hardly saw the hallway as she ran away. Away from the painting that proved her greatest fears. Away from Tristan's voice as he confirmed he was a willing participant in Devlin's schemes. Away from her broken heart, though she didn't seem to be able to run fast enough to escape that pain.

She heard Tristan's office door open and then close, and she glanced over her shoulder. He was coming her way, and there was no way she would escape without him seeing her if she continued scurrying up the hall. Instead, she slipped into a darkened doorway and flattened herself against it.

She held her breath as his long, sure strides approached her position. He passed by without noticing her. She watched his retreating back as she struggled to catch her breath. Her heart threatened to explode and her ears rang with the whoosh of blood.

She wanted to weep. She wanted to chase Tristan and pound her fists against his chest in anger. She wanted to scream out her frustration until she brought the house down around her.

But she couldn't.

Instead, she turned to her training for calming exercises. Slowly, by focused breathing, she was able to control her ragged emotions, then carefully fold them away. She had no doubt she would revisit them later.

But for now she had a job to do. One she could no longer avoid or pretend was a mistake. She had a letter to write. A missive that would be in London by daybreak thanks to her connections.

When he examined the hated painting, Tristan had said it would be over soon.

And it would be. All of it.

Chapter 16

Meredith thought she had experienced torment before: after the deaths of her parents, during one long night before Tristan arrived to rescue her from her own folly, even during the early days of her training, when her sheltered body revolted against the pain of physical exertion.

But she realized now those pains had been mere annoyances. The true definition of torment was the anguish roiling inside her while she sat at the supper table waiting for the inevitable.

After she'd snuck back to her chamber the night before, she'd written her letter . . . the hated letter condemning Tristan to a fate she did not wish to consider. Her driver had taken it to a contact waiting in Carmichael. The roads were good and the moon was full, so he had probably arrived in London early enough that Charlie had read her letter over breakfast. Her superior never wasted time when the moment for an arrest came. She had no doubt he had departed for Carmichael within hours.

She looked at a clock in the corner of the dining room. How much more time did she have before Charlie arrived?

Her gaze moved to Tristan, sitting at the head of the table, chatting with another gentleman. He had no idea the end was near. Still, he looked tired. Wrung out. His green eyes lacked some of the warmth and light she'd come to expect from their stare, and his skin was sallow, with dark smudges beneath his eyes.

"Lord Carmichael, a few of us were wondering where your friend has gone?" said one of the ladies farther down the table.

Meredith saw that it was the portly Lady Blankensheft, whose daughter Hester had come out two years before. Her ladyship had been in constant pursuit of a bridegroom ever since.

"My friend, my lady?" Tristan asked blankly.

"Mr. Devlin. A few of us noticed his absence today at our game of Pall Mall, and I see he is not with us tonight," Lady Blankensheft clarified.

Meredith's eyes widened as she scanned the table. She had avoided the Pall Mall game because she couldn't bear to pretend to have a good time when she knew what was about to transpire. Tonight she'd been so involved with her tangled thoughts, she had hardly noticed any of the party guests, including Devlin.

Now she was paying the price. When Charlie came to collect Tristan, she would have no intelligence as to where Devlin had gone, or even how long it had been since he'd departed. Once again she was too caught up in her emotions to effectively do her duty.

She watched Tristan carefully for his answer. At least she could garner some evidence from that, if nothing else.

His eyes lit up with a little more life than he'd been exhibiting previously. He looked . . . triumphant, actually. As if he had finally won a long-fought battle. With Devlin? If that were true . . . over what?

"Mr. Devlin was called out of Carmichael on business," he said. "He will not return, I'm afraid."

Terror gripped her. Had the painting already been exchanged? No, that was not possible. If the painting was moved, Devlin would have been forced to depart Carmichael in a carriage. Her driver and groomsman would have notified her of such suspicious movement. Versus, if Devlin had simply departed on horseback, which was the report on how he had arrived, her driver might have thought he was only going out for the day.

Since she had been hiding like a coward, she

hadn't spoken to him yet. Something she would correct as soon as she could break away.

Lady Blankensheft's face fell with disappointment. Apparently she had been considering Devlin as a potential match for her daughter. Happily for her, she hadn't received her wish.

" 'Tis a pity," she sighed, then immediately turned her attention back to the next potential suitor.

"Yes." Tristan swirled the liquid in his glass. "A pity."

Meredith cocked her head at his tone. She was fairly certain the painting had not been removed, so why would Devlin leave without it? And why would Tristan be so pleased by that fact? Last night he seemed eager to rid himself of the landscape. The web he had spun was so complicated, she wasn't sure what to think. She certainly didn't understand his reasons for what he'd done. She could only pray someday she would hear what they were. Perhaps that would give her peace.

Somehow she doubted it.

Tristan seemed to sense her eyes on him, and he looked in her direction. For a moment his stare burned with heat and emotion, desire and disappointment, then he turned away and returned to his conversation.

Meredith frowned as anger flared inside her. *Why* had he done this?

Tristan claimed he wanted to protect her, but

what kind of protection could he provide when he surrounded himself with such treachery? It ate at her core and nicked at her heart so much that she hardly heard Lady Carmichael rise from her place and announce that the ladies would retire to the South Parlor while the men went to play billiards and have their port.

Relief washed over Meredith. She took her time in rising as the other members of the party made their way out of the room. She tried to look occupied as Tristan passed on his way out. His stare burned her, but he chose another lady to escort. Finally, she was the last remaining and got to her feet.

She had no desire to join the women. In her current state of mind, she doubted she'd be very good company, and she didn't trust herself not to show her emotions. Aside from which, she needed to speak to her driver as soon as possible.

She slipped into the hallway just as Lady Carmichael left the parlor where the ladies were gathering. Meredith could already hear their laughter and talk buzzing in the hall.

"There you are, my dear," Lady Carmichael said with a genuine smile. Meredith was surprised to see the expression. Surely, Constance knew Meredith had refused Tristan's offer of marriage. She had expected the lady to be coolly polite, not openly warm.

In fact, she had counted on it. Despite the necessity of her duty, she felt no pleasure about ruining the Carmichael name and family. And she hadn't had the nerve to face the other woman since Constance had come upon them in the parlor the day before. Her cheeks heated with the memory of her ladyship's intrusion . . . and the pleasure of what she had intruded upon.

"Good evening," she said with a weaker version of Constance's smile.

"Do you not intend to join us?" Constance asked.

Meredith sighed. "I'm afraid I am feeling a bit under the weather again—"

Before she could finish, Constance raised a slender hand. "I won't force you to come up with an excuse if you don't wish to join the fray, but might you share a moment with me before you slip away?"

Meredith's heart thudded. "Of course."

Constance motioned to a sitting room nearby. As they entered, she closed the door behind her. Meredith glanced over her shoulder with caution. So Lady Carmichael wanted to be alone.

"By your expression, it appears you believe I mean to eat you." Constance laughed. "I assure you, I have no intention to do so."

Meredith couldn't help but smile, and this time it wasn't forced. "Of course not, my lady."

"I think the reason for your worry is that you've refused my son's offer of marriage, and you fear

I judge you harshly for that? Or for the actions I witnessed yesterday afternoon?"

Meredith drew back. She couldn't believe Lady Carmichael would be so . . . so blunt!

"I admit I am embarrassed by what transpired yesterday," she said softly. She wasn't lying. Being discovered in such a delicate position was not something she would ever have desired. Especially since she knew how shocking a lady such as Constance Archer must have found it. "And I wouldn't blame you for being upset that I refused Tristan's proposal."

Lady Carmichael's face softened. "My dear, I am not angry. I hoped you would accept Tristan's offer, but I don't know what reasons you have for your refusal. I would not dare judge them. Or you." She smiled. "But I hope you did not judge Tristan too harshly either."

She jolted. If only Constance knew how harshly he had yet to be judged. "Judge Tristan?"

"I know he can seem distant sometimes. But I hope you realize what a true heart he has." Constance met her gaze evenly. "My son is as honorable a man as I ever knew. He may not express his emotions well, but he feels them keenly. Deeply. That is why his sorrow over his brother's death has troubled him so long. Only you removed the emptiness from his eyes, Meredith."

Meredith pulled away from her touch. From the words that affected her so deeply. There was the war of emotion and evidence again. Every time she was with Tristan, she felt the same way about him as his mother described. That he was honorable. Decent. Passionate in his feelings, though he hid that passion beneath a cloak of propriety.

And yet all evidence pointed to him being the worst kind of man. It said those feelings weren't real.

But they still existed. In her mind. In her heart.

"I won't speak to you of this again," Lady Carmichael assured her. "And if you choose to let your refusal stand, I won't hold it against you. I do hope you'll come to visit me from time to time and accept me when I call on you."

"Of course," Meredith said hurriedly. "I would never turn you away."

Constance smiled. "I hope you won't turn my son away either. Time in this life is so short. Regret is a terrible burden." She withdrew to the door. "I must tend to my guests. If you join us later, I'll be very pleased. If not, then I wish you good night."

"Good night," Meredith whispered. She turned away when the door shut.

"Time in this life is so short," she repeated.

Lady Carmichael didn't know how true that statement was. Meredith's time with Tristan was coming to a rapid close. She had to make the best of the few moments she had left. She would have enough regret to lie heavy in her heart when this case was over.

With a feeling more certain than she'd had in a long time, she hurried from the room to take care of her last duties before she allowed herself one final moment with the man she loved.

Tristan paced his office. Tangled thoughts kept him from enjoying the happy group in the parlor below. They played cards, the ladies took turns on the pianoforte, couples danced informal country jigs, and the talk was so loud he'd closed his door to force it from his ears.

He might have stayed, despite his discomfort in such situations, except Meredith wasn't in attendance. She had slipped away sometime between supper and when the men rejoined the ladies an hour later. His mother wouldn't say, but he had the impression she'd spoken to Meredith. And knowing his mother, probably encouraged her on his behalf.

But Meredith was not there. She didn't want him.

He sat down at his desk and scrubbed a hand over his face. The only hope he held on to at present was that he'd finally taken care of the other problem in his life. Now he was free to hand over that blasted painting to Devlin.

With a sidelong glance, he caught sight of the portrait he'd had made of his late brother. Edmund was his reason for all he'd done. It seemed fitting that his brother's face hid the last piece of the puzzle that would finally grant him access to Devlin's group.

The bastard hadn't been pleased when Tristan sent him off to fetch the leader of his sect. But he'd had little choice. Devlin had no idea where his precious painting was hidden, and without it, he couldn't perform his next act of treason. Until Tristan got what he wanted, an introduction to the man behind Devlin's treachery—Devlin wouldn't get what he desired either.

He couldn't help a smile. Soon this would be over. He could shut the book on the worst part of his life. Start over. In time, perhaps he could even convince Meredith . . .

No, now wasn't the time for such thoughts. Now he had to put all his energy, all his time, all his emotion, into completing his revenge. That was all that mattered.

If only his heart would listen. It kept protesting that a future with Meredith was worth more than living in the past. That his brother would not wish him to throw away everything to even the score.

The door to his office opened, but he didn't look up.

"I don't need anything," he said, steepling his fingers at his chin as he kept his gaze on the portrait of his brother, cut down in his prime.

"Nothing?"

The sound of Meredith's voice made him pivot in his chair. There she was, as if his earlier musings had called out and she'd come in answer. He wanted to take her in his arms. Instead, he rose to his feet and stayed behind the desk. He had opened himself to her once. Not completely, but as much as he was able when secrets hung over his head like a guillotine. She had refused him. He didn't desire a second dose of that pain.

"Meredith." He motioned to the chair opposite his.

Instead of joining him, she strolled across the room to the fireplace. Her gaze slipped up and she flinched when she saw his brother's portrait, as if seeing it hurt her as much as it sometimes did him. But why? She'd only met Edmund in passing as a girl. She had no cause to be visibly moved by seeing his image.

She turned, and the desperation in her eyes stopped his wayward thoughts. "I realize I hurt you when I refused your proposal."

His heart pounded furiously, and he gripped the corner of the desk.

"I won't deny that," he answered, measuring his tone carefully. If she wasn't here to alter her decision, he had no desire to make a fool of himself.

She dipped her head. "I also believe that, whatever else may be true, you offered for me with good intent."

He wrinkled his brow. "You doubt me in other ways?"

Again she flinched, but ignored his question.

Her blue stare came up to meet his. Unwavering. Her earlier desperation was gone, but she so often masked her emotions. He wondered why she hid so much of herself behind the guise of a social butterfly.

"Tristan, soon things will happen that will only increase whatever anger or hurt lies between us." She stepped toward him. "Things will happen that will change both our lives forever."

He shook his head in utter confusion. "What things?"

"But before they happen, I ask one boon of you."

She moved closer, gliding toward him slowly, evenly. Her gaze never left his, even when she brushed against him. Even when the floral heaven of her scent surrounded him. When her light filled him. Her warmth made him whole.

"What do you want?" he asked, his voice hoarse from desire and emotion.

"One last kiss." Her voice broke and tears began to glitter at the corners of her eyes. "Just kiss me one more time. Before—Before it's too late."

He didn't understand the ominous nature of her request. Perhaps she intended to leave without seeing him again. Perhaps she thought her refusal had done irreparable harm to their fragile bond. Or perhaps the thing that made her hands tremble was even more dire than anything he could guess.

But he didn't care. She offered him heaven, and even though it cost him another piece of his heart, he took it. But he took his time to savor it. If this was to be their last kiss, as she claimed, he would make sure neither one of them ever forgot it.

Slowly, he let his fingers brush through her hair. With one hand, he cupped her cheek, while he let the other drift lower. He glided along her arm until she shivered, then cupped her hip and drew her closer than she already was.

She sighed, but her breath shivered out like a sob. She tilted her chin, offering her mouth, but he ignored that for the moment. He brushed one soft kiss at the corner of her eye, tasting the saltiness of tears she had already shed, of others she held back. He kissed her cheek, brushed his lips against her ear. He pressed a kiss on the tip of her nose.

It seemed the moment hung between them, stretching forever as he finally let his lips touch the corner of hers. Then he moved in and pressed them firmly against her. Her second sigh was just as ragged, if more relieved. Arching, she opened her mouth and deepened the kiss.

He tasted her as he had the first time. Learning her flavor, testing her responsiveness. In some ways this "last" kiss was like the first. Unknown. Unexpected. And something he feared he was imagining. But her warmth assured him it was no addle-minded dream.

The desperation Meredith had been masking came through again. She clung to him, hands clenching, grasping handfuls of his tailored jacket.

She tangled her tongue with his, begging for more, demanding more.

He gave her what she wanted. The kiss deepened, but this time it danced on the edge of losing control. His body could only take so much before he wouldn't be able to keep himself from claiming her in the most elemental way.

He might have given in to that desire, except he felt her hold back a piece of herself. If he asked to make love to her, he knew that she would pull away. He didn't want to lose her now, so he tried to rein in the out-of-control passion she inspired.

Noise echoed from the hallway, disturbing the pleasant oblivion he found in her touch, but he pushed the sound aside to continue to explore her lips. She, too, allowed one more kiss, then moved away. Away from his lips, out of his arms. Somehow he didn't want to let her go. Some part of him cried out that if he released her, he might never hold her again.

But she insisted and they broke apart. Her eyes were glazed with need and more unshed tears.

"Tristan," she whispered on a soft breath. "I hope you'll understand."

"Understand?" Now he was distracted by the noise in the hallway. Closer. Footsteps, voices.

"Yes."

As she said the word, the door to his office flew open and several men stepped inside, followed by his butler and two footmen. Tristan stiffened at the way the men simply interrupted without a proper announcement.

There were three intruders. All were dressed well, if a bit wrinkled from travel, but they were clearly part of the upper middle class. Not of his rank. Not of the rank required to barge into a man's home without leave. He didn't recognize any of them. One was a portly man, starting to bald. He appeared to be the leader of the three, as the other two men simply stayed at his side, watching the servants and Tristan.

"I'm sorry, sir." His butler pushed in front of the men. "They forced their way in, I couldn't stop them."

"It's all right, Jensen," Tristan assured his servant. "These men look like they have business here. Or at least, they believe they do."

The butler folded his arms and stood in place, ready to escort them out by their ears if it were required. Tristan smiled at his servant's loyalty, but then his smile fell as he caught sight of Meredith. She stood near the door, but she looked anything but shocked or frightened by the sudden interruption. In fact, she seemed resigned.

Stepping forward, she spoke softly to the servants. To his surprise, they stepped from the room. Meredith closed the door behind them, then turned to face him. His eyes met hers and he saw . . . *guilt* flash in them.

She knew these men. And she knew their purpose.

"Who are you?" Tristan asked, straightening to his full height.

"My name is Charles Isley, Lord Carmichael," the balding man said, coming forward.

Tristan shook his head. The name meant nothing to him. "And why have you barged into my home and interrupted my private gathering at this late hour?"

Isley frowned. "My lord, I am an agent of the War Department, working for the Crown. I've been given the duty of taking you into custody. You must return to London with me right away."

Tristan's world collapsed. Custody? That meant he was being charged with some crime. The blood began to drain from his cheeks, though he forced himself to straighten up with a smirk of confidence. He could not let them see that he'd dreaded this very moment for over a year.

"Take me into custody?" he asked, and was pleased his voice didn't waver. "Am I to understand I'm being charged with some kind of crime?"

"Yes, my lord." Isley nodded once, curt and with only the slightest hint of civility. "You have been charged with treason against the Crown."

Chapter 17

❦

The word "treason" cut through Meredith. It wasn't a surprise to hear it. She'd expected it, known it, *proven* it . . . but when Charlie said the word, she couldn't help but flinch away from what it meant for Tristan . . . for herself.

Tristan flinched too, almost at the same moment she did. But like her, his face registered no shock at the charge. There was anger in his eyes, yes. Frustration. But something else.

Resignation.

On some level, in some dark place in his heart, he had expected this moment to come, even if he'd dreaded it. And that confirmed the evidence more than anything except an outright confession.

She watched Charlie explain the situation to Tristan, watched Tristan argue, but the words were like some foreign language. She didn't comprehend what they said because she was assailed by images.

Of Tristan as a boy, playing at her aunt and uncle's home. Later, of the night she ran away and he found her in that dirty pub. She thought of his face when he realized the identity of the girl he had saved from rape or worse. And the fury with which he had attacked her assailant. Her protection had been his main concern, both from the man who would have attacked her and from the ramifications of running away from her aunt and uncle. He'd never told anyone the truth about where she had been and why, even when he turned away from her.

What had changed since then? What had turned him from her noble knight to a vile traitor against all she held dear?

And why could she not keep herself from giving a damn what had changed Tristan? Pain ripped through her and she loathed it. She cursed herself for the weakness of emotion and the tingling of tears at the back of her eyes. She wanted to dismiss him and move on.

She couldn't.

Because there were new memories now. Memories of the tenderness of his touch when he kissed her. Of the pleasure when they made love. And also of the time they spent together when he made her believe he was still decent, still good.

Charlie's voice pierced her emotional haze. "I'll need to bind your hands while we escort you to the carriage, my lord."

Tristan's eyes widened and he shook his head. "No. My mother is down the hallway, along with a roomful of guests. I couldn't hide that I was being led away in shackles!"

The two agents with Charlie stepped forward. Each one grabbed Tristan's shoulders. Of course he fought. She knew he would. He twisted in their grip, sending elbows backward as a defense against them.

Her heart lurched. If he didn't stop, he could be killed.

Stepping forward, she held up her hands. "Wait, Charlie!"

At the sound of her voice, everyone in the room stopped and turned to look at her. Tristan's face was filled with her betrayal. Charlie arched an eyebrow. She had never interfered with an arrest before. In fact, she normally didn't attend them, in order to protect the secrecy of her identity.

But there was nothing *normal* about this arrest.

"Meredith, what is it?"

She slipped between Charlie and Tristan, keeping her back to the man she had betrayed because she could not bear to face him. "Lord Carmichael is correct. If you bind him, everyone here will notice his arrest."

Charlie shook his head. "And why does that matter?"

"Because Devlin slipped away. If we hope to catch him, it might be best if he doesn't know his newest partner has been arrested for crimes against the Crown." She allowed herself a glimpse over her shoulder. Tristan's arms were folded as he glowered at her. "Take Lord Carmichael quietly, let him tell his family he's been called away on business to protect them from the truth. We could determine what kind of information he has about Devlin and his group without letting the world know about his arrest."

"And why would a traitor like him give us information about other criminals?" Charlie asked with a glare at Tristan. "At any rate, Meredith, the truth will come out. Whether tonight or next week or next month. We can't keep it a secret forever."

She touched Charlie's forearm. "Please, I have never asked anything like this of you. *Please*."

He drew back in surprise. Then he looked at Tristan again, but this time with a more appraising stare. Probably he wondered what kind of spell his suspect had cast on his spy.

Meredith wondered that too.

"You're involved with these men?" Tristan asked

from behind her, his voice filled with horrified disbelief. "You did this?"

Meredith turned. His eyes bore into hers, piercing her soul and demanding nothing less than the truth. He reached for her, but the two agents behind him grabbed his elbows to keep him away. She found herself aching for the touch they withheld, even as she snapped, "No, *you* did this!"

Tristan recoiled, no longer leaning against the men who held him from being nearer to her.

Charlie touched her elbow. "Very well, perhaps you're right. I will do what you ask and keep the arrest secret as long as I can." His voice grew harder. "I assume that is what you wish, Lord Carmichael. For secrecy?"

For a moment Tristan only stared at Meredith, then he broke his gaze. "Why would I wish secrecy when I don't understand why I'm being arrested?"

Meredith winced. How could he deny the truth? Well, she wouldn't allow it any longer. Slowly, she walked across the room to the portrait of Edmund Archer. Reaching up, she found the releases hidden along the picture's frame. With a snap, she slid it out of the way and revealed the stolen landscape.

Turning back, she motioned to the hated painting with one hand. "This, Tristan. It's all about this."

His face paled, and the denials it seemed he was preparing fell away. A breath passed before he murmured, "Yes. I would appreciate discretion in this matter."

Charlie nodded and stepped aside to talk for a moment with his men. Meredith came forward, moving toward the door in case Tristan made a dash for it. Instead, he looked at her. Evenly.

"Tristan," she murmured, somehow wanting to explain herself, as though she had been wrong when all she'd done was perform her duty.

He shook his head. "There is nothing to say, is there? You've already decided what is true and what's not."

She clenched her fists at her sides. "The evidence is in front of me." She motioned to the painting, but he did not look at it. "What am I to believe?"

He shrugged. "That not everything is what it seems."

Before she could reply, Charlie returned. "We must leave quickly and try to arouse as little suspicion as possible. If we're able to take leave of the house without questions, I'll allow you to send a message to your family explaining you were called away on sudden and urgent business. Will that keep them at bay?"

Tristan looked away from her. "Yes. My mother will have questions, but she won't neglect her guests in order to pursue me, if that's what you mean. She's scheduled to visit my sister and her family in Bath after this event. She wouldn't cancel that trip. My sister recently had a child."

"Good." Charlie motioned to the door. "If your guests interfere, you'll say the same. That you've been called to London on urgent business. If you make any move that implies you intend to escape or send some kind of secret message, I will put you in shackles and drag you out. Is that clear?"

Tristan's eyes narrowed. As she had when they made love, Meredith saw the imprisoned rake within him come out. A man not used to being ordered around. Not by anyone.

His lips thinned. "I have no choice."

"No, you don't. Meredith has given you a respite from public censure, which is more than I would have done." Charlie motioned toward the door. "Once we reach London, we'll keep you somewhere that won't receive excessive attention."

"Thank you," Tristan managed to grind out between clenched teeth.

He allowed the guards to escort him to the door. Meredith watched them and was surprised when he turned back to pin her with a stare. He wasn't the man who had wooed her, made love to her, proposed to her any longer. The hard glint in his eyes made it clear any feelings he may have had for her had been crushed.

"Don't forget what I said, Meredith. Everything is not what it seems." He looked her up and down.

One last acknowledgment of betrayal and utter contempt. "You are proof of that."

"You must eat something."

With a start, Meredith looked away from the rain-streaked window at Emily's London home. She was so tangled in her thoughts, she'd all but forgotten that Emily and Ana were present.

Her two friends sat having their tea, but they looked at her with concern plain in their eyes. As plain, she feared, as her own twisted emotions. It seemed she had lost her ability to hide her feelings. That could be a fatal flaw in a spy.

"No," she said. "I'm not hungry. Thank you."

Emily pushed away from the table and came to the window. She grasped Meredith's shoulders and physically guided her to the table, where she "helped" her into a seat. Ana placed a steaming cup of fragrant tea and a scone before her.

"You have been moping since your return to London two days ago," Emily said, sitting down and folding her arms. Meredith guessed that sharp look in her friend's eyes was much the same as the one she gave suspects in interrogation. No wonder Emily was so successful in obtaining secrets.

"Yes," Ana agreed. "We're worried about you."

Meredith shook her head. She didn't want to discuss what made her heart hurt, not with them. Not with anyone. She just wanted to forget what had happened in Carmichael. She had tried, but memories continued to haunt her. As well as Tristan's final volley as he was led away to imprisonment.

"Don't be silly," she managed on a shaky breath. "I'm right as rain. Just a bit low after the end of a case. You know how it is. A month or so of excitement makes it difficult to return to normal until we're assigned something new. London is . . ." She hesitated. "It's not the same."

Nothing was.

Ana pursed her lips as she shoved little wire-rimmed spectacles up her nose. They were the ones she wore while she worked in her area downstairs. She had forgotten to take them off, a common problem.

"It's more than that," Ana insisted. "Even in the field something was off about you. You've been distracted and troubled ever since you were told you would be investigating Tristan Archer. It has only been worse since your return. You've been so quiet."

"Not yourself," Emily agreed with a nod of her head. "You've hardly told us anything about your case. And you don't seem pleased with its resolution."

Meredith picked at the scone in front of her. "What is there to be happy about?"

She sighed as she thought about the report that had been waiting for her in London when she managed to break away from Lady Carmichael's party.

"Whatever evidence might have been hidden in the painting had already been removed before we retrieved it. Now we cannot find it. For all we know, it was handed over to Devlin before he left Carmichael."

"Yes, but—" Ana began.

Meredith waved her off. "Because of *my* stupidity, my distraction, we don't know where Devlin is now either. And Tristan—"

She stopped herself. There was no need to rehash that portion of her regret. She did that enough in her empty bed when she lived and relived every stolen moment they had spent together.

Emily stood up and came beside her. She reached out a hand and stroked it over Meredith's hair. Meredith glanced up at her friend in surprise at the tender gesture. Normally Ana was the nurturer and Emily was stern, tough. She'd had to be.

"What happened?" Emily whispered. "What are you keeping from us?"

Meredith sighed. It was such a heavy burden to bear. She wanted to tell her two closest friends, her sisters in spirit, so much.

Ana's smile was soft and genuine. "It might help if you told us."

She nodded. There was no denying them when they worked together. She drew in a few breaths as she gathered herself.

"I—I—" she stammered, searching for a way to say the words. To reveal the truth. But there was only one. "I fell in love with him." Hearing the statement for the first time brought tears to her eyes. Ones she had been hiding, denying herself. Now they fell freely. "I fell in love with a traitor."

The corner of Emily's lip tilted. She lifted her eyes to Ana. "You owe me a pound."

Meredith snapped her gaze to Emily with a frown. "A pound? Wait, did you place a *wager* on my feelings for Tristan?" She shook off Emily's comforting hands and got to her feet. Stomping over to the fire, she folded her arms. "No wonder you wanted me to tell you the truth so badly."

"Come now," Emily insisted. "You know that isn't the reason."

"Yes, we really are worried about you!" Ana said as she hurried to Meredith's side to put her arms around her waist. "We guessed you had deeper feelings for the man, especially given the tone of your missives home while you were in the field. But we take no pleasure in your pain. You know that, don't you?"

Meredith looked at Ana, but she couldn't hold her scowl for long. Not when her friend was looking at her with such genuine concern. "I know you don't."

"Now, tell us everything," Emily said with a sigh.

Meredith rubbed her eyes with her fingertips.

How could she explain what she, herself, didn't understand?

"I don't know how it happened," she began. "I had feelings for Tristan as a child. Feelings that ran deeper than the mere friendship he showed me. But I never thought those things would return. Not with my training, not with the knowledge of what he might have done."

"But they did," Ana supplied with a little sigh.

Romantic that Ana was, Meredith could see she appreciated the passion of the situation, if not the pain. "Yes," she admitted. "They did. Almost immediately, there was a deep attraction between us. But it went beyond a spark of desire. I—I still *liked* Tristan. I liked talking to him, I found myself sharing things with him, things I hadn't told anyone."

"Even us?" Emily asked, both her eyebrows arching.

"Believe it or not, I still have—or had—some secrets, Emily." Meredith shook her head. "I realized my emotions were getting out of hand, especially when more and more of the evidence pointed to his guilt. But I still played close to the fire, kept coming to him when my investigation didn't require it. We—We made love. He even asked me to marry him."

Both Ana and Emily gasped their shock. Meredith nodded. "I know. And I wanted to say yes. I wanted to forget what I knew and surrender to the life he offered, even if it was a false image."

She frowned. Even now she couldn't tell her friends everything. She couldn't tell them how she had nearly burned the letter Ana sent her with the decoded information before reading it. How she almost threw her duties to the wind and gave in to her heart's desire.

"And how do you feel now?" Emily asked softly. "Now that you know for certain Tristan stole the painting? You know the information we sought was removed, probably by him, and hidden . . . or worse, turned over to Devlin and his group?"

Meredith walked to the window to look outside. She thought about Emily's question. One she'd been avoiding. She didn't want to face the truth.

"Before Charlie and his men took Tristan away, he said something to me. He told me my case wasn't what it seemed. And I believe him. Or—Or I want to believe." She covered her face. "I just don't know anymore! I can't trust myself."

"Why?" Emily prodded.

Meredith pressed a palm against the cold window. "Because the evidence points to him, but my heart and my feelings tell me differently. He doesn't seem like the kind of man who would barter men's lives for a few pounds. I battled with that fact the entire time I was in Carmichael. It hasn't changed since I returned to London."

"Perhaps you should see him," Ana suggested.

"See him?" Meredith's heart lurched to her throat. How many times had she thought of doing just that, but resisted because she knew how painful it would be?

"It's not a bad idea." Emily tapped her index finger on her chin with a thoughtful expression.

Meredith's eyes went wide. "You too?"

Ana nodded. "If you saw him, you might be able to sort out the evidence from your heart. And know if your emotions were still involved."

Emily waved off that comment. "More importantly, you might be able to do what Charlie and his men haven't since they arrived in London. Get Lord Carmichael to tell them where the evidence he removed is now."

Meredith shut her eyes. Facing Tristan was a terrifying prospect, even though she knew her friends were each right in their own way. She needed to see him to purge herself of the love that tormented her. Seeing him in whatever prison he inhabited might bring the reality of the situation to her.

And she wanted to know where the hidden evidence was. Without it, it seemed she had pursued the case in vain.

"Where are they holding him?" she asked quietly.

Ana smiled. "Charlie's home, in the small holding cell. He felt it would reduce suspicion for as long as possible."

Meredith sighed. "I'll go this afternoon."

"Would you like one of us to accompany you?" Emily asked, her brow wrinkled in concern.

"No," Meredith said. "I started this alone. I must finish it alone."

Chapter 18

"**L**ord Carmichael, your cooperation in this manner would help your cause enormously. It could mean the difference between transportation and death."

Tristan looked at Charles Isley with a carefully neutral expression. He didn't hate the man as much as he had expected to when Isley stormed into his home a week before and stole Tristan's chance at revenge . . . his chance at any future at all. Since they had arrived in Isley's home in London, he'd found the man to be a fair and gentlemanly jailer.

But he couldn't give Isley what he wanted. Tristan desired private justice, the kind the government could not provide with a swift trial.

"There is little difference between the two for me," Tristan said, meeting his jailor's eyes. "I will be dead in every sense of the word once the news of my arrest becomes public. And I'll have killed my family as well."

He flinched at the truth of his dramatic statement. Once the word "traitor" was linked to his name, his fortune would be decimated, his family destroyed. His entailed estates would no doubt be transferred to the closest cousin, his mother thrown into the street. His sisters would take her in, but she would never again be accepted in good society.

Worse, no one would ever understand *why* he had done what he'd done. The *ton* was eager to believe the worst. Getting such a salacious piece of gossip about a man like him, when he'd been so careful to avoid even a hint of scandal, would be an even bigger boon. Society would talk about his fall from grace for years.

His head pounded.

Isley's eyes narrowed. "Meredith asked me to protect you. Do you realize what a gift that was? That you would throw it back at us like this, refuse to give any information about where the hidden evidence is or even *what* it is . . . I don't understand."

Tristan sat down on the small bed in the corner of the room and pondered the uneven floorboards. Meredith. He had tried not to think of her since he'd left Carmichael. When his thoughts did veer in her direction, the anger, the betrayal, the utter heartbreak that burned in his chest were too much to bear.

She had *lied* to him. Used him and the feelings he had for her. And all to bring him to his knees, like he was now. Nothing between them had been true. Her kiss, the emotions in her eyes, they were nothing but weapons in her arsenal.

His anger bubbled and boiled, but he shoved it back. Showing those powerful emotions would only land him in Newgate all the sooner. And venting his rage changed nothing.

"I did not ask Meredith to protect me, nor you, Mr. Isley," he said with a frown as he lay back to stare at the ceiling. "And I have told you everything I intend to. What you believe is not the truth. I've tried to explain to you about my brother—"

Isley rolled his eyes. "Please don't waste my time telling me about your quest for revenge, my lord. The evidence states otherwise. It would do you better to be truthful instead of coming up with elaborate explanations for your behavior."

Tristan clenched his fists. Isley was a pragmatic man. He clearly didn't understand the heat of emotion or the power of hate. "I see no point in going further if you won't hear the truth."

Isley let out a string of curses as he stormed to the door. There, he hesitated. "If you won't help yourself, then I have no choice but to remove you from these comfortable quarters into a real prison. There will be no stopping the news from becoming public then. You understand that, don't you?"

Tristan shut his eyes, tried to block the pain. "I understand perfectly."

The door clanged shut and he heard the lock slide into place.

With a sigh, he looked around. His room was like a shabby gentleman's chamber, but it was his prison cell. It was a room in Isley's own basement, with no windows for escape and the door locked from the outside. It was comfortable . . . at least, more comfortable than he imagined Newgate would be. Soon enough he would find out.

What would his family think when they heard the news?

Voices echoed from the dark, narrow hallway outside. He recognized the sound of his guards, who treated him with as much respect as Isley did, another courtesy he assumed he would lose once he was moved to a real prison. But then he heard another voice. A female voice.

Meredith.

Isley might be pragmatic, but he was also intelligent. Of course he would send for Meredith. The man was aware of Tristan's weaknesses. Ones he would now be forced to fight, along with his rage. Somehow he thought it would be much harder to mask his fury when the woman who betrayed him was standing mere feet away.

His body clenched at the sound of her low murmur. Her words were indiscernible, but he would have recognized the lilt and tone anywhere. It took all his willpower to stay on the narrow bed.

The door opened and her footsteps hesitated when she saw him. Still, he did not turn his head. From the corner of his eye he watched her stare for a long moment and sucked in a breath. By God, she was beautiful. He'd hoped he could forget that fact, but it slapped him in the face as she pushed a loose strand of hair away from her cheek.

She looked around the little chamber, then whispered something to the guards. He was surprised when they backed away, closing the door and leaving them alone.

"Hello, Tristan."

His body reacted to her voice of its own accord. Blood rushed hot to every place where she had ever touched him. He was stunned by his own reactions. That was *need* that filled him. What the hell was wrong with him?

He pushed away the desire with force. This woman had deceived him. He could not allow his baser needs or deeper emotions to control his interaction with her. That was far too dangerous a trap.

With difficulty, he remained silent as she came farther into the room. She examined the books stacked on the little dresser, then stepped toward him.

He turned his head to face her, let her know he was watching. She faltered under his intense gaze.

"You—You look tired," she said softly. "Are you eating?"

His lips thinned. "Do you care?"

He stifled a curse that he had replied to her question, and with such vehemence that she must know her answer mattered.

"Of course I care." Hurt flickered in her eyes, but was it real? Or just another trick?

"Do you?" he said softly before he sat up and turned. In one swift motion he got to his feet and took a long step toward her. To his surprise, she didn't back away from his angry advance, merely stood looking at him. Wary, but unafraid.

He halted in his tracks. No. He would not give her the satisfaction of watching him lose control one more time. He would be as collected and uncaring as she managed to be. She was merely an enemy now. No matter how his hot blood called to her.

He folded his arms. "Tell me, how did you leave Carmichael?"

She shifted at his directness. "All was well."

With a snort of disgust, he turned away. "No one was surprised by my sudden departure, then?"

She hesitated. "Most of the guests were disappointed, but no one was suspicious."

"Even Philip?" he snapped. Despite his letter of explanation, Tristan knew his best friend wouldn't believe that he'd suddenly disappeared on business. Business his man of affairs knew nothing about.

Her face paled, but she gave no answer. His heart sank as the silence stretched between them. "Meredith?"

She sighed. "Philip became problematic after your departure. He didn't believe your letter and began inquiries. To protect your privacy and the chance of catching Devlin, we—we took him into custody."

Tristan stumbled back as horror expanded in his chest. "You arrested him?"

She nodded wordlessly.

"But he did nothing!" he cried.

Meredith pursed her lips. "He was aware of your activities. He aided you. Charles and the other agents felt he could provide information you've been unwilling to share."

Tristan scrubbed a hand over his face. Nausea threatened to overwhelm him at the thought of his friend in prison because of his own transgressions. "And has he?"

She frowned. "No."

"Idiot!" he barked. Philip would sacrifice himself before betraying him. Somehow he had to help his friend.

But first . . .

"Tell me, how is my mother? Have you arrested her as well?"

She paled. "Of course not! I left her well. She was confused by your sudden departure, but believed it was because I refused your proposal a second time. I allowed her that belief." Her face changed as if she were remembering something painful. "She has since departed to Bath and expects you to follow when your business is complete. She even invited me to join you for a fortnight."

He scowled as anger pulsed inside him, bubbling out. "She doesn't know she invites a snake into the henhouse." He clenched and unclenched his fists at his sides. "I'm sure you reassured her, placated her. Made her believe you cared. What a heartbreak it will be for her when she finds out the truth about you."

She flinched as if he'd physically struck her, then erased her emotions. "I *do* care for her, Tristan. That was not a lie."

He snorted out a laugh of disbelief. "You care for me, you care for my mother. Interesting how you can claim to have such deep feelings for us, then destroy us, along with everyone else in my family."

Now it was her turn to frown. Hot anger flashed in her eyes, and it reminded him of how she looked when she reached the heights of pleasure. He pushed the traitorous thought aside. That was over.

"If anyone destroyed your family, it was *you*, Tristan," she snapped. "*Your* actions are why you are here, not mine."

He cringed. There was truth in that statement. So much truth. And he'd spent a long time preparing for the day when he was in this very position. He'd always known he might be caught. Imprisoned.

But what he had *not* prepared for was that someone he loved—or thought he loved—would be the one to cause his capture. That someone he cared for would do everything in her power to bring him to his knees and make him crawl.

Her lack of faith cut him as much as her lies infuriated him. In her mind, she'd already convicted him. Only the evidence mattered, not the time they had shared. Was it even worth it to try to defend himself?

For his family, if not himself, it was. So he drew a long breath and looked her straight in the eyes. "Tell me the truth." He broke the stare as he paced away to the low fire near his bed. The fire tools had been removed in case he would use them as weapons, so he couldn't stir the coals. "You are clearly a part of all this. Tell me exactly how. Why?"

Her breath caught and he looked at her over his shoulder. She stared at him for a long time, silent, as she considered what he'd asked.

Finally, she nodded as she took a seat on one of

the uncomfortable wooden stools that had been provided for him.

"I do owe you some kind of explanation, yes," she admitted. Her voice was soft, but not weak. "After my husband died, I struggled with my place. I had no desire to remarry—"

He frowned as he remembered her refusal of his proposal. Of course, now he fully understood her reasons.

"But a woman of my station has so little she can do to occupy her time if children and a husband are not part of her life," she continued. "I was looking into charitable work when I was approached by Charlie."

"Mr. Isley?" Tristan asked.

She nodded. "Yes. He explained a woman of rank was putting together a group to aid the cause of widows and orphans who couldn't fend for themselves. She wished to remain anonymous, but thought I would make a good addition. I agreed because I had been both an orphan and a widow. I knew how lucky I was that I hadn't been put in financial straits by either event." Her face drew down. "Once I involved myself, I realized there was more to Charlie's offer than met the eye. He revealed that this mysterious woman was not just putting together a ladies aid group, but a group of female spies."

Surprise tempered Tristan's anger and disappointment temporarily. Female spies. The more he considered that, the clearer the benefits of such a group became.

"Women have access to society that men may not," he reasoned, more to himself than for her benefit. "They are told gossip and secrets a person might keep from a powerful man. And, of course, no one suspects a lady of doing something so bold."

She nodded and for a brief moment seemed pleased that he understood the group she was part of. Then she remembered herself and her smile fell.

"Yes, quite right on all accounts. That was Lady M's rationale exactly. I was hesitant at first. The life of a spy is dangerous and unpredictable. But as I trained, I grew more excited about the prospect of helping my country, of *doing* something thrilling and real."

Her eyes lit up when she spoke, shining like sapphires. Tristan's body reacted, warmed though he willed himself not to be moved by her beauty. Her excitement. Those were the very things that had landed him in this cell.

"A little less than a month ago, Charles came to me with a new case." Her excitement faded. "He told me about the robbery at Genevieve Art House, about the possibility of secrets hidden within the painting that could be passed to the wrong people." She drew in a breath, as if the next part pained her. "And then he told me *you* were the prime suspect in the investigation. I was to pursue you to determine your innocence or guilt, and do my best to retrieve the painting before whatever was inside was passed to the wrong hands."

Tristan flinched at the calm, straightforward way she explained her role. As if it had been so easy. Just a part of her everyday life. He hated this.

"Well, I suppose that's better than what Philip believed," he sneered. "You *were* out to destroy me, but you weren't working in league with Devlin."

She recoiled.

He calmed himself before he continued, "My only question is, why were you chosen for this rather than any other spy, male or female?"

She swallowed. "Because of our prior relationship."

"Because we were childhood acquaintances?" he asked, unable to keep the acid from his tone. "Because I saved your life?"

She did not flinch again. In fact, her countenance changed, but not with sadness or regret. This time anger flashed in her eyes.

"Yes, Tristan, that is exactly right." Her tone was just as harsh as his own. "Are you angry I used our prior involvement to further my investigation?"

"Yes, damn it!" he said, finally letting his emotions show as he slammed a hand against the narrow mantel above the fire. He wanted to rip the room apart. To show her exactly how furious he was with her, with the situation, with himself.

She gripped her hands into fists as she jumped to her feet. "Well, so am I! I'm angry you forced this course of action. I hate that you put me in this situation. That you turned against everything you were, everything I believe in. And for what?"

Without realizing it, Tristan found himself moving toward her. But this time he could find no control to keep from touching her. The moment he caught her arms, drew her against his chest, though, his anger faded. Despite everything, her warmth was the same. And so was his reaction. She had used her body against him, but he still longed to kiss her until she begged for more.

"I didn't!" he insisted as he released her. Touching her was too intense. It burned him, made him want things he knew now he would never have again. "I didn't."

She backed away, her face pale. She smoothed her fingertips over her upper arms with an almost imperceptible shiver.

"No?" she asked, her voice trembling. "Then how did you end up with the stolen painting in your home? Explain that."

He drew in a breath, watching her carefully. He had tried to tell Isley the truth and the man had not believed him. But Meredith had been in his bed. She admitted part of why she was assigned his case was because she *did* know him. Perhaps, just perhaps, he could convince her of the truth.

But that would mean opening up to her. Telling her something about his heart. He was wary to share that with a woman who'd already proven herself a liar. How could he know she wouldn't use his confession against him?

He couldn't. He would just have to go on faith this time. One last time. At this point, he had nothing to lose.

He closed his eyes as he expelled a long breath to calm his suddenly racing heart.

"It all started with the death of my brother."

Chapter 19

Tristan drew another deep breath. He hadn't realized it would be so difficult to confess the truth. Meredith knew him well enough that he couldn't gloss over the details. With her, it was all or nothing.

"I'm sure you know I didn't want Edmund to join up with the army and go to the Continent to fight." Tristan couldn't help but think of the arguments he'd had with his brother. Edmund didn't want to live an idle life. Tristan hadn't wanted to lose him. Their screaming could have brought down the house.

She nodded. "You wanted to protect him."

"Yes. I somehow forgot he was a grown man,

capable of making his own decisions. We had a terrible row before he left and almost came to blows. I've always regretted we left things that way."

He gathered his emotions before he continued, and Meredith waited. When he looked at her, she regarded him with an appraising glance. Nothing on her face told him if what he said moved her.

"When we were informed of Edmund's death, my world shattered." He flinched as memories assailed him. "I wanted to shut myself away from everyone. I wanted to drink myself into oblivion, but I had responsibilities. Ones that had been on my shoulders since my father died. My mother was destroyed. My sisters were brokenhearted. I had to tend to their needs. Instead of grieving, I turned to anger." He looked at the fire. Watched it crackle. "Anger I can control. Anger I can master."

She nodded as if she understood. Thinking about her childhood, he thought she actually might. She, too, had been helpless to control her fate. That must have played a part in her decision to begin a dangerous life of service to the King.

Memories took over again. Images and feelings assailed him. Ones he had pushed aside for so long. Now that he was with someone who knew him and knew some of his desperate secrets, they threatened to overwhelm him.

"I demanded information about my brother's death," he continued, clenching his fists. "I called in favors, wrote to every officer I could think of. I even went to the War Department offices and waited for two hours to speak to anyone who granted me entrance to his office. No one could tell me anything except that Edmund's regiment was attacked, ambushed. But there was something about the tone, the looks they gave me. I knew there was more to the story."

Meredith gave a small, sad smile. "And, of course, you could not let it go."

"Not until I knew the truth. If only to satisfy my need to understand why my brother was taken from us." He flexed his fingers. "Finally, one of his superior officers was able to see me. He admitted the assault was orchestrated. The French soldiers responsible couldn't have known their regiment's position without secret information. The only way they would have come by it was through treason."

He spat out the last word. The word he hated above all others. The word now associated with his own name. Or would be if he couldn't convince Meredith to help him. Believe in him.

She drew back but didn't seem surprised. Of course she would know. The information he had sought for months had probably been easily at her fingertips when she began her investigation. It was part of the damning evidence she collected against him. Probably it led her to believe he was an enraged man, seeking revenge against the government that had failed to protect his brother.

That was, after all, how he'd convinced Devlin to accept him.

She cocked her head. "And?"

He realized his musings had gone on too long. "I was enraged. Livid. I wanted to find the man responsible for my brother's death and rip his heart out with my bare hands. Instead, I channeled my anger into an investigation of potential suspects. Again and again my resources led me to Augustine Devlin. I considered simply killing him, but I found out Devlin wasn't the leader of his group, only the gateway to the man in charge. And that is the man I want."

"Want for what?" she whispered, eyes widening.

He ignored her question. "I befriended Devlin, provided him with capital for some of his legitimate ventures, introduced him to prominent people. I gained his trust, then approached him about his group. Of course, he was wary at first. But slowly he allowed me further into his circle. He told me some of his secrets and asked favors of me . . . tests, he called them."

Her face twisted in horror, and he realized she was thinking of the atrocities Devlin and his associates had committed.

"I sabotaged his schemes whenever I could. And I have the information on the plans he involved me in."

She opened her mouth, but he interrupted with a wave of his hand. He wasn't ready for questions yet. For her demands that he turn over evidence. Not until she heard the rest of his story.

"It went like that for a year. Slowly, he let me in further and further, but he wouldn't reveal who led his group. But when he talked to me about stealing a painting from Genevieve Art House, he told me this would be my final test. If I completed that task, I would have full access."

Meredith's eyes grew wide and she was no longer able to control the emotions that flashed across her face. Surprise, empathy, but most of all, hope. She *wanted* to believe him. She wanted him to be innocent, to have done what he did not because he was a conspirator, but because he wanted to *stop* a traitor. The anger bubbling inside him faded a fraction at that realization.

"That was why I had the painting, Meredith." He stepped toward her, unsure if he wanted to shake her or kiss her into having faith in him.

"So you wish me to believe you did all this just to meet the leader of Devlin's group?" she asked.

He nodded wordlessly.

She gripped her hands at her sides, her inner struggle clear. "And what will you do when you meet him?"

He straightened. He had already told her so much of the truth. If he hoped to escape from this prison, he could do no less than tell her all of it.

"I will kill him."

* * *

Meredith gasped at the cold tone of Tristan's voice, recoiling from his sure, even promise to take another's life.

His claims tore at her. If he was being truthful, it meant he wasn't a turncoat. In fact, he was working toward the same goals as her own group. Destroying Devlin's organization, stopping the treason that threatened the Empire's troops, their supplies, even their leaders.

But that also meant the driving force in Tristan's life was vengeance. He was calculating, patient, ready to reward violence with more of the same. He had spent a year cultivating a plan to destroy another man.

"Do you believe me?" His eyes were wild with emotion, which turned them a deep, vibrant green that pulled her in.

She drew a breath. Her heart was so torn, she didn't know how to answer. "I—I'm not sure."

The anger he had displayed earlier flashed across his face, but she also saw a stronger emotion in his expression.

Defeat.

Her heart ached. How she *wanted* to believe . . . But that was the problem. Her desire to exonerate Tristan came from her heart, not her head. How could she know for certain she wasn't being a lovesick fool?

"I need to know more," she said softly. "Can you tell me something?"

His gaze came up. "Perhaps."

"Where is the evidence we believe was hidden in the painting?"

Charlie had demanded that Tristan reveal the truth about the evidence, without success. If she could retrieve it, perhaps it would prove his honesty. It was the only hope she had.

Immediately, he said, "I removed it. I told Devlin he wouldn't receive his prize until I met with his leader. That was why he left Carmichael before I was arrested. He came to London to arrange it. I was to meet him tomorrow night."

Her heart soared, but her doubts remained. Perhaps Tristan was giving her a show of faith in the hope of one in return.

But perhaps he was all too aware of how much she wanted to hear his claims of innocence. Perhaps this immediate revelation of the "truth" was part of some greater trap.

Still, the details rang so true . . .

He reached out and caught her hands. For the second time, her body heated with his touch. But now she couldn't stay immune. His hands on her skin reminded her of all they had shared. Of everything she wanted to trust.

Tristan stroked his thumb across the sensitive webbing between her thumb and forefinger. Instantly, her body grew heavy with desire. "I tried to explain my position to Isley, but he won't hear it."

She shook her head. Of course Charlie wouldn't believe Tristan. Charlie believed in hard facts, evidence. All the evidence said Tristan was guilty.

"I need to be out of this cell in order to complete my duty, Meredith," he said, his voice low and husky. "You know me. You cannot believe me capable of desiring the deaths of more men like my brother. Won't you help me?"

She hesitated. Doubts nagged at her even as everything in her soul begged her to give in. To help him. To convince Charlie that Tristan was innocent.

His face fell when she didn't answer. A hard edge came into his eyes as he released her hands. "If you won't assist me because of your heart, then perhaps I can call in a favor?"

"A favor?" she asked with a wrinkled brow.

"Yes. Do you remember the night I found you in that pub?"

Meredith shut her eyes. Even after more than ten years, it was a night she tried not to think about, though it had haunted her more and more since she'd resumed contact with Tristan. She remembered the lewd catcalls of the men in the bar. The heat of a stranger's dank breath on her cheek as she tried to struggle away from his iron grip.

But mostly she remembered the sense of relief that filled her when someone yanked her attacker away. And the shock when she realized her savior was none other than Tristan Archer, the boy who made her heart lighter.

She also remembered Tristan's rage when he realized who the man had attacked. He'd nearly killed her assailant in his need to avenge her. That was why his dismissal of her later had been so hurtful and confusing. His emotions had seemed so strong that night. So real.

Like they did now.

"I remember," she said softly. "I remember everything."

He nodded as if he understood. Did memories of that night haunt him as well?

"Then you'll also remember as we rode home on my horse, you asked me to make a promise."

She nodded. "I asked you never to tell anyone the truth. I told my aunt and uncle I was staying at a friend's home for the night. I didn't want them to know I tried to run away."

"I kept my promise."

She lifted her eyes and found herself lost in mossy green. "You did."

"Then make a promise to me tonight. Help me escape. Set me free. Just long enough to avenge my brother."

She drew back. "You compare a childhood vow to this? If I did what you ask, it would destroy my future in The Society. I would most likely be arrested."

"I do not compare the vows," he said softly. "But I ask you to take that promise I kept all those years ago as proof I am a man of my word. And I give you my word that I am innocent. If I don't meet with Devlin tomorrow night, all will be lost."

Her breath caught and her eyes filled with tears as she considered his words. He was asking her to believe *him* over her evidence. Asking her to have faith. She wasn't sure she had the ability.

She spun away, her head pounding as she went to the door, where she turned back. "I—I don't know."

Then she opened it and ran into the hall. She didn't dare look back, but felt Tristan's eyes on her until the door blocked his view.

The last thing she heard was his long howl of frustration.

Meredith shifted. The wooden floor was hard under her backside, almost as uncomfortable as remembering her encounter with Tristan. But remember was all she could do. She glanced around. She was surrounded by piles of paperwork, notes and evidence, the things she and other spies had gathered while investigating Tristan.

All things that proved he was lying, proved he truly was a traitor. But her heart insisted. Wouldn't the same evidence exist if he was telling her the truth? To infiltrate Devlin's inner circle, Tristan would have to be convincing. Couldn't her evidence only be proof of that and not real intent to do wrong?

She glanced to her right, at Ana flipping through some papers. To her left, Emily did the same, making encoded notes on a sheet of paper with a quill pen, her face long and drawn. Meredith could only guess her own expression was just as serious. Certainly she felt the weight of the world on her shoulders.

Emily sighed as she looked up. "You're right. All the evidence points to Tristan."

Ana removed her spectacles and set them on the floor as she rubbed her eyes. "I looked and looked, but I found nothing to corroborate Lord Carmichael's story that he stole the painting in some bid to infiltrate Devlin's group. And no evidence to prove he's innocent in any way."

Meredith nodded. She had known that would be the outcome of this final search. She'd read over the evidence so many times, she could recite it from memory.

Her heart sank. She so wanted to believe him. But perhaps that was exactly what Tristan wanted. If he truly were a traitor, he might be using her feelings against her.

But as she thought of the fire, the desperation, and the desire in his eyes, she had a hard time believing all that was an act only meant to deceive her. After all, Tristan would not leave any evidence of his innocence, for then Devlin might well have discovered his subterfuge.

Her mind spun between the claims of the man she loved and the facts of her case.

She pushed to her feet and dusted off her gown. She paced the room, needing to move so the pain didn't catch up to her. "The evidence has always been against him."

Ana and Emily exchanged a look. Ana stayed on the floor, leaning back on her palms. "The physical evidence, yes. But there is other evidence we haven't examined."

Meredith cocked her head. "Other evidence? No, this is everything I gathered for my report, as well as that collected by officials outside our organization." She motioned to the mess spread across Ana and Emily's sitting room. "If there was more, trust I would have reviewed it."

Ana smiled gently. "I'm talking about how you feel, Merry."

Emily barked out an incredulous laugh as she got to her feet.

Meredith froze. "My feelings." She shook her head. "They're not evidence."

Ana scrambled to her feet and grabbed Meredith's hands. "Don't say that. When we were trained as spies, one of the first things we learned about was intuition. Charlie told us to trust the voices in our heads that told us to go right when we were supposed to go left. That told us someone was dangerous when they appeared to be safe."

"Oh, please!" Emily snapped, taking a long drink from the tumbler of sherry she'd poured herself. "There is a huge difference between intuition about whether a person is dangerous and 'feelings.' " She motioned to Meredith. "She *feels* like Tristan is innocent because she wants to believe it."

Meredith hesitated. Was that true? It was what she'd been telling herself, but hearing the statement out loud made her doubt it. Was she only seeing what she wanted to see, or was there truly something more there?

She drew in a breath. "Emily may be right. My love for Tristan could be clouding my judgment, not letting me see the truth."

Ana snorted as she shot a glare at Emily. "I don't believe that for a moment. Tell me, have you made a habit of falling in love?"

Meredith drew back. "No, of course not."

"Have you *ever* loved anyone before Tristan?"

Meredith felt like a dagger was being stabbed into her chest and twisted. She swallowed, trying to measure her tone. Trying not to lose control of her emotions. That was the very thing that had gotten her into this mess in the first place.

"No," she said softly. "I have never loved a man before."

Ana's expression softened. "Feeling is based on

intuition, Merry. You have danced with other suspects, you've chatted with them, flirted with them. So has Emily. Some of them were handsome, accomplished gentlemen, just like Tristan. But you haven't ever fallen in love with them, because your intuition told you they weren't good men. I don't believe for a moment you would fall in love with someone if you truly thought he was wicked."

Meredith stared at Ana. Normally, her friend didn't involve herself in the deeper elements of cases. She was happy to stay in her cellar, inventing new devices and making and breaking codes. But when she wanted to, Ana could make a powerful argument.

Still . . .

Meredith shrugged. "I don't know anymore."

"If you're not sure of yourself, then tell us," Ana said. "Obviously Emily and I fall on opposite sides of the argument. Together, we are completely neutral."

Emily's brow wrinkled, but she gave a reluctant nod. "That is true, Meredith. With us, you won't have to worry about emotion involving itself. We may be able to help you sort out the truth from what your heart wants to believe."

Slowly, Meredith nodded. That made sense. If she explained why she believed Tristan, perhaps her friends could advise her.

She sat down in the settee closest to the fire. When Emily motioned to the decanter of sherry, she nodded. She definitely needed a drink.

"Taking love out of the matter—because it does cloud my thinking—there have been elements to this case that have troubled me from the start."

"Such as?" Emily asked as she offered her the tumbler.

Meredith took a sip of the drink and let the burning sensation wake her senses. "It never made sense to me that a man of such wealth would turn to desperate acts. Tristan has been known as a quiet man, even a proud man. We all know from our dealings in the field that often men who are involved in treachery want to be the center of attention. They like to feel smarter than everyone around them, like they're pulling a trick on society or breaking the rules beneath the noses of the authorities and even their friends."

Emily pursed her lips. "That's true. But Tristan had a different motivation than many of those men. Not money, but revenge."

"Because of his brother's death?" Meredith asked. "Yes, that was what I believed at first. That Tristan only knew his brother had been killed in combat and somehow wanted to punish the government for that loss. But today he told me he knew about the ambush. He knew traitors were involved." She looked at the fire as she remembered the anguish on his face when he recounted that tale. "He discovered that fact *before* he became involved in Devlin's group. I verified it with the War Department after I left him. If he loved his brother enough to take revenge, why would he take it on the government when he knew a group like Devlin's—or even Devlin's itself—had been responsible?"

Ana's eyes lit up. "A man who knew his brother was killed due to information sold by traitors would be loath to involve himself in the acts of those same men."

Even Emily had to nod reluctantly. "What else?"

"He kept trying to . . . protect me," Meredith whispered. A stab of pain accompanied the statement. "From Devlin. Whenever I got too near the man, Tristan whisked me away and chastised me. He wouldn't tell me why he thought Devlin was dangerous, but he didn't want me near him."

"That could be because he didn't want you to find out the truth about his misdeeds," Emily said.

Meredith shook her head. She'd thought about that too. "I don't believe so. Tristan was utterly shocked when he discovered I was a spy. If he didn't suspect I was probing into his activities, there would be no reason for him to suspect a lady of society would uncover his betrayals."

"If you were a regular lady, yes," Ana said. "Did he tell you he wanted to protect you?"

She thought about the afternoon she and Tristan

were caught by his mother nearly making love. That day he had confessed he told Devlin they were involved in an affair to keep him from pursuing her. And because he wanted it to be true.

She shivered. "Yes. He lied to Devlin about our relationship. Even though it put him in danger, even though Devlin would have been enraged if he'd found out."

Ana took her hand. "I can tell by the pain on your face that you don't only *want* to believe Carmichael is innocent, you *do* believe it. What he told you today about his drive to destroy Devlin's group from within made sense. If he felt the government was doing nothing to avenge the death of his brother, he may have thought infiltrating the group responsible was the only way to find justice."

Meredith lifted her gaze to Emily, who was finishing a last gulp of sherry. "And what about you? Do you think my intuition could be right? Or do you still believe I'm blinded?"

"I admit, some of what you say makes sense." Emily sighed. "And I trust your integrity. You wouldn't want a traitor to walk free simply because you loved him."

Ana smiled in triumph. "Then the only question that remains is what do you wish to do about this? Are you going to confront Charlie and try to have Tristan's name cleared?"

Meredith considered that question. It could take

weeks to convince Charlie and the others in the War Department to hear her pleas for Tristan's life. Many would dismiss her as an emotional woman who became too involved with a suspect. Doing so could endanger the very existence of The Society.

Aside from which, during the time she pleaded for Tristan's life, he would be transferred to Newgate. The charges against him would become public. Even if she could convince the War Department that the evidence was wrong, Tristan and his family would be ruined. And Devlin would slip through their fingers yet again.

It wasn't good enough. She had to do more. She had to do the one thing that terrified her more than anything. She had to have faith. In herself. And in Tristan.

"I'm going to follow my instincts." She braced herself with a deep breath. "I'm going to help Tristan escape and accompany him when he confronts Devlin with the evidence he removed from the painting."

Chapter 20

◯◯◯

A sense of peace filled Meredith the moment she said she would help Tristan. It was the correct decision. Or at least the decision she wanted to make. Only he could prove if it was right or wrong.

Her friends stared at her, but they didn't seem surprised. She bit her lip.

"I realize this goes against protocol, against everything we do," she said. "But I must do this. I understand you cannot help me. I would never ask you to do so."

Ana's eyes went wide. "But you need us. This will be a difficult plan to execute with three, let alone one."

Meredith shook her head. "I don't want to force you to break any vows. There will be consequences to my actions tonight, no matter the outcome. I won't bring those consequences down on your heads."

Emily folded her arms, and for a moment terror gripped Meredith's heart. Normally it was Ana who fought for the keeping of rules, but Emily had been the one arguing against Tristan with the most passion. Unlike romantic Ana, she didn't believe love would conquer. And Emily was entirely capable of stopping Meredith in ways Ana wouldn't imagine.

"Do you truly think you can keep us from helping you?" Emily asked with an unladylike snort. "Please. The vows I made were to you and Ana. We're sisters and we fight together. Of course I'll help you."

Ana nodded. "And I know I go on about rules and regulations, but if your heart says this man is innocent and can help us end Devlin's reign of terror, I trust that. I'll help in any way I can."

Relief and love for her friends filled Meredith to her very toes. She hadn't wanted to think about storming Charlie's miniature prison alone. Now she wasn't forced to. Her friends had come through for her . . . as they always had in the past. And she believed together they could execute this daring escape.

She hugged both, clinging to them tightly to let

them know how much their sacrifice meant to her. Then she stepped back and swiped her eyes.

"Tell us what you need," Emily said, and Meredith thought she saw a few tears in her eyes as well.

She nodded. "Ana, last year you suggested we secretly purchase that little town home near Southwark. A place only we would know about and could hide if we needed to."

Ana nodded, and she could see her intelligent friend was three steps in front of her. "I'll make sure the house is ready for you and Tristan. The department knows nothing of the purchase. You should be safe there tonight."

"Very good. Once that is done, you'll need to be ready to retrieve the evidence Tristan removed from the painting. Emily can help you with that once she and I are finished."

Emily gave a little smirk. "And whatever shall *we* be doing?" she asked, fluttering her eyelashes sweetly.

Meredith laughed as the first happiness she'd felt since returning to London flooded her. "You and I are going to Charlie's home. We have a prisoner to escort."

"There was only one guard when I came earlier today," Meredith said as she finished binding her hair into a severe style. "And Charlie told me he was meeting with Lady M after his briefing with the War Department. He shouldn't be home until after midnight."

Emily nodded as she slipped a form-fitting crocheted cap over her blonde locks. "Let us assume all Charlie's servants are home, but probably above stairs now in their chambers at this late hour. That is one butler, a housekeeper, and a parlor maid. But they'll all be easily subdued if it comes to that."

Meredith winced at the thought even as she pointed to the gate in the alleyway. "We must also presume there may be another guard."

Emily popped the alleyway lock with no difficulty. "We'll make our move on the guard by the prison room first. While you free Carmichael, I'll do a quick sweep of the house and clear your escape route. If you need me, signal and I'll come back."

She swung the gate open and the two women rushed across the dark courtyard, staying in the shadows when possible. They hurried to the window of a back parlor. Ana had remembered Charlie mentioning something about the latch being broken a few days before. Meredith hoped that was still true. Otherwise, they would have to break in, and that could cause all kinds of trouble.

"I have the serum," Meredith whispered as Emily glided black-gloved fingertips along the windows of the parlor, looking for the loose one. "I think we should at least attempt to use it."

Emily shrugged. "I still vote for using the neck technique, but I'll try your way first. Aha!" Her friend laughed as she gave the last window a push and it swung in. "Charlie needs to follow his own recommendations of security. This place has at least five breech points!"

Meredith rolled her eyes as she ducked under the open window and found the floor inside with the tip of her toe. "Write a report about it after this is over . . . *if* we all still have jobs."

Emily slipped in behind her and closed the window. "Don't talk that way, Merry! You must believe this will work out. I do."

Meredith glanced over her shoulder as she made her way out of the parlor and into the hall. As she reached the cellar stairway, she whispered, "You? Optimistic? Will wonders never cease?"

"Shush and prepare yourself," Emily said, sticking her tongue out.

Meredith straightened her shoulders as she took the first few steps down the stairway. She said a silent prayer, then strode down the hall, Emily at her shoulder, as if they had every right in the world to be there.

The guard who had been leaning on the wall outside Tristan's chamber, a book in hand, straightened up in surprise. "Lady Northam, Lady Allington, I wasn't told you would be coming tonight."

Meredith arched a brow and looked the guard

in the eyes. She felt a droplet of sweat trickle down the back of her neck. "That was an oversight. Mr. Isley gave us permission to see the prisoner."

The guard's brow wrinkled. "I'm sorry, my lady. You know protocol. When Isley isn't in residence, no one sees him who hasn't been cleared."

Meredith folded her arms. "You weren't here earlier, were you?"

He shook his head. "No, ma'am."

"Isley cleared us with . . . Wilson, isn't that his name?"

"Wilson is still here, ma'am," the guard said, setting the book down on a chair that was beside the door. "In the kitchen having a cold supper before he goes home. I'm happy to ask—"

Emily exchanged a brief glance with Meredith before she held up her hand. "You can't leave your post, you know that. *I'll* fetch Wilson. You stay here with Lady Northam."

As Emily turned to go back upstairs, Meredith could have sworn she saw her friend wink. It looked like Emily would get to use her neck technique to drop a man tonight after all. Well, it gave Emily some pleasure to utilize the combat training. But that left Meredith to deal with the young man before her alone.

She smiled and he returned the expression. Now to make him comfortable.

She withdrew a little flask from her reticule and

opened the top. Her smile grew when the guard's eyes widened.

"It's frightfully hot out tonight," she said, then swung the flask up and pretended to drink. "But it's worse in here. I imagine you must get thirsty."

He nodded, still shocked by her behavior. "Er, yes, my lady."

"Would you like a drink? It's a very nice scotch."

He seemed to consider her unorthodox offer for a moment before he took the flask and downed a drink. He held it back out toward her, but she shook her head. "No, no. I've had plenty tonight. I need a clear head for my interrogation. Feel free to finish it. You've worked hard, you've earned it."

"Thank you, my lady."

Within a minute he had drained the bottle. Within five he'd hit the floor in a heap.

Tristan lay on his back staring at the ceiling overhead. He couldn't actually see it, as the room was nearly pitch-dark, but he knew it was there. Just as he hadn't allowed himself to feel the pain of Meredith's rejection, but it was there. Waiting for him beneath the surface.

Meredith, however, was not. It had been hours since she'd run from his cell, ignoring his pleas for assistance, never telling him if she believed his innocence. If she hadn't returned by now, she wasn't coming back.

If after all they had shared, after all she knew about him, Meredith wouldn't believe him, he had no doubt he would be convicted. Transported. Hung.

When the young night guard had come on to replace his day jailer earlier, Tristan heard them talking about moving him to Newgate tomorrow. Once that happened, all his work would be for nothing. His family would be destroyed. The group Devlin and his mysterious leader controlled would be free to continue its treacherous activities. More men like Edmund would die.

He could only imagine how devastated his mother would be when word reached her in Bath. And such news would travel like lightning. He was sure some "kind friend" would be compelled to whisper it to her, along with the filthy details.

He fisted his hands. His mother had trusted Meredith as much as he had, and now she would suffer for the betrayal he had allowed through his lack of control. Damn the woman for lying. And damn her for making him love her.

He barked out a humorless laugh. With all he was facing, he couldn't believe what tormented him most was Meredith Sinclair. But she did. She'd changed him from a man bent on only vengeance to someone who might have a future worth living. She had reminded him there was light and love.

Only to snatch it all away. To make it a falsehood.

Noises echoed from the hallway outside, and he sat up on his elbow to check his pocket watch. It was far later than anyone usually bothered him. If Isley wanted more interrogation, he could bloody well wait until morning, until Tristan was transferred to prison. He was certainly in no mood to defend himself tonight.

He rolled over on his side and feigned sleep as the lock on his cell clanged and the door creaked open. He measured his breathing, hoping whoever intruded would just go away. Instead, light footsteps entered the room, moving toward him. He tensed.

"Tristan?"

He spun on the cot to face the feminine voice. Meredith stood over him, dressed in dark clothes. Her cheeks were flushed with excitement and her eyes lit with emotion.

Once again the anger he felt toward her mingled with an unsettling joy. She'd come back . . . but for what?

He struggled to a seated position. "What are you doing here?"

She lifted a finger to her lips. "Shhh. I've taken care of the main guard, but there are probably others. We don't want to wake the servants or other agents who may be in residence."

He dropped his voice to a whisper. "What are you talking about? Are you saying you're here to—"

She locked her gaze with his, and he was lost in blue. "I'm here to take you away."

In her eyes he saw fear, anticipation . . . and hope. It stirred a fire in his chest that had gone out long ago. His own hope flamed from the embers.

He got to his feet in a flash.

"You said you took care of the guard?" he asked as she motioned for him to follow. "How?"

She gave him a look over her shoulder. "I am a spy, you know. I'm capable of removing a threat when need be."

He hesitated. "You killed him?"

"No!" Her voice went up a notch before she dropped it. "Of course not. These are my fellow agents. I wouldn't hurt them . . . uh, permanently. I used a special brew made by Ana to put this guard"—she waved her arm toward the motionless man as they hurried past him—"to sleep."

He glanced over his shoulder. The giant of a guard was snoring.

She smiled. "Don't worry. Ana assures me it is perfectly safe. He'll suffer from no more than a headache when he wakes in a few hours."

"But—"

She flashed him a nervous smile. "No more questions. You can ask me anything you like when we are away from danger."

He drew back. Meredith had told him she was a spy, and he'd seen proof that it was true, but he hadn't fully comprehended what that meant until now. By her calm expression, this was an every-day occurrence for her. He wasn't sure whether to be impressed or horrified that she would put herself at such risk.

But tonight she had done it for him. When he remembered that fact, he stopped worrying about her past and their future as he followed her up the dark, winding staircase leading to Charles Isley's foyer. He barely recalled making that journey in the opposite direction a few days before. He'd been in too much of a fog. Now he wished he had paid closer attention so he could be on the lookout for danger.

Meredith held up a hand to slow him as they approached the servants' area of the house. She cracked the door and peered around. He couldn't see the hallway to know what she was observing, but soon enough she waved for him to follow.

Slipping behind her, he moved down a narrow hallway. Twists and turns took them past room after room. At each door, Tristan's heart thudded as he waited for someone to burst out and catch them in their escape. But finally they were at a back entrance. Meredith slipped it open silently and they crept outside.

Isley's town house was not enormous, and its cramped back garden fit the house. A worn door was hidden amidst the shrubbery along the far wall. It led to the street.

Tristan had a sudden urge to run. Run past

Meredith and never look back. But he didn't, if only to satisfy his curiosity. Why had she come back to him when it seemed so clear mere hours ago that she believed him guilty of the worst kind of treason? Why she had aided him when she'd been the one to put him in prison to begin with?

She flipped the latch on the gate and they moved into a dark alley. There was a carriage, its windows darkened by heavy curtains and its doors unadorned by identifying crests. He pursed his lips as he wished he'd had such a rig when he'd taken the painting from Genevieve's. When his carriage was identified, it had been one of the first things that brought agents of the Crown to his door.

Brought Meredith to his life.

She reached for the carriage door, but he grabbed her wrist. She wore no gloves and her skin was like hot satin beneath his rough fingertips. God, she felt good. Better than he remembered in the dreams he'd tried to block out since his arrest. She was no more immune to the touch than he. She hissed out a breath at the contact of skin on skin as her eyes darted to his with wariness.

"I am still a gentleman, my lady," he said softly as he reached for the carriage door and opened it. "No matter what anyone thinks."

She hesitated as if pondering the prudence of entering the vehicle before he did. Then she stepped up and took a place in the carriage. He followed and settled beside her, pulling the door shut as he did so.

The carriage was dark, but he felt Meredith shift as she pounded the wall behind them to signal their driver to move.

"Would you care to explain?" he asked in the darkness.

A rasp of flint met his question, and the rig filled with dim lamplight. Across from him sat another woman, as different from Meredith as she could be. Her hair was blonde, done in a loose chignon that framed her pretty oval face. Her eyes were blue, but light and icy, not the midnight depths of Meredith's. The main difference, however, was the utter lack of warmth in her expression. She looked at Tristan like she would kill him in a heartbeat if he gave her cause.

And judging from the pistol she aimed at his heart, that expression was no lie.

Meredith followed Tristan's line of sight and drew in a sharp breath when she saw her friend's tiny pistol pointed directly at his chest. She glared at Emily.

"Good God, put that thing away."

Her friend pursed her lips, but did as she was asked, though Meredith noticed she situated the weapon so it was within easy reach.

"Tell me you didn't use that on the guard upstairs!"

Emily gasped in disbelief. "Of course not. I simply want his lordship to be absolutely aware of his position."

Tristan folded his arms with the air of a bored rake. "You could not make it clearer, madam. May I inquire the name of the woman ready to take my life?"

Meredith pulled back the curtain on the carriage window to ensure they weren't being followed as she answered. "Tristan Archer, this is Emily Redgrave."

His eyebrows arched. "The Dowager Countess of Allington?" His mouth quirked. "Forgive me, my lady, I didn't recognize you."

"You have cheek for a man being threatened on all sides," Emily said with a cock of her head as she gave Tristan an appraising look. "I'm not sure whether to applaud you for your gall or shoot you for it."

Tristan let out a bark of laughter. "I vote for the former."

"I'm sure you do."

Meredith scowled as she let the curtain fall back into place. "You didn't have to help me, Emily. And I would appreciate it if you didn't threaten my—my—"

Tristan turned his gaze on her. "Your what, Meredith?"

An interesting question, but one she did not have the time to answer while they were escaping capture, or the inclination while one of her best friends looked on.

"Ana will be ready for us by now," she said instead, strumming her fingers on the carriage seat.

She was uncomfortably aware of Tristan's proximity. His body heat seeped through her silk dress and his leg brushed hers as they rounded a corner. It was maddening to be so close to him yet not be able to do anything about it.

Not yet. Not until they resolved a few things. After that . . . well, she wasn't ready to face the future yet.

Tristan seemed unmoved by their closeness. He hardly looked at her as they rode. As she had earlier, she felt the pulse of his anger pounding beneath the surface. It matched her own. They would have to resolve that as well.

She shifted as tension arced between them. Finally, she slanted a glance at Emily, who was staring back at her with an arched brow.

"Do you think we were detected?" Meredith asked to fill the silence.

Emily shook her head. "No. My guard was unconscious before he knew I was a threat. And I'm sure I would have heard if yours put up a struggle."

"He drank Ana's brew happily and collapsed into a very large heap," Meredith said.

"I'm certain if Isley knew I was a free man,

he would be galloping after me already," Tristan said. "It isn't often a member of society is caught in a web like this."

Meredith turned on him. "Do you think that gives Charlie any pleasure? Trust me, it doesn't. When members of the *ton* are involved, it makes all of our jobs more difficult."

"But he's right," Emily said, though neither looked at her as they glared at each other. "We wouldn't have been allowed to come so far if we had been seen."

Meredith hardly heard her. Behind the angry, accusatory fire in Tristan's stare there was something else. Something that drew her in. Something she wanted desperately.

The carriage pulled to a stop and she forced herself to look away as Emily pushed the door open. Tristan climbed down first and surprised Meredith by turning back to offer Emily a hand out. Her friend seemed surprised by the gentlemanly action as well, but took his offering of assistance. Meredith followed.

When their palms touched, her skin all but sizzled. A streak of awareness cut through her, and her entire body felt the aftereffects. The things this man did to her . . .

He seemed to sense her reaction as he drew her a fraction closer than he had Emily. She fought the nervousness in her chest with a rusty laugh.

"I'm surprised you offer to help us, Tristan. Is that a gentlemanly habit?"

He shrugged as he released her fingers. "Perhaps it's the knowledge that Lady Allington has a gun and I would wager she knows how to use it. A man would be foolish not to be gentlemanly in such circumstances." He turned away and called back over his shoulder. "Or perhaps I'm not the scoundrel you and your friends think I am, after all."

She hesitated, longing to tell him she believed him. Or *wanted* to believe. But she needed something first. A final test of faith. But it wasn't the time yet.

With a sigh, Meredith looked up at the little house Tristan and Emily had just entered. It was small but tidy, well cared for but not at all fancy. It was simple by design. Drawing attention to themselves in any way could bring her and her friends harm when they stayed here. So when they came, they dressed plainly, did not allow their driver to assist them, and made sure no one in the neighborhood suspected they were anything but lower-middle-class women who occasionally came to town and let this home.

Inside, the apartment was just as unadorned. Meredith welcomed it. In the past few days her extravagant home on St. James Street had seemed stifling in its formality. The simplicity of the small parlor just off the tiny foyer was a welcome change.

Except Tristan seemed to fill the space completely.

Shaking that feeling off, Meredith called out, "Ana? We're here."

Anastasia hurried in from the hallway with a smile. She was wiping her hands on a dish towel, and the smell of baked goods wafted in behind her.

"I'm so glad you made it unharmed," she said as she briefly hugged her two friends. Then she folded her arms as she looked Tristan up and down. "This is him, is it?"

Tristan's lip twitched like he wanted to laugh. "Yes, I am, apparently, *him*. Tristan Archer, Lord Carmichael."

Immediately, Ana held out her hand. "Anastasia Whittig, a pleasure to meet you."

"*Lady* Whittig?" he repeated, eyes widening as they had when he realized Emily was titled as well.

She smiled. "Yes. I did not think anyone in Society remembered me."

He turned to Meredith with a shake of his head. "Please do not tell me that every lady in Society is involved in this group of yours. Are there spies surrounding me daily? Are my sisters secret agents to the Crown?"

Emily was trying to scowl, but Meredith saw her hide a laugh at his comment. She couldn't hide her own.

"I'm afraid spies are more prevalent than most

people know, yes. But we are lacking in female spies."

He leaned closer. "And my sisters?"

"Even if they were in our group, I could not tell," Meredith said with a light laugh as she realized she was *teasing* him. They had just come through an escape from prison, she still wasn't sure of his intentions, and yet she was engaged in word play with him as if they were flirting at a ball, not in the midst of a serious situation.

Ana and Emily seemed as surprised as she was, for they watched with unreadable expressions. Finally, Ana stepped forward with a tiny shake of her head. "The kitchen is filled with food. The beds are made up. Once you have the—" She glanced at Tristan warily. "—the final information we discussed, send word back to the house with Henderson. He'll wait with the other carriage. Emily and I will make the final arrangements and meet you tomorrow."

Tristan's eyes went wide as the three women said their good-byes and Ana and Emily headed for the door. Meredith ignored his unspoken questions as she followed her friends into the foyer. After Ana hugged her good-bye and moved toward the carriage, Emily looked her up and down.

"Be careful."

"You still doubt him, then?" Meredith whispered, wrinkling her brow with worry. What if her judgment was wrong?

Emily shook her head. "I don't doubt he means a great deal to you. And there are more than physical ways to be hurt."

As her friends departed, Meredith shut the door and leaned back against it. "Trust me, Emily. I know that as well as anyone. Perhaps better."

Straightening up, she moved into the sitting room to face Tristan. To face a night alone with him where nothing would be hidden, nothing would be secret, and everything was at risk.

Chapter 21

Meredith watched Tristan devour another slice of cake. They had barely said two words since she'd offered the food Ana had brought for them. The kitchen table they sat at was old, but sturdy and comfortable. Yet at the small table in the equally small room, there was nowhere to hide.

Tristan looked at her and the point was underscored. She felt cornered by the focus and heat of his stare. Judging from the way he slowly wiped his mouth and folded his napkin, he was ready for discussion.

"Excuse my terrible manners."

She shook her head. "You were obviously

hungry." She hesitated as an awful thought occurred to her. "They did feed you while you were in custody, didn't they?"

One eyebrow came up. "Do you doubt the kindness of your employers?"

She shook her head. "No. Charles Isley is the best of men."

He looked incredulous. "I was fed. I simply had very little appetite."

"And now you do?"

"The chance at freedom will do that to a man." He rose to his feet and warmed his hands over the fire that burned brightly in the kitchen.

She watched his tense back. From the jerky way his muscles moved, she could see he was still angry.

He spun on her with a frown. "We have been avoiding the subject long enough. Certainly at some point we must face it. *Why* did you help me escape? You clearly have some plan for me now involving your friends. What is it?"

She drew in a breath, but willed herself to remain seated. Calm. "It must be obvious to you that I helped you escape because a part of me believes what you told me. Or—Or part of me wishes to believe it."

His nostrils flared. "And what is your plan?"

"That depends on you."

He clenched his fists. "Ah, so it comes down to proving myself some more, does it? Giving more information, explanations, and apologies? Well, my darling, what about you? Where are *your* explanations?"

His tone mocked, his eyes flashed. Accusation was in his every word and gesture. Her own anger bubbling to the surface, she surged to her feet.

"And what have I to explain? I was assigned a duty to protect my country. Your clandestine activities showed you to be a suspect in a treacherous plot. I did my job."

He moved toward her, heat rolling before him like a dangerous wave, bringing a storm of desire and equally potent rage. "Yes, you did, didn't you? You not only wormed out the details of my life, but you lied to me. You even lied to my mother."

She shook her head. "I never lied to Lady Carmichael."

"You led her to believe you were at her party as a friend, even that you were beginning to care for me. You encouraged her matchmaking . . . why? So you could use her feelings against me?"

"No!" she protested as pain smashed into her.

He snorted his derision. "I spent an inordinate amount of time in Isley's prison wondering about your methods of 'investigation.' Do you make love to every suspect or is there a criteria they must meet? Where do you draw your lines, my lady?"

Hot blood burned her cheeks, but she forced herself not to turn away. "You know what happened in Carmichael meant more than that."

"Do I?" He barked out a laugh. "When I touched you, I thought I felt something between us. I thought your emotions were as strong as mine. But now I see what a competent liar you are, and I wonder how many of those emotions were real."

She opened her mouth in protest, but he continued, as if he could not stop the flow of angry words.

"I applaud you. In some ways, a female spy is preferable. After all, you were able to use my heart and your body as deadly weapons against me in a way no man could have. You came to my bed and had me surrendering without firing a shot."

"Coming to your bed was never part of my investigation!" Fisting her hands at her sides, she fought tears. "I know you're angry, but I am putting my life, my position as spy, and my country on the line in order to help you. Can't you have some faith in me?"

He laughed, just as hollow and ugly as before. "Like the faith you had in me when you gathered evidence against me? When you pretended to care?"

Her tears came now, flowing despite her efforts to hold them back. "I never *pretended* to care. Despite the evidence, despite the suspicion, I fell in love with you. And that is the truth."

Tristan bit back his next sentence as Meredith's words sank in. She fell in love with him? Even as she investigated his every move? Even as she compiled evidence that could send him to his death?

If that was true, it meant she'd gone against her own training. It meant that everything they had shared was real, not some twisted fantasy meant to ensnare him.

But *was* it true? Or just more trickery?

"Why should I believe that?"

With the back of her trembling hand, she swiped at tears. "I can't tell you why, but I can tell you that every single day, I fought to find evidence to prove you were innocent of the crimes you were accused of committing. I searched for other suspects. I spent a few days praying I could find Philip guilty instead—"

Tristan jolted as he thought of his imprisoned friend. "Philip? You thought *Philip* might be responsible for all this?"

She nodded. "I hoped he was. The pieces were there. He had access to everything required to entrap you, to act on your behalf without your knowledge." She sighed. "But as hard as I tried, those pieces wouldn't fit. So I shifted my focus to other explanations of why you became involved in treason. I fought to prove you were being blackmailed by Devlin or misled into doing something you didn't understand."

He folded his arms, but the hard shell of his anger was beginning to crack in the face of her explanation. "I'm pleased you had such faith in my intelligence."

"I would rather believe you were naïve than a liar and a killer," she snapped, eyes flashing. "But those hopes were dashed at every turn."

"And so you turned me over to the authorities?"

She nodded slowly. "For my own sake as much as the investigation. My heart was so involved that I—I—" Her voice broke as she turned away.

Tristan caught her arm and gently pulled her to face him. He couldn't let her escape. He needed to look into her eyes, see her expression. He needed to judge whether her words were true.

"What did you do?" he asked, loving how she trembled at his touch. He began to hope, once more, that the tremor was real. That she wanted him. Cared for him.

Loved him.

She dipped her head as a flash of something dark and ugly filled her eyes.

"My heart became so involved that I began to disregard the evidence completely. I started to care so much about protecting you from Devlin, from my own superiors, that I tried to ignore what I found. I even wanted—" She shivered. "I wanted to destroy it. Emily and Ana sent me a piece of evidence and I nearly burned it. For a brief moment I considered pretending it didn't exist and trying to convince you to run away with me instead."

Tristan drew back as he realized what the dark emotion on her face was. Shame. Her love for him had driven her to the edge of everything she believed.

Two emotions washed over him. The first was horror. Horror that his drive for revenge had taken her so far. His lies, his plots nearly made Meredith turn against her own conscience.

But a second emotion lurked behind the horror. It was powerful and pure, and it felt better than anything he remembered experiencing since before his brother's death. Joy.

Meredith had nearly sacrificed everything for him. She had been willing to love him no matter what he'd done.

He cleared his throat and forced himself to press her further. "Why *didn't* you burn the evidence?"

A tear slipped down her cheek, and he caught it with his thumb. She shivered and turned her face into his hand. "I knew I couldn't destroy the evidence and turn against my friends and country. Not if I wanted to be happy. That doubt I felt would have tormented me and destroyed my love after a time."

He nodded. Though he might have preferred running away with her, what she said was true. The secrets that lay between them would have become too much to bear after a while. Now they were out in the open, but could the past be overcome?

"I went to your office the night before you were arrested with every intention to tell you my true purpose for being in Carmichael and confront you with the evidence. I planned to offer my help." She shivered. "But you revealed the stolen painting before I could alert you to my presence. I heard you say you were turning it over."

She lifted her gaze, and her eyes pleaded for understanding. Tristan was surprised to realize that he did understand. And he loved her all the more for her goodness and honor. With the company he'd kept lately, he'd almost forgotten those things existed.

"I thought of all the pain and death turning over evidence to a known enemy would bring, and I couldn't allow that to happen," she whispered. "So I sent emergency word to London and called Isley and his men to collect you before any damage could be done." She clutched her hands in front of her chest as if the mere memory pained her. "It broke my heart, Tristan."

He nodded, unable to speak when such powerful emotions tore at him.

"That was why, when Charlie arrested you, I pleaded for privacy. And why I helped cover up the truth so your mother wouldn't find out until the last possible moment. I wanted to protect you, even though I had proven to my superiors that you were the worst of men. Something in me whispered that you weren't, that I couldn't destroy the man I loved."

"And that is why you helped me tonight," he said.

It was a statement, not a question, but she nodded. "The story you told in your cell this afternoon . . . I wanted to believe it."

Tristan wrinkled his brow. She *wanted* to believe in him, and that meant everything to him. But *did* she believe him? Or was this just her heart leading her when her head told her to have faith in her evidence?

Her mouth drew down. "By setting you free, I've probably destroyed my career as a spy. My friends were involved, so I have endangered their futures as well. If the faith you claim I do not have in you is misplaced, I could be walking into a trap. My life could well be forfeit." Her face hardened. "So please don't tell me I haven't given you my trust. It's a gift I learned early not to give, yet you have it. Whether you acknowledge that or not."

For the first time, Tristan realized how completely vulnerable she was making herself. On only the strength of his vow that he was innocent, she risked everything. What had he given her in return?

"I understand, Meredith," he said on a sigh.

She smiled and more hope blossomed in her

expression. But there was still hesitation. She continued to hold something back. "But do you trust me as I have trusted you?"

He thought about that. Yes, she had lied. She had used his heart to obtain evidence. But she had done it without malice. She had done it to protect the things she held dear.

"I'm here, aren't I?" he asked, longing to draw her into his arms. To take away any lingering doubt with a kiss.

She shivered, but shook her head. "I need more than that. I need something that tells me the faith and trust I've put in you are not in vain."

He cocked his head. "What proof do you need?"

"The evidence you removed from the painting, Tristan," she said, her voice even. "Tell me where it is."

The warmth he was beginning to feel froze again and mistrust returned. Doubt. The evidence from the painting was the only leverage he had left, both with the War Department and with Devlin. If he gave it to Meredith, he could very well lose everything.

"Faith, Tristan," she whispered as she reached out to touch his hand. A spark of desire jolted through his aching body. "Isn't faith what you demand of me? You have fought this battle alone for a long time. Have faith in me and know my deepest desire is to help you win."

He let out a long breath he hadn't realized he'd

been holding. Meredith was offering to be his partner in the battle he'd waged for so long. She'd given him her trust and her heart. Now she asked for the same in return.

They were things he couldn't deny her now that the shadow of secrets no longer stood between them.

"The evidence is a collection of battle plans, troop assignments, and arsenal locations," he found himself saying. Her fingers curled tighter around his hand. "When I removed them from the painting, I sent the information to my town home in London with instructions for them to be hidden in a secret compartment in the stables. My favorite mare's stall has a false floor in the east corner. The evidence is there. She's skittish with strangers, so be sure whomever you send is prepared for her sass."

"You don't know what this means," Meredith whispered with a sigh of relief.

He hesitated. "No, I don't. What will happen? Will you and your friends be solely responsible for Devlin's future? Or will I be allowed some part in what began the night my brother died?"

Her face softened and she lifted his hand to her lips. "I know how important this is to you, Tristan. I wouldn't leave you out of the resolution you've sought so long. Trust me, you will have your role." She smiled as she let him go. His fingers tingled where they had been tangled with hers. "I must send a message to Emily and Ana, but it won't take a moment."

He nodded, numb from the emotional exchange. And strangely light, as if the weight he had carried on his shoulders for so long was gone. Telling her the truth was a balm on the burns in his soul.

She hurried from the kitchen. Tristan scrubbed a hand over his face as he made his way into the hall. He climbed the stairs to explore the rest of the home, his heart pounding.

Meredith gave her faith by setting him free. He had returned that faith by telling her the location of the evidence. But there was still a wall between them. Despite her declaration of love, she held back. He felt it. He had felt it in Carmichael too, but now he understood the cause. And he wanted nothing more than to take down that final wall, brick by brick. He wanted to see the future without any impediments.

In the dim upstairs hallway were three doors. He opened the first, to find a master bedroom with an attached sitting room. Tristan stepped inside, eyes wide. It would have been a simple room except someone had turned it into a romantic escape. Candles glowed along the mantel, on every spare inch of every tabletop, even in the windowsills, while a roaring fire warmed it and a sinfully silky coverlet graced the bed.

"Are you tired? I can—" Meredith's voice came

behind him. She cut herself off abruptly when she entered the room.

"It seems someone went to a lot of trouble for us," he said as he turned. Meredith's face was soft in the firelight. The candles made her skin luminescent and her eyes dance. He longed to touch her. To make good use of the bed.

"Ana," Meredith muttered, with a secret smile that made blood rush hot in his veins. "She is ever the romantic."

"So she believes in my innocence?" he asked, finally allowing himself to move toward her.

She caught her breath as he reached for her. "Ana believes in my intuition. My heart."

Tristan trailed his fingertips down her arms before he caught her elbows and drew her closer. "And what about you?"

"What about me?" she repeated, eyes glazing with hot desire. He had no doubt if he took her to bed, she wouldn't resist. But he wanted more.

"You said you fell in love with me," he whispered. "Do you love me still?"

Her breath hitched, but she answered immediately. "Yes. I love you still."

He shut his eyes and let the pleasure of her confession fill him body and soul. Then he met her gaze a second time. "You also said you *want* to believe in my innocence. But do you? Do you think I'm a traitor?"

Slowly, she slid her hand up his chest, leaving

fire in her wake. She cupped his cheek. "If I did, we wouldn't be here. I would have left you in Isley's prison cell, even if it broke my heart. I believe in your innocence, Tristan."

The joy Tristan felt nearly took him to his knees, but instead he drew her closer. There was her answer, her leap of faith. He drew a long, deep breath and gave her his own.

"I love you, Meredith Sinclair. I have loved you since that night so long ago when I rescued you from the inn. I tried to deny it, to avoid you so I wouldn't feel it. But I couldn't. I can't now and I don't want to. I love you, and tonight I'm going to prove that to you."

Chapter 22

    Tristan dropped his mouth to Meredith's and a thousand starbursts of pleasure exploded before her eyes. His kiss was like coming home, filling a void she hadn't been aware existed. She clung to him, his declaration of love still ringing in her ears as her body molded to his.

It was as if the bud of a rose in Ana's garden had finally opened to the sunlight. Everything was revealed. There were no more lies, no more walls, just the feeling of his arms around her. Only now did a lifetime like this seem possible.

She opened to him and their kiss deepened, slowed. It turned from the passionate expression of love to a deeper, more sensual promise of what was to come. From experience, she knew that was a night of overwhelming passion. But this time it wouldn't be just one stolen night together. It would be the first of many nights to come. Once they brought Devlin to justice and cleared Tristan's name, they could face that future. Together.

Tristan drew back, looking into her eyes. "I missed touching you so much."

She smiled through fresh tears, this time joyful. "I missed you too. I dreamed of you every night and I worried about you."

He pulled her back toward the bed. "You may have to examine me to ensure I wasn't harmed."

She laughed as she found his buttons with seeking fingers. "With pleasure, my lord."

She pulled his shirt free until it hung loose around him. He was just as beautiful as she remembered, and her body reacted as it always had. Hot blood warmed every sensitive part of her. Her nipples tingled in anticipation, and beneath her underskirts humid desire warmed her thighs.

She released an anticipatory sigh before she let her fingers caress his bare chest. His eyes fluttered shut and he let out a low, hungry groan that set her knees to trembling. She stroked his collarbone in long swishes, gliding her fingertips lower with each graze.

Tristan's grip on her arms tightened and the evidence of his desire stroked her belly as his steely erection rose to attention. She arched her hips, shivering at the touch of his length and knowing what he would do with it once they were free of these troublesome clothes.

The feel of Meredith writhing against him was almost more than Tristan could take. His fingers shaking, he reached around and yanked at the buttons on her dress. They popped loose, one flying across the room, but he didn't care. Once he had her naked, he would use finesse. He would take his time.

If she was troubled by the loss of her button, she didn't show it. Arching her back, she granted him greater access. Finally, he slipped his hands beneath her gown. Her chemise was fine silk, but not as soft as her skin. With a tug, her dress fell forward.

He let it bunch around her elbows, imprisoning her in the fabric as he bent his head to press his lips against her skin. Her pulse pounded hard, quickening when he darted out his tongue to caress the hollow of her throat. Her breath came ragged as she struggled against her gown, but he held steady, moving his lips on a slow, easy trail toward the edging of her chemise.

Meredith let out a low sigh as he caught one flimsy strap and let it join her dress at her elbow. Carefully, he peeled the silk lower until he revealed her breast. He reveled in her perfection for a moment: how beautifully her nipple puckered in anticipation, how perfectly she filled his hands, but then he couldn't resist any longer. He captured the little bud between his lips.

Her cry was primal, echoing as she clawed his shoulders and her hips bucked. He took his time, stroking her with his tongue, swirling around the nipple until it was rosy from his attentions.

He switched sides, drawing Meredith's chemise down but still leaving her gown at her elbows, where it limited her movement. She shivered, attempting to lift herself for his lips, but unable to do so when she was hindered by her dress.

He dipped his head and gave her the relief she was silently demanding, laving her nipple as her moan turned to a scream of pleasure. But it wasn't enough. He hadn't yet made her shiver in release or beg for more.

With a tug, her clothing pooled at her feet. Without breaking contact from her pebble-hard nipple, he grasped her hips and lifted her onto the bed. Immediately, she wrapped long, lithe legs around his back. Her wet heat pressed against his chest, telling him how much she wanted him inside her, how ready she was.

He leaned up to capture her lips, gently sucking her tongue as he palmed her thighs and spread her wide. She let out a cry into his mouth as he brought his hand up to cup her sex, brushing the weeping entrance to the core of her desire gently, letting his thumb play across the little bud of her pleasure.

Pressure blossomed at the point where Tristan's fingers touched. Spreading, arcing, it built in a crescendo. But every time Meredith started to slip over the edge of pleasure, Tristan withdrew, keeping her close to completion without ever giving her release.

She leaned on her elbows, letting her head dip back over her shoulders and shutting her eyes as he continued to tease her, toy with her. Then his mouth moved. He slid down her body, sucking, pleasuring, until his mouth and fingers met.

The moment his tongue swept across her, Meredith exploded. Her hips jolted, pressing against his steadying hands as he tongued her mercilessly, bringing her through her tremors and even after the last shakes of her release were over.

Trembling from the force of her climax, she met his eyes. "Please."

He nodded wordlessly as he slipped from his trousers. Her body ached in response to seeing him exposed, to seeing his erection at full and complete attention. Soon she would have him inside her.

She scooted back to let him climb onto the bed. He knelt between her legs, draping her knees over his elbows. The tip of his manhood nudged her, jolting her awareness up a notch as he surged forward to fill her to the hilt.

Her fingernails dug into the satin sheets for purchase as sensation assailed her. She reached for him as he withdrew, only to fill her with another sure thrust. Her hands clutched his arms, clinging to him as he took her.

His thrusts began as long, sure, controlled strokes meant to drive her mad. Meant to claim. She met them in kind, lifting her hips to his, massaging his muscles in encouragement. The pressure of her impending release built in her lower belly, spreading and expanding each time he stroked within her.

But as he continued to thrust, his eyes glazed and a fine sheen of sweat broke out on his forehead. Meredith watched him struggle to maintain control. Just seeing the veins in his neck strain with pleasure, the focus in his eyes as he held her gaze and took her again and again, drove her over the edge.

Her pleasure peaked, and she was falling a second time, pressing hot kisses against his skin as she rode out the waves of completion.

"Now, Tristan," she moaned. "Now!"

He roared out his pleasure, his arms straightening and his back arching as he poured into her. His cries merged with hers as she let out her own final scream of completion and went limp with satisfaction against the pillows.

Tristan's elbows buckled as he collapsed on top of her. Her arms came around him, feeling every part of him she could reach, reveling in the fact that he was finally hers.

Until tomorrow, when their lives would be in danger again.

Tristan shut his eyes. The light outside was starting to dim as the sun dipped in the west. Already, streetlamp lighters were doing their jobs.

Which meant he had to do his.

He had waited nearly two long years for this moment. The time when he would meet face-to-face with the man responsible for cutting his brother down. He had lived and breathed his quest to discover who killed Edmund. It had driven him to dance along the edge of madness and ruin. It had nearly cost him everything . . . and still could. But avenging his brother was the one thing that mattered. He had pictured the meeting so many times. Imagined every detail. Anticipated it.

But now, on the cusp of getting what he desired most, reluctance filled him.

Rolling over, he looked at Meredith. She was tangled in the sheets, the satin just barely draped over the tantalizing slope of her breasts. One shapely leg hooked over the covers, crooked in a way that made him want to trace the curve with his lips.

She was the reason for his reluctance. They had spent the previous night and most of this day making love, except when Meredith was making arrangements for their meeting. The meeting she insisted on attending with him, despite his protests. But he knew her too well. If he refused her, she would only follow.

She looked at him. "You seem very serious. Much like that troubled man I encountered at the ball before we left for Carmichael."

He nodded. There was no use hiding his emotions. "It's growing late. We'll be meeting with Devlin soon."

Her expression tightened and the lines of worry creased her forehead in the firelight. "Yes."

"Tonight will be very dangerous," he continued. "I don't want you to go."

Her face grew even more tense as she shook her head. "I told you the first ten times we had this discussion, my attendance is not up for debate."

"Are you certain you aren't coming along because you don't trust me?"

She leaned up, cupping his chin before she kissed him. Her lips clung to his for a moment, then she pulled away. "I trust you completely, but Devlin is dangerous. I can only imagine the man in charge of his group is even worse. You'll need the assistance of someone trained. And we won't be alone. Emily and Ana are our reinforcements. Everything is in place. All we need to do is find a viable explanation for my presence."

He sighed at her insistence. "Actually, I've been thinking about that, and I've come up with a plan."

She drew back in surprise. "Really? Do tell me."

"It will require more faith," he said, his gaze flitting over her face.

She didn't hesitate. "You have it."

Warmth flooded him. "You will appear to be my prisoner. I'll tell Devlin that's why I came to London so suddenly. That you were delving into secrets best left kept hidden in your fervor to marry a marquis."

She laughed. "Ah, yes. Everyone knows what a mercenary I am when it comes to marriage."

"I'm known as a catch, my love," he answered with a brief kiss on her nose. "That a woman would push her way into my business in an attempt to sketch my worth might not be so unbelievable."

"I believe it utterly," she teased.

His smile fell as he thought again of the danger she would be in, especially in the guise of his hostage.

"Devlin will see my bringing you to him as another test passed. A matter of trust that I would ferret out a danger to his organization."

Meredith looked at his face evenly, comforting him with her understanding expression. She didn't look afraid. If she were an ordinary lady, he wouldn't be able to accept her help. But Meredith Sinclair was no ordinary lady. She was a spy. And her skills would protect her even as he did everything in his power to do the same.

"You know," she said, her smile soft and loving,

"*that* is a wonderful plan. I think we may make a spy of you yet."

"If we survive the night, we can talk about my becoming a spy," he said as he rose to ready himself.

She caught his hand, drawing it to her cheek. "Don't worry, Tristan. Everything will be fine."

He nodded for her benefit, but in his heart he remained unsure. Tonight would be the most dangerous of his life. He could only pray he would survive, and be able to protect Meredith. Only then could he dare to hope for a future in her arms.

Chapter 23

Though it was summer, a brisk breeze blew off the Thames. Meredith shivered as she and Tristan stepped from their carriage onto the Southwark docks. The worn-down port in a poor and often violent part of London was the place Devlin had designated for their meeting.

Part of her chill had nothing to do with the temperature. She had reassured Tristan about their safety because he was afraid for her life, but in truth she wasn't sure of anything. In a case like this, in a meeting place not of her choosing, she knew very well they could be walking into a trap.

Tristan grabbed her arm without sparing her a glance. She longed for the comfort of his smile, but that wasn't possible. Since they could be watched, they had agreed he would treat her as his captive from the moment they stepped from the carriage. It was the only way to be sure their cover stayed intact.

As they walked along the docks, she caught sight of a woman, a lightskirt, hawking her wares in front of a rough tavern. As they passed, the woman touched her hand to her lips. It was the signal Emily used to reveal herself to her sister spies when she was in disguise.

That meant Ana was also close at hand, hiding herself and probably shaking in terror since she so rarely ventured into the field. But Meredith knew that when she had to, Ana would defend her friends to the best of her abilities.

Meredith shook her head in awe. Ana was brilliant and Emily was a master at covering her true identity. She was aligned with two of the most gifted women in the Empire. And she was glad they were on her side tonight.

She made a show of pulling away from Tristan, and he responded as they had rehearsed, yanking her back.

"The lightskirt in front of the pub is Emily," she whispered, twisting her face as if she were arguing with him.

To his credit, he did not look at her or turn back to observe the woman she pointed out, but she could tell he was surprised when he sucked in a breath.

"Truly? Well, she is a wonder, isn't she? I never would have recognized her."

Meredith hid her smile. "She is. And you're doing very well."

He nodded, though his expression never softened from its hard, gruff resignation. "I hope so. If we're being watched, I would hate for a misplaced expression to do us in before we reach our goal."

Meredith shivered and she didn't have to force the reaction. Their goal.

Her goal was to bring Devlin and his group to justice in the courts. To make sure they never betrayed their country again. Her goal was to obtain enough evidence through this encounter to clear Tristan of wrongdoing.

Tristan's goal was much simpler, and in a way, at odds with hers. He wanted to take a life for the life that had already been lost. And she wasn't sure she would be able to stop him when the time came. She wasn't sure if she *wanted* to take his chance at revenge away. Not after all he'd sacrificed for it.

They neared the area in the dock where Devlin had told Tristan to meet him. It was a darkened spot near the end of the line of shipping ports. The warehouses there were quiet. Some even looked to be abandoned or only used during certain seasons. The perfect place for a clandestine meeting.

Or an ambush.

In this part of London, no one saw anything that didn't directly affect them. And no one interfered if things turned violent. She cleared her thoughts to focus entirely on the situation at hand.

Tristan slowed his pace and his hand tightened on her arm. This time it was for comfort and protection, not show. He must have sensed her worries. She had to admit, feeling him by her side, ready to protect her, was a blessing.

"Devlin!" he called out, his voice full of cocky certainty.

Silence greeted them. The tension in her chest mounted, building as she waited for Devlin's reply. From the lines visible on Tristan's face in the dim light of a few flickering lamps, she could tell his anxiety was as high as hers.

"Augustine Devlin!"

"Lord Carmichael," came the familiar, bored drawl from behind a pile of stacked crates. From the smell that hung in the air, the boxes had once stored fish.

Meredith sucked in her breath as Devlin came into view. Even on the dirty docks, he looked calm and pulled together. Not one blond hair was out of place and his clothes were extravagant. He looked like a bird of paradise who had flown too far south and ended up in hell. But beneath that perfect, handsome exterior lurked the Devil himself.

"What is she doing here?" he barked as he caught sight of Meredith. "I told you to come alone, and you bring your whore?"

Tristan stiffened at the slur, and Meredith rushed to speak in the hopes he would gather his emotions and remember their plan.

"I beg your pardon," she snapped in her best Offended London Miss tone. "I never asked to be brought here. One moment I was having an evening drink in my town home, the next I was whisked into a carriage by this—this brute!"

"Shut your mouth," Tristan replied, his tone as cold as ice. If Meredith hadn't known it was an act, he would have frightened her. As it was, she obeyed on instinct.

"Answer me, Carmichael," Devlin repeated. "Or so help me God, I will have her shot where she stands."

As he spoke, four men emerged from where Devlin had been hidden. Meredith tensed. Five against two; five against four, including Ana and Emily. Not bad odds, but terribly dangerous. At such close range, even the worst shot could get lucky.

Tristan's breathing changed the moment the other men stepped into view, and Meredith realized he was sizing each one up, wondering who was in charge of Devlin's organization. Which one had caused his brother's death.

She looked them over herself. Two were large, with dim eyes. Brutes. Not meant to lead, but to carry out orders.

But the other two were distinct possibilities. Intelligent faces, menacing stares. And by the way one withdrew a pistol from his jacket and leveled it at her chest, they were men who had killed before and wouldn't hesitate to do so again. Even if their victim was an unarmed woman.

Tristan hesitated when the gun came into view. She prayed he would continue to carry out their plan, even though she was being threatened.

"You want to kill her?" he asked. She heard the strain in his voice. "Go ahead. But I'd question her first."

Devlin's eyes darted to her, then back to Tristan, narrowing with suspicion. "Why?"

"I was forced to return to London when I found out someone was digging into my business practices. I discovered it was Lady Northam."

She struggled in his grip again for show.

"Really?" Devlin's even stare returned to her. "And why would you do that, my lady?"

"Apparently she desired more than a turn in my bed," Tristan sneered. "She was marriage minded and wanted to make sure my fortune was as large as rumored. But the minx uncovered too much."

"Lies!" she protested, putting terror on her face, which came more easily than she would ever admit. "Mr. Devlin, you cannot believe I would be so mercenary! Surely you'll help me!"

Devlin let out a low chuckle. "Really now, my lady. I always sensed there was more to you than met the eye, but investigating a man's business in order to secure a good marriage?" His attention returned to Tristan. "How much did she uncover?"

"Enough," he spat.

Meredith shook her head. "He's wrong, I know nothing."

Devlin stepped forward, cupping her cheeks in one large hand. Tristan tensed, but she admired how he stood still, following the plan they'd mapped out earlier. Devlin searched her stare.

"You're a liar," he hissed as he yanked her from Tristan's hold and pushed her toward his men. "And once Lord Carmichael and I finish with our business, I'll delve into just how much of one."

Meredith caught Tristan's eye. His gaze briefly flickered to her and she felt his terror for her safety, but then it was gone, flashing too quickly for anyone else to have noticed.

"Consider her my gift to you." Tristan waved her off as if she meant nothing. "One last bit of proof that I'm worthy of your trust."

Devlin nodded, seemingly impressed by the callousness of Tristan's demeanor. "Yes, you have proven yourself. Now do it one final time. The materials that were retrieved from the painting, if you please."

Tristan touched his jacket pocket, the one that contained what Devlin desired most. As much as they hated to do it, Meredith knew they had no choice but to bring the real evidence, in case Devlin examined it.

But Tristan folded his arms instead of bringing it out to hand over. "Not this time. You know my terms, Devlin. I made them perfectly clear in Carmichael. I'm tired of being your lackey. I want to meet this man who leads your group. I'll turn over the evidence to him and him alone. Where is he?"

Devlin hesitated, looking Tristan up and down in a slow sweep. Meredith tensed as she watched him, praying he wouldn't kill them both and take what he desired. A man like him was capable of it.

"You want the man responsible?" he asked. A smile broke on his face. "You're looking at him, Carmichael. You've had access to him all along. *I* am the one you want."

It took all the strength and control Tristan possessed not to let his mouth drop open in surprise and stumble back. *Devlin* was the man in charge after all? Tristan had spent so long with this man, had done so much . . . when all along what he was searching for was right at his fingertips. He could have killed Devlin a hundred times.

But then, that was exactly why the man kept his identity secret. There was a long-standing belief that Devlin was someone else's minion. The authorities watched him, but didn't move on him because they wanted him to lead them to someone bigger and more dangerous. And men like himself, who had lost everything to Devlin's schemes, never spent their fury on the man because they believed he was only the conduit to someone else.

If rage hadn't been building in his chest, overwhelming reason and all other emotion, he would have congratulated Devlin on a well-played hand.

"You're pale," Devlin said with his signature smirk. "You did not expect my news?"

Tristan let his gaze flit to Meredith. She was being held by one of Devlin's men, watching him with wide eyes. From her expression, she was as shocked by this information as he. But as much as he wanted to strike out, he had to remain unruffled. If he did anything now, Meredith could be injured.

"No," he said as calmly as he could manage. "I did not. You told me again and again that you would allow me access to the man responsible for your group's actions. I assumed he was someone separate from yourself."

Devlin nodded, smug pleasure in his gaze. "The mask I wear as Augustine Devlin is nothing like the man I truly am. You'll soon see what I mean, once you pass a final, little test."

Tristan tensed. "Another test? Do you mean turning over the evidence?"

Devlin's smile grew. "No. I know you'll do that. You wouldn't come all this way, do everything you've done, only to refuse the easiest part. I want you to do something I think will be much harder. Kill her." He motioned over his shoulder at Meredith.

Rage made everything in Tristan's sightline turn red at the thought. He could no longer control those ragged emotions. Threatening him was one thing. Turning those threats on the woman he loved was another.

He stepped forward, ready to confront Devlin, but Meredith's voice stopped him. "Oh, Tristan, no!"

She seemed to be begging for her life, but when he glanced at her, he saw the message in her eyes. This was their opportunity. She had more than enough evidence for her quest for justice. And he had more than enough for his own search for vengeance.

He pulled his pistol from his pocket and slowly raised it to aim at Meredith . . . or at least at a spot just slightly to her left. The men behind her backed away so they wouldn't be hit by a stray bullet, and he realized just how brilliant the woman he loved was. Without her in the line of fire, he could easily shift the situation.

"I'm sorry," he said. "But you know what I have to do."

With a quick flick of his wrist, Tristan turned the gun on the ruffian who had his weapon drawn. He pulled the trigger and the man staggered back, his gun falling to the wooden dock with a clatter, as the bullet pierced his heart.

At the same time, Meredith dropped to her knees and rolled backward toward the protection of the stacked crates where Devlin and his men had hidden. Tristan saw her snatch the gun that had dropped at her ankles as she disappeared behind the crates. Dear God, she really *was* a spy, with the physical training to back it up.

Then all his attention was drawn to his own safety as he dove to his left. Devlin's men scrambled for their weapons, and the sounds of pistol blasts greeted him as he made his way around the crates, reloading as he went. He popped up and fired again, barely missing another of Devlin's men. That sent them scattering to their own hiding places.

Easing his way along the line of boxes, he kept his eyes on Meredith. She popped up, firing. He heard the hollow grunt of a man being hit and smiled. Of course she would be a perfect shot. Why not? She was seemingly perfect at everything else.

She reloaded with the swift efficiency of a soldier in the field, only pausing to cast a brief glance his way. She popped up and fired again.

"Damn, missed," she said as she dropped back, her gaze slipping to him. "You were wonderful."

"You were nearly killed!" he argued before he cautiously peered over the crates and fired a shot. "Where the hell is Emily?"

"On her way. I saw her slipping up from behind. She has to be careful or she could be caught in the cross fire."

"And I'm right here," came another voice behind them.

Both turned to see Ana making her way along the docks in a low crawl. She had her gun out, but didn't seem as comfortable holding it as Meredith did or Emily had in the carriage.

"Good, we need all the help we can get," Meredith said with a smile for her friend.

"I heard everything." Ana shook her head. "All this time, Devlin has been toying with every investigative branch of the government."

"I could have killed him a hundred times," Tristan muttered. "I never had to do anything he asked. I could have ended this a year ago."

Meredith moved closer, taking his hand as a stray bullet ricocheted near them. Ana pursed her lips and came up to fire her pistol.

"Tristan, with all the work you did, all the evidence you can provide us with, you will do much more to avenge your brother's death than if you had simply cut Devlin down a year or more ago." She squeezed his hand. "I realize you want his blood, but it won't wash away Edmund's blood. It won't bring your brother back."

She cursed as another bullet rained shards of wood down on them. Popping up, she fired, and a man cried out.

"He won't shoot using that arm again," she muttered as she began to reload. Her blue eyes recaptured his, holding his gaze. "Tristan, do you understand what I'm saying?"

He pondered her words. She didn't want him to take Devlin's life only to avenge his brother. But that had been his goal for so long. How could he rest if it wasn't done? He let his gaze focus on her again. She was watching him intently, waiting . . . and, he could see hoping as well.

Before he could answer, Ana whispered, "No more shooting."

Tristan lifted his head.

A woman stood behind the crates, leveling a pistol at the remaining men who were not injured or worse. It was the lightskirt Meredith had pointed out as they journeyed down the dock earlier. Emily in disguise.

Emily shook her head, though her eyes never left her prisoners. "Are you coming out to help me, or are you going to take up residence behind those crates?"

Meredith jumped to her feet and hurried around to assist her friend. Tristan watched her go, Ana trailing behind. He sighed as he followed, craning his neck to see which of the men had been injured or killed.

The man he shot first was definitely dead, lying in the same position where he'd fallen. One of the men Meredith hit was also dead, but the second cupped an injured arm while he howled like a baby.

Devlin and the other man were unharmed, scowling up at Meredith and Emily. Devlin's eyes darted to Tristan. "You bastard."

"Me, the bastard?" Tristan smiled as he thought of the fate that awaited Devlin. "I don't think so. You're the one committing treason. You're the one responsible for my brother's death."

The other man's eyes went wide with surprise.

"That's right, Devlin. I climbed my way into your organization, made you believe I was on your side, and all along I was against you." His smile grew. "Remember when your arms shipment sank? *I* was the one who anonymously passed the information of its location to the right people. Or when the courier with that large payment went missing?"

"You!" Devlin burst out, struggling as if about to get to his feet. When Meredith's gun moved level with his face, he returned to his seated position against the stacked boxes.

"And now you'll pay for all your crimes," Meredith added. "Ana, go send for Charlie. I'm sure he'll want to take these men to Newgate where they belong."

"With pleasure," Ana said, hurrying down the dock.

Devlin's focus moved from Tristan to Meredith. His eyes narrowed, and Tristan could have killed him for the violent malice in his stare.

"Who are you?" he asked, low and dangerous.

"You're not the only one with secrets," Meredith replied with a little smile. "*I'm* the woman who is placing you under arrest. For crimes against King and Country. For treason. Emily, bind his hands."

"With pleasure," Emily said as she finished with Devlin's partner, then stooped to deal with Devlin.

It only took a moment, just a flash, for everything to change. As Emily bent, Devlin abruptly rose up. His forehead hit her chin with a jolting blow, powerful enough that she staggered forward. Devlin caught her with one arm, her gun with the other, and got to his feet before Tristan or Meredith could take a step forward.

Meredith bit back a scream of horror as Devlin carefully maneuvered away from them. Emily was limp in his arms, unable to fight or run. Meredith couldn't tell how badly she'd been injured.

"Let her go, Devlin," Tristan cried.

"Release her or I swear I will blow a hole in you," Meredith ordered. Her gun remained steady, but her voice trembled.

"And risk my shooting her first, or my using

her as a shield?" Devlin's old smirk returned. "I think not."

Tristan and Meredith exchanged a glance, and she saw the empathy in the eyes of the man she loved. Devlin was right, of course. Even though both of them had their pistols raised, they couldn't risk the danger to Emily, who couldn't protect herself in her unconscious state.

Devlin dragged her back along the dock, keeping his gun trained on her head. Meredith moved forward to follow when a clatter echoed behind her. Her fan had fallen from the folds of her skirt where it had been hidden. She saw Tristan's eyes go wide at the sight of the six-inch blade protruding from the base.

She dropped down to scoop the weapon up, hiding the blade in her palm in the hopes Devlin hadn't noticed. He seemed too busy gloating as he made his escape.

"If you take one step closer, I *will* kill her," he promised.

Meredith raised her hands. "No! I'm putting my weapon down." She sent a look to Tristan and whispered, "Don't let go of yours."

He nodded, lowering his gun to his side as she let hers rest on the dock, leaving the fan as her only weapon.

As she straightened, she watched in helpless horror as Devlin moved even farther away.

"How can we stop him?" she whispered.

Tristan quickly took in the scene, his gaze darting around like that of a highly trained spy.

"Devlin is about to come even with that pillar on the right," he said softly, glancing at her. "When he does, I'll shoot it."

"No," she insisted with a shake of her head. "If you shoot, he might kill Emily! Or the bullet could bounce the wrong way."

He turned to face her while he watched Devlin from the corner of his eye. "If he gets out of our range, do you doubt he will kill Emily the moment he makes an escape?"

She hesitated, then her eyes dropped. "No, he'll kill her the instant she is of no further use to him."

Tristan lifted his weapon. "Once I distract him with my shot, throw your knife. I assume you have good aim with that thing."

She nodded even as she stared at him. Tristan's weapon was leveled on Devlin. Her heart skittered. Would he take this last chance at revenge, even though it could end her best friend's life?

A ragged breath escaped her lips. "I have faith in you."

He glanced her way from the corner of his eye. "I know."

Then he pulled the trigger.

Chapter 24

Meredith released her held breath in relief when the worn wooden pillar beside Devlin's head shattered. He yelped, turning away from the spray of splinters that flew in every direction. She said a short prayer, then threw her knife.

She watched the weapon circle end over end in the air before it hit its mark. Devlin's exposed throat.

The gun clattered from his hand as he let out a sickening gurgle. He dropped to his knees, and Emily's limp body hit the dock with jarring force.

Meredith took off running, with Tristan at her heels. Kicking the weapon far from Devlin's reach, she sank down and gently lifted Emily's head into her lap.

"Wake up," she whispered, frowning at the ugly bruise already forming on Emily's chin and the other that would certainly darken on her cheek. How badly was she hurt? A head injury could kill.

"Please," she murmured, stroking hair away from her friend's face. "Please."

Tristan placed his hands on her shoulders as she stared at her still motionless partner. Tears stung her eyes while she waited, praying for some sign. Then, finally, Emily stirred and her eyes fluttered open.

"Did you stop him?" she whispered, wincing when she tried to sit up.

"Shhh," Meredith soothed her. She glanced at Tristan and caught her breath. He stared at Devlin's body. Could this be enough to fulfill the duty he believed he owed Edmund?

"Meredith?" Emily croaked.

She nodded, bringing her attention back to her friend. "Yes. He's dead."

Emily smiled as she shut her eyes.

Within moments a flurry of activity descended on the dock. Tristan was shoved aside as Ana returned, swiftly followed by Charlie and his men. There were questions to be asked, arguments to have.

Finally, Meredith made her way to Tristan. He

stood on the edge of the dock, staring out over the murky water. She hesitated before she touched his arm.

"I'm sorry," she whispered. "I hope you don't feel I stole your revenge."

He turned and his potent green stare held hers. "You were right, Meredith. His blood won't bring Edmund back. My brother rested easy long ago. My quest to kill Devlin was about *my* peace, not Edmund's."

She bit her lip. "And can you find your peace now?"

His expression softened. "I found you. *You* are the one who brings me peace."

Her eyes filled with joyful tears. "I love you," she whispered as she curled her fingers into his hair and brought his mouth down on hers. "I love you."

Charlie stacked a mound of paperwork on his desk with a nod. His eyes came up, snaring Meredith's first, then Tristan's.

"I believe everything is in order here. Lord Carmichael, it appears your story was correct. And while I don't condone a gentleman involving himself in matters better left to officials, I do appreciate what you did to assist us." He stood and offered a hand. "I hope you'll accept both my thanks and my apologies."

Meredith held her breath as she watched Tristan

rise. His face remained stern. "There is still the issue of Philip Barclay to be resolved. Have you removed the charges against him as well?"

Charlie nodded. "Your friend has already been released and escorted to your town home, where he awaits your arrival."

Tristan's face relaxed and he took Charlie's offered hand. "Thank you, Mr. Isley."

Her superior's gaze came to her. Slowly, Meredith got to her feet. It had been over twelve hours since their encounter with Devlin and his men. Emily now rested comfortably, with no worse injury than a blackened eye and a pounding head. This was the final obstacle to overcome.

Charlie scowled. "I want to make it perfectly clear that Lady M and I do not condone what you did. I've had a stern discussion with Emily and Ana as well."

She nodded. "I hope you realize this was all my doing, Charles. If a severe punishment is required, please let it rest solely on my shoulders."

He opened his desk drawer and withdrew a letter. Her heart sank. Surely it was the notice of her dismissal. Then she caught sight of Tristan, watching the scene with silent concern. If she had lost her position, it had been worth it.

Charlie's face softened. "This is from Lady M. It is her thanks for a job well done."

Meredith reached for the letter with trembling hands and clutched it to her chest. "I—I'm not dismissed?" she whispered as tears wet her cheeks.

"No. Your instincts were best, after all. That is why you were chosen as a spy." Charlie touched her hand. She thought she saw moisture brighten his eyes before he cleared his throat and returned to his seat. "You shall be very busy, you and Ana and Emily. The evidence we obtained from Devlin's surviving cohorts, his town home, and the information Lord Carmichael shared with us shall keep you working for months to come. I hope you're ready."

She nodded. "We're always ready, Charlie."

He looked at Tristan again. "Is there anything else we can do for you, my lord?"

Tristan nodded. "Yes, Isley, actually there is."

"Name it."

"Give Meredith and her friends a few weeks holiday before they start disseminating the evidence. Give yourself a little time as well."

Meredith wrinkled her brow, confused. Charlie did the same.

"And why is that, Lord Carmichael?" Charlie asked.

Tristan's gaze moved to her, and the love she saw sparkling in his eyes warmed her to her very toes. "Because we're all going to be very busy planning a wedding. If we start reading the banns this Sunday, we could be married within the month."

Meredith gasped, her hand coming up to her lips. "You—We . . . ?"

He smiled as he dropped to one knee and took her hand. "I have never succeeded in asking you this in a romantic setting," he said with a laugh. "But the sentiment is real. I want you to be my wife. And this time, I will brook no refusals."

Joy lifted Meredith until she felt she could fly. Everything she ever desired, yet feared to hope for, was looking at her, embodied in Tristan.

She laughed even though tears streamed down her face. "You will hear no refusals, my lord. Yes, I will marry you, Tristan."

As Tristan's face lit up, she turned to Charlie. "I suppose I must tender my resignation."

Tristan was on his feet in a heartbeat. "What?" He clenched her shoulders and forced her to look at him. "Why?"

"I will be a marchioness," she answered. "No longer a widow. I assumed—"

He cut her off by slipping his arms around her. "I would want no other person protecting my country than my wife. You cannot give up your work, Meredith."

Her heart swelled with joyful emotion. "Only if you fight by my side, Tristan."

He smiled. "I will always be on your side." His mouth came down to hers. "Always."

Next month, don't miss these exciting new love stories only from Avon Books

His Mistress by Morning by Elizabeth Boyle
An Avon Romantic Treasure

When Charlotte Wilmot wished that Sebastian Marlowe, Viscount Trent, loved her as she loved him, she meant it with all her heart. She never thought her wish would come true—with her as his mistress when all she wanted was to be his wife.

Hysterical Blondeness by Suzanne Macpherson
An Avon Contemporary Romance

Patricia Stillwell is on a mission to put her wallflower ways behind her. But when a weight-loss drug turns her hair from drab brown to sparkling blonde, Patti's new world starts spinning out of control. Will blonde hysteria *really* go to her head?

No Man's Bride by Shana Galen

An Avon Romance

Catherine Fullbright has no interest in marriage, but her younger sister must remain unwed as long as Catie does. Determined to win his younger daughter a spectacular match, their father engineers a plan that lands Catie in bed with Quint Childers, Lord Valentine.

The Perfect Seduction by Margo Maguire

An Avon Romance

Norman lady Kathryn de St. Marie has been exiled from her people after a kidnapping attempt by the Scots. Forced to rely on Edric of Braxton Fell, the Saxon who rescued her, Kathryn finds herself falling in love with the brave warrior, who is far more interested in rebuilding his estate than catering to the woman he saved.

Visit www.AuthorTracker.com for exclusive information on your favorite HarperCollins authors.

Available wherever books are sold or please call 1-800-331-3761 to order.

REL 0806

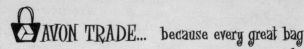

AVON TRADE... because every great bag deserves a great book!

0-06-052228-3
$12.95

0-06-082388-7
$12.95 ($16.95 Can.)

0-06-089005-3
$12.95 ($16.95 Can.)

0-06-089930-1
$12.95 ($16.95 Can.)

0-06-077311-1
$12.95 ($16.95 Can.)

Visit www.AuthorTracker.com for exclusive
information on your favorite HarperCollins authors.

Available wherever books are sold, or call 1-800-331-3761 to order.

ATP 080